The Power of

Jewish Holiday Stories

Their Meaning for Our Time

Rabbi Dov Peretz Elkins

Winner of the National Jewish Book Award
and NY Times Best-Selling Author

Mazo Publishers

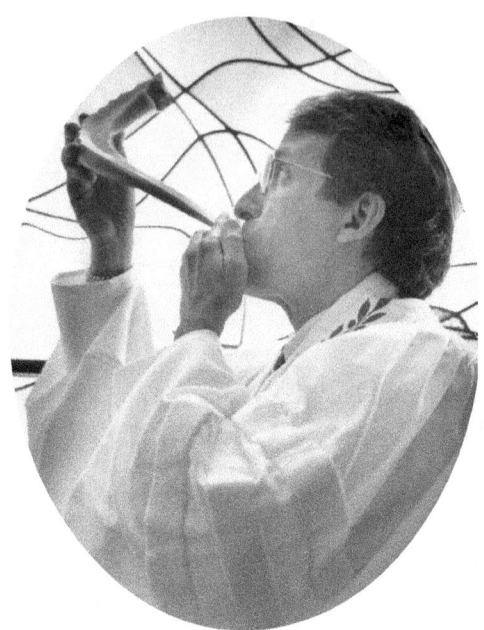

The Power of Jewish Holiday Stories

ISBN 978-1-956381-696
Copyright © 2024 Dov Peretz Elkins

Contact the Author
RabbiElkins@gmail.com

Mazo Publishers
Website: www.mazopublishers.com
Email: mazopublishers@gmail.com

Some stories included in this book have been retold over many generations and original sources are not known. We attempted to contact other sources for inclusion. We apologize for any omissions and will update notices in the next edition.

For All My Colleagues
Who Enjoyed Hearing These Stories
For The First Time.

Contents

The Author

Rabbi Dov Peretz Elkins is a nationally known lecturer, educator, workshop leader, author, and book critic. He is a popular speaker on the Jewish circuit.

Rabbi Elkins is a recipient of the National Jewish Book Award, and the author of over 63 books. His *Chicken Soup For The Jewish Soul* was on *The New York Times* bestseller list.

His most recent books are: *The Power of Hasidic Stories: Their Meaning for Our Time; Judaism: Ideas, People, and Rituals; Rabbi Sabato Morais: Pioneer Sephardic Rabbi of Early American Judaism; The Battle Between The Menorah And The Magen David; Rabbi Alexander Goode: The Rabbi and His Three Fellow Chaplains Who Went Down with the USAT Dorchester; The Founder of Hasidism: Wisdom and Tales of the Baal Shem Tov; Peter Bergson – The Jewish Lobbyist Who Advocated To Save Jews During the Holocaust; The Friendship That Shaped Jewish History; Bialik: Israel's National Poet; The Power Of Human Speech – In The Jewish Tradition; FATE; Jewish Ethical Wisdom From Pirkei Avot; To Climb The Rungs – Memoirs of a Rabbi; Jewish Stories from Heaven and Earth: Inspiring Tales to Nourish the Heart and Soul; Tales of the Righteous, Simple Actions for Jews to Help Green the Planet; Heart and Scroll: Inspiring Stories from the Masters; In the Spirit: Insights for Spiritual Renewal in the 21st Century; For Those Left Behind: A Jewish Anthology of Comfort and Healing* and *A Treasury of Thoughts on Israel and Zionism.*

Among Rabbi Elkins's other books are *Rosh Hashanah Readings: Inspiration, Information and Contemplation, Yom Kippur Readings,* and *The Wisdom of Judaism: An Introduction to the Values of the Talmud.* Other books by Dov Peretz Elkins are available on Amazon.

Rabbi Elkins served in several outstanding congregations in Rochester, NY, Cleveland, OH, and in Princeton, NJ, before retirement. He earned a doctorate in pastoral counseling in Rochester, NY.

Dr. Elkins lives in Jerusalem with his wife, Maxine (Miryam). They have six children and twelve grandchildren.

Acclaim For Rabbi Elkins's Previous Books

The author has a remarkable knack for choosing those statements in the wide sea of the Talmud that best express the human values of Judaism. Even as a collection of moral and ethical aphorisms, the book will be outstanding. Add to that the author's elaboration and explication of the values inherent in these dicta in a charming and literate style, and you have a book that is not only worth reading and studying, but also sharing with others.

Rabbi Dr. Norman Lamm, Chancellor, Yeshivah University

Here is a collection of gems – each essay sparkles with knowledge and originality. Whether he's showing the Jewishness in Thoreau's thinking or tackling knotty questions about Divine revelation, Rabbi Elkins approaches his subject with authority, clarity and utter honesty. Read and learn. This book opens up new worlds to explore.

Francine Klagsbrun, author of Lioness: Golda Meir and the Nation of Israel

Here is a distillation of a lifetime of reflection, learning and encounter – real earned wisdom from a wise man. A book to turn to again and again.

Rabbi David Wolpe, Senior Rabbi, Sinai Temple, Los Angeles

Amongst rabbis, Dov Peretz Elkins has long been a legend. Upon entering the rabbinate, one of the first books I was told to buy was his book of sermons and essays, *A Tradition Reborn.* That was in 1973! Here it is in 2023 and I still turn to it for his insights and perspectives that are still relevant. He has the gift of bringing together the Jewish perspective on a variety of topics. How appropriate that his newest book bears the title, "Judaism: Ideas, People, and Rituals." Contained within it are messages and wisdom that relate to all of us ... every man and woman. The ancient religion is brought to life for the contemporary seeker. Who else but Dov Peretz Elkins could cover in one book subjects ranging from "human sexuality" to "hearing the sound of the Shofar". See how he does that, and much more! It's really brilliant!

Rabbi Mitchell Wohlberg, Beth Tfiloh, Baltimore

In Judaism: Ideas, People, and Rituals, Rabbi Dov Peretz Elkins demonstrates once again why he has been one of the greatest teachers and rabbis of our time. He has here culled together sermons and portraits of figures and movement to display and share his wisdom with us, his readers and students. This work truly displays the knowledge, breadth, and insights of his learning that he shares so clearly and brilliantly. We are all the beneficiaries of his teachings!

Rabbi David Ellenson, Chancellor Emeritus, Hebrew Union College-Jewish Institute of Religion

In this important collection of his writings, Rabbi Dov Peretz Elkins explores how Judaism offers us a path to meaning, purpose, belonging and blessing. He mines Jewish tradition, introduces influential teachers, and shares his own unique and powerful rabbinic voice. A must read!

Dr. Ron Wolfson, Fingerhut Professor of Education, American Jewish University, author of Relational Judaism

This is the kind of book in which you say to yourself after reading it, "Why did it take so long for someone to think of doing this?" [*Jewish Ethical Wisdom From Pirkei Avot*] Pirkei Avot – Ethics of the Fathers has had centuries of commentaries, but now, for the first time, multiple commentaries on many of its passages are arranged according to topic. This will make it much more user friendly, just as the Mishnah made Jewish law more accessible by organizing it by topic. Furthermore, the wealth of commentaries that Rabbi Elkins has amassed on each topic, including classical, medieval, and modern voices, makes what the original Mishnah says all the more relevant and meaningful. We all should be grateful to Rabbi Elkins for writing this book.

Elliot Dorff, Rabbi, PhD, Rector and Distinguished Service Professor of Philosophy, American Jewish Univ.

Rabbi Dov Peretz Elkins tells the heroic story of Peter Bergson (born Hillel Kook) who understood, before most, Nazi Germany's genocidal intentions, and devoted great efforts to mobilize the United States, in particular, to save European Jewry. Written in a manner accessible to young people and also of great interest to adults, Elkins reminds us that Germany's intentions were no secret, that American Jewry did not do enough to help, and that one man can make an extraordinary difference. Especially in light of the resigned cynicism that often meets claims of human rights

violations today, the story of Peter Bergson is important to retell.
Dr. Jeffrey Herbst, President, American Jewish University

Dov Peretz Elkins has written an important book for young people. It is the heartbreaking story of a neglected Jewish hero, Peter Bergson (born Hillel Kook), and his desperate efforts to rally the United States government and people to make a significant attempt to save Jews from the Nazi "Final Solution" exterminations program which engulfed European Jewry.

The apathy of President Franklin D. Roosevelt and the Administration, and their unwillingness to act is vividly portrayed. The shocking indifference of mainstream American Jewish organizations and the callous policies of not rocking the boat pursued by Rabbi Stephen Wise are exposed. The spiteful attacks on Bergson and his various organizations and their allies by do-nothing organizations are ever more devastating to read.

Elkins describes the one success of all the rescue efforts – the appointment of a War Refugee Board which saved as many as 200,000 Jewish lives. One could argue that Elkins gives all the credit to Bergson and that Secretary of Treasury Morgenthau and his team's role is downplayed. But this would be nitpicking. All in all, this book is an important moral contribution. It pays a long overdue debt to Peter Bergson, to history and to memory. Tragically, it makes clear that human failures enabled the Nazis to operate with little resistance from America (as from the Allies and bystanders in Europe.) This book deserves a wide readership.
Rabbi Irving (Yitz) Greenberg Dr. Greenberg served as Executive Director of the President's Commission on the Holocaust, which recommended the creation of the U.S. Holocaust Memorial Museum, and later as chairman of USHMM (2000-2002)

Peter Bergson (Hillel Kook) was among the first Jews in America to internalize the idea that the Germans were implementing the Final Solution to the Jewish Problem, murdering Jewish men, women and children throughout German-occupied Europe. He understood that this was not a time for business as usual and he raised a ruckus, pulling out all the stops to call attention to the plight of the Jews and to plead for their rescue. He organized, he publicized, he cajoled, he yelled, he planned, and he tried idea after idea.

History has vindicated his radicalism, his activism, and his boldness. Dov Peretz Elkins has made an important contribution in bringing Bergson to life, portraying him for a new generation, where he can become a model, an inspiration.

Dr. Michael Berenbaum, Professor of Jewish Studies Director of Sigi Ziering Institute: Exploring the Ethical and Religious Implications of the Holocaust. American Jewish University, Los Angeles, CA

My family reads these stories out loud to each other. We laugh. We cry. A family that eats chicken soup together will remain culinary Jews. A family that reads *Chicken Soup for the Jewish Soul* together will remain part of an enduring tradition that has transformed the world with its humor, passion and generosity of spirit.

Alan M. Dershowitz, Felix Frankfurter Professor Emeritus of Law, Harvard University Law School

Rabbi Elkins has written an engaging book, involving discussions among four rabbis of different religious movements. Through these conversations, readers gain insight into major – and minor – issues in Judaism. It's an opportunity for readers to "eavesdrop" on rabbis who are on the front lines of Jewish life ... to agree or disagree with them, to engage in their discussions.

Rabbi Marc D. Angel, Founder and Director of the Institute for Jewish Ideas and Ideals, and author of many books

In the Spirit is a lovely and accessible compendium of Jewish virtues that draws on our traditions of wisdom from the Bible to modern writers. Rabbi Elkins's own stories and comments make this book a valuable guide that can accompany the reader on many occasions.

David Ariel, PhD, former President of the Oxford Centre for Hebrew and Jewish Studies at the University of Oxford

Four Rabbis at Lunch is a marvelous discussion sprinkled with seriousness, humor and a great amount of important information about what rabbis have to deal with whatever their denomination and struggles. Much to learn from, to have a good laugh, and think about what Judaism is all about and why it is of crucial importance. The most important message of this book is that rabbis with very different ideas about Judaism can sit together, listen to each other and have an actual discussion. A hopeful sign!

Rabbi Dr. Nathan Lopes Cardozo, Jerusalem

Rabbi Dov Peretz Elkins is a leading spiritual figure in our time, and all his writings are of high quality.

Rabbi Zalman Schachter-Shalomi, author of Davening: A Guide to Meaningful Jewish Prayer

Imagining, visualization, and meditation have been part of Jewish prayer and life for the longest time. In the Talmud we read that the early Hasidim would spend an hour before prayer in order to direct their minds to God. In his book on guided imagery, Dov Peretz Elkins helps the Jewish community recapture this grand tradition and practice. This guidebook will assist all who dare experience a new way of Jewish growth and development.

Rabbi Samuel K. Joseph, Ph.D., Professor of Jewish Education, Hebrew Union College – Jewish Institute of Religion

Few friendships in all of American Jewish history have been as impactful for Jews as the one between Eddie Jacobson and Harry S. Truman. Dov Peretz Elkins ably recounts the story of that friendship and what it meant for the emerging State of Israel. An inspiring story.

Jonathan D. Sarna, University Professor and Joseph H. and Belle R. Braun Professor of American Jewish History, Brandeis University

Since the 60s, I have cherished the books by Rabbi Elkins. He is generous and brave, traditional and cutting edge. He is a great teacher because he is a great student. Rabbi Elkins is a gifted Rabbi and teacher and writer. I always purchase his new books sight unseen, and I am always grateful for what he has written.

Arthur Kurzweil, author of On the Road with Rabbi Steinsaltz and From Generation to Generation: How to Trace Your Jewish Genealogy

"What Rabbi Elkins does in this one volume window in the heart of the world's greatest Book [*The Bible's Top Fifty Ideas*] is truly amazing. His discussions are engaging, inspiring, comprehensive and scholarly. I have found his book to be exceptionally accurate, thorough and comprehensive. This is a veritable treasure. I cannot praise this wonderful book enough."

Prof. Shalom Paul, former Chair, Dept. of Bible, HU, Jerusalem

Through the lunch-table conversation of four imaginary rabbis, *Four Rabbis at Lunch* offers the reader an original perspective on the Jewish community and Jewish religious leadership in our time by a master rabbi drawing on his decades of experience in the Jewish community. The book's unprecedented fictional format provides the layman with a witty, anecdotal, and memorable entree into the complex, sometimes contradictory intellectual, moral, and social currents that lie behind the polished words of the preacher and the wise counsel of the pastor.

Raymond Scheindlin, Professor Emeritus, Jewish Theological Seminary

A most creative application of guided imagery techniques to Jewish education. If my Hebrew school teachers had used these tools to involve me personally and emotionally in my Jewish heritage, I would not have had to reach my thirties before coming to accept and prize my Jewishness. These activities are interesting, enjoyable, practical and useful with young people and adults.

Howard Kirschenbaum, co-author, Values Clarification

Dr. Elkins has compiled an exceptionally interesting and uplifting collection of essays and articles on the meaning and practice of the Jewish Sabbath. Readers of this book will be rewarded not just with new information, but with the kind of education that will help mold their character and forge their spiritual values.

Prof. Harold T. Shapiro, President, Princeton University

Rabbi Elkins has written another creative, useful, and user-friendly book that will help teachers, groups workers and Rabbis enrich their teaching of Jewish subject matter.

Audrey Friedman Marcus, Executive Vice-President, A.R.E. Publishing

What a treat! Dov Elkins has compiled a rich collection of guided imagery scripts, with invaluable suggestions for implementation.

Dr. Mel Silberman, Prof. of Organizational Development, Temple University

Dov Peretz Elkins is one of the most spiritual people I know. His creative work in education and nourishing human beings is known throughout the world. He has made another useful contribution through this marvelous collection of spiritual quotations. His work continues to be chicken soup for my soul.

Jack Canfield, co-author, Chicken Soup For the Soul

"So, four rabbis walk into a deli..." Sounds like the beginning of a joke, but fortunately for us, it is actually the set up for a compelling peek behind the closed door of the rabbi's study. These thoughtful colleagues bring all sorts of fascinating questions to discuss as they grapple with the key Jewish questions of our time: Jewish practice, intermarriage, fostering welcoming and inclusive communities, The rabbis may be fictional, but the brilliant Rabbi Dov Peretz Elkins is sharing truths stranger and more meaningful than fiction. If you've ever wondered how rabbis make decisions, grab this book. You'll find it hard to put down!

Dr. Ron Wolfson, Fingerhut Prof. of Education, American Jewish University

This magnificent collection touches on the soul and secret of Jewish survival.

Sherwin B. Nuland, MD, author of How We Die

"It's fun to learn the real meaning of Biblical texts. Rabbi Dov Peretz Elkins is a great teacher."

Edward I. Koch, former Mayor, New York City

"Dov Peretz Elkins is a gifted rabbi and teacher who has authored a number of books which are very popular among his colleagues. They will find this volume particularly appealing. It is a wonderful text."

Professor David L. Lieber, President Emeritus, University of Judaism

Rabbi Dov Peretz Elkins has devoted his career to collecting wisdom from the Jewish tradition and making classical and contemporary Jewish ideas accessible to learners and leaders.

Rabbi Lauren Berkun, Vice-President, The Hartman Institute

"Find yourself a teacher," *Avot* advises. In these pages, I find Rabbi Dov Peretz Elkins to be an erudite and elegant teacher of Jewish ethics. Rabbi Elkins organizes *Avot* in an accessible way and provides a wealth of sources from both inside and outside of Jewish tradition to gently guide us to the ethical life.

Professor Ari L. Goldman of Columbia University, author of The Search for God at Harvard

Wise and accessible, this is a book that shines. Everything you need to know about how to be a "mensch" – a fully evolved, caring human being – is here in this treasure trove of practical inspiration.

Joan Borysenko, Ph.D. author of Inner Peace for Busy People, and A Woman's Journey to God

A reservoir of rabbinic insights into how we should live our lives – in relationships, family and community. Helps all of us in our struggles with the enduring questions we face as human beings. A must read for anyone who reflects on what it means to live lives of holiness and goodness.

Dr. Norman Cohen, provost, Hebrew Union College – Jewish Institute of Religion; author, The Way Into Torah

Beautifully shows the eternal wisdom of our sages in our contemporary world. Elkins' personal wisdom is interwoven with ancient texts to illuminate so many issues with which we are faced today. A valuable resource for anyone interested in understanding the great worth of the Talmud.

Rabbi Judith Z. Abrams, PhD, founder and director, Maqom: A School for Adult Talmud Study

Clearly and beautifully elucidates important teachings on spiritual concepts like love, charity, kindness and companionship – plus some of life's sticky issues like greed, sin, and belief. A great book for anyone wanting to dip into the pool of Judaism's timeless wisdom.

Rabbi Elyse Goldstein, editor, The Women's Torah Commentary and The Women's Haftarah Commentary

Filled with wise guidance on the dilemmas humans face every day, mixed with gems from the Jewish tradition. A great book.

Rabbi Sid Schwarz, founder/president, PANIM: The Institute for Jewish Leadership and Values; author, Judaism and Justice: The Jewish Passion to Repair the World

For those of us unable to tackle the multi-volume Talmud, this thoughtful and well-written book gives us the essence of Jewish wisdom on a variety of topics relevant to our lives today.

Ron Miller, chair, religion department, Lake Forest College; coauthor, Healing the Jewish-Christian Rift: Growing Beyond Our Wounded History

A sturdy craft for sailing the sea of Talmud, and Rabbi Elkins is a fine navigator. His choice of text is solid, his commentary is insightful, and his style is both enlightening and engaging. This is a book to come back to over and again.

Rabbi Rami Shapiro, author, Ethics of the Sages: Pirke Avot – Annotated and Explained

Dov's involvement in Israel-oriented teaching is part and parcel of his larger spectrum of Jewish engagement. His many books on Jewish learning – from Bible, Talmud, history, holidays, Jewish educational methodology, to Jewish environmentalism and Soviet Jewry – have informed Jewish professionals and laypersons throughout the world.

Rabbi Haskell M. Bernat, D.Min., D.D.

All the timely issues of the day are illumined by the timeless insights of a great tradition. Rabbi Elkins speaks in a clear and straight-forward fashion directly to his generation.

Rabbi Dr. Robert Gordis – Professor of Bible, Jewish Theological Seminary

Telling stories is what makes us human, providing us with meaning. In this marvelous collection, Rabbi Elkins offers dozens of short, profound Hasidic stories, which he then applies masterfully to our life today. This book will inspire, delight, challenge and surprise you, page after page. Keep a copy by your bedside, and give another to a friend!

Daniel Matt, translator of the Zohar; author of The Essential Kabbalah, God and the Big Bang, and Becoming Elijah

Dov Peretz Elkins has given our generation the gift of renewed access to the wisdom of Hasidic story-telling. With keen spiritual insight, Elkins chooses stories that speak to the needs of this time, reminding us of why early Hasidism revolutionized Jewish devotional life. His wise commentary helps unveil the complexity behind the deceptive simplicity of these tales and parables. This is a manual for anyone seeking to draw closer to God and to the heart of Jewish spirituality.

Yossi Klein Halevi, senior fellow, Shalom Hartman Institute, author of Letters to My Palestinian Neighbor

An entertaining and informative presentation of

important archeological data illuminating the stories of the Bible. In addition to the discussion of ancient materials there is a lively account of the circumstances and personalities involved in the discoveries.

Prof. David Noel Freedman, Department of Near Eastern Languages and Literature, UC, editor of The Anchor Bible, and The Anchor Bible Dictionary

This valuable book successfully presents the findings of archeology in clear nontechnical style. Readers of all ages will find it informative, interesting and useful.

Dr. Nahum M. Sarna, Professor of Biblical Studies, Brandeis University

What an amazing book. Dov Peretz Elkins brings Hasidic wisdom to light, sharing the wise, clever, often humorous stories that are the way the Hasids taught. He emphasizes the value of story as metaphor, a way to help people look differently at the world. He offers direct interpretations of each story, emphasizing what he sees as its core lesson. And he marshals comparisons to other thinkers, analysts and writers who have taught the same lessons differently, sharing their words to make the teachings of the Hasids central and relevant.

This book is truly a guide – if not to the perplexed, then to those who can benefit from a little guidance for how we might best live our lives. Elkins takes ancient teachings of the Hasidic community that were themselves presented inside of clever and creative stories, draws out what we have to learn from each story and makes it come alive for today.

As Elkins teaches us, the Hasidic stories offer us all the wisdom we need about being ourselves, about harnessing the best ways of looking at the world, about understanding the many ways in which we can move forward even in moments of uncertainty or confusion.

This is the kind of book you want to carry in your pocket for a daily dose of wisdom, for the opportunity to look at the world with new eyes, understand yourself better and set a course for being the best you can be.

Ruth W. Messinger, Global Ambassador, American Jewish World Service

Dov Peretz Elkins amplifies the impact of powerful and surprising Hasidic stories by bringing them into conversation with a rich range of contemporary sources, including psychology, philosophy and his own commentary, to offer guidance for how we may live with integrity and wisdom on our day.

Rabbi Deborah Waxman, Ph.D., President and CEO, Reconstructing Judaism

In The Power of Hasidic Stories, Dov Peretz Elkins connects the reader to the stories of the Hasidic masters created during the 18th and 19th centuries. The stories use counter-intuitiveness, surprise, and humor as ways of teaching some of life's most important lessons. Rabbi Elkins draws upon the wisdom found in each artful story to call attention to a particular value or life-challenge worthy of consideration. Using his knowledge of Jewish texts, values, and practice, he offers both his own understanding of the stories and the valuable insights of thinkers,Jewish and non-Jewish, that relate the lesson of each Hasidic masterpiece. Both the Hasidic stories and the accompanying commentary of this volume make The Power of Hasidic Stories a most welcome and valuable resource for considering the contemporary concerns of life that inspired the masterful story tellers to create the stories found in this volume.

Rabbi William Lebeau, former VC, Jewish Theological Seminary of America

Dov Perez Elkins's interpretive wisdom enriches the powerful tales of the Hasidism in ways that will both make you laugh and seriously ponder about how to live a good life.

Rabbi Sandy Eisenberg Sasso, author of Midrash – Reading the Bible with Question Marks and I Am Not Afraid – Psalm 23 for Children

Fascinating and useful, not only to young people. Anyone who is not a professional archeologist will learn things he did not know before and will feel enriched. Absorbingly written.

Dr. H. L. Ginsberg, Sabato Morais Professor of Biblical History and Literature, the Jewish Theological Seminary of America

Dov Peretz Elkins' excellent anthology reminds us that accepting ourselves is the only way of affirming the human spirit and our faith in each other. It is a celebration of our goodness and our potential for growth. The sense of celebration is stretched by the beautiful photographs. The weight of its meaning is balanced by the lightness of this book's beauty.

Joseph C. Zinker, author, Creative Process in Gestalt Therapy

Dov Peretz Elkins has made a most valuable contribution to the search for self. These readings will supply endless hours of fascinating debate, inquiry and values clarification.
Dr. Sidney B. Simon, author, Values Clarification

This remarkable book manages to capture in each and every Hasidic aphorism the spiritual audacity, deep humor, and moral wisdom of a great tradition. It has enriched my life.
Rabbi Harold M. Schulweis, Valley Beth Shalom, Encino, CA

The wisdom of the Hasidic tradition distilled into folk proverbs, presented with much warmth and humor....a great gift.
Dr. Arthur Green, Founding Dean of the rabbinical program at Hebrew College, Boston

The Bible's Top Fifty Ideas is smart, well-written, and particularly useful to those for whom Jewishness is more familiar than Judaism.
Bret Stephens, Columnist, The New York Times

Introduction

The story is the main vehicle in Jewish literature to convey important ideas. Of course, it is not the only such vehicle, but no other medium transmits Jewish values and ideas as powerfully as does a story.

There are laws, there are poems, there are prayers and there are ethical treatises, but none of these modalities compare with the power of a story.

Let me illustrate this point with a story.

A Story About Stories: It happened that Rabbi Yisrael Baal Shem Tov was traveling with his students and was chatting with them about fear of heaven and worship of the Creator. The sun was setting. They approached a tree. The Besht got down from his wagon and stood near the tree. He stood and swayed with deep feeling. Then he ordered his student, Rabbi Leib ben Sarah, to dig a hole in the tree and put a burning candle inside the hole. Rabbi Leib ben Sarah did so. The candle burned and the Besht stood near it, and whispered a prayer with awe, until the fire was extinguished. At that moment the Besht raised his eyes to Heaven, and called out in a voice filled with joy:

Thank You, Blessed One, thank You, Master of the Universe. They returned to the wagon. The sun set. The moon glowed. After a prolonged silence the Besht stirred from his deep thoughts and said:

Blessed be God, Blessed be God, Who saved our people, B'nai Yisrael, from an evil judgment, Heaven forbid. The students understood that by the merit of the burning candle, the evil decree that was about to come, was canceled.

The Besht and his students got down from the wagon, broke out in inspired dancing to the light of the moon, and sang merrily.

Salvation and comfort to our people, B'nai Yisrael, salvation and comfort!

After many years Rabbi Dov Ber, the Maggid of Mezritch, told this story to his friends: In one of his travels he got down from his wagon, near a tree, ordered to have a hole made in the tree and put in it a burning candle. Then he began to shake a lot, and recited this prayer:

Master of the Universe: it is clearly known to You, that I am not accustomed to deal with long meditations as Rabbi Yisrael Baal Shem Tov. Therefore I ask You that his merit will stand for me, as I recite before You these special prayers, and cancel from Your holy Jewish People the evil decree.

Then Rabbi Moshe Leib of Sassov during his travels with the circle off his friends paused once near a tree on the road, and after he told them the story of the burning candle in the tree, which canceled the evil decree in the days of the Besht and in the days of the Maggid of Mezritch, pleaded:

My masters, the holy Baal Shem Tov knew the secret of the burning candle, and had great power with the special prayers. The Rav Rabbi Dov Ber also knew the secret of the lit candle, but the wisdom of the special prayers was forgotten. We, the generation who know much less, small-hearted that we are, we do not know the secret of the candle or the special prayers.

Our only choice is to rely on the story of the burning candle, the special prayers, that our holy rabbis used with their powers to avert the evil decrees upon the seed of Avraham, Yitzhak and Yaakov, and we hope that mercy from Heaven will come to us and stand for us, and the merit of our great rabbis will stand for us to have the story annul the evil decrees. (From "Knesset Yisrael", Warsaw, 1906.)

The cornerstone of Jewish literature, the Torah, begins with a story. It is the story of God's creation of the world: "In the beginning..." (Genesis 1:1).

From that story to the most recent story in our time, it is stories that carry all the important values, events, history and deep concepts that are the warp and woof of Jewish religion, ethics, - all the important things we learn when transmitting Jewishness.

If we look through the history of Jewish literature, stories have found important places in many different periods: biblical, rabbinic, medieval and modern.

This book is a selection of the stories which I consider having some of the most powerful ideas I have encountered over the years.

It is, of course, the story's relevance for our present-day lives that encourages us to mine the worth of these stories.

My hope is that the presentation of these stories will enrich the days and years of the lives of all who read them.

Dov Peretz Elkins, Shavuot, 5785, Jerusalem
The fifty-seventh anniversary of the reunification
of the Holy City of Jerusalem
The seventy-sixth anniversary of the reborn State of Israel

The Power of

Jewish Holiday Stories

Their Meaning for Our Time

Elul

There is a custom to devote more time during the month of Elul to prayer and the reciting of Psalms. The founder of Hasidism, the Baal Shem Tov, instituted the custom to read three extra chapters of Psalms each day, beginning from the first of Elul until Yom Kippur (including 36 chapters recited on Yom Kippur itself) – thereby concluding the entire book of Psalms.

The King is in the Field

When Berel Gartner was 12, before World War II, he was one of the children who left Germany through the Kindertransport. He arrived in England and was taken to an orphanage. He spent most of his days crying and asking his caregivers when he would see his parents again. As hard as they tried to make him happy, he could not be consoled.

One day, Berel's caregivers found out that King George VI would be passing through their village, as he frequently did during the early years of his reign. When they told Berel that they would be seeing the king pass by that day, it was the first time in weeks that he stopped crying. Berel had a secret plan.

Berel and the other Jewish children were taken to the town square and stood behind a barricade as they waited for the king to pass by. As the royal carriage came closer, Berel jumped the barricade and ran with all of his might towards the king's carriage. As soon as the royal guards saw him, they grabbed him and carried him back to the barricade. The king asked his guards what was going on. When they told him about the boy who ran towards his carriage, he invited Berel to come closer.

The king asked Berel, "Why did you run towards the carriage? Is there something you would like to tell me?" Berel broke down crying and told the king how much he missed his parents who were still back in Germany. He then wiped the tears and said, "Please. Please help bring my parents here."

King George responded, "Young boy, we are at war with Germany. It would be impossible for me to do that."

"But you're the king of England!" Berel cried. "You can do anything! Please bring my parents to me."

The king looked at the boy with compassion and said, "Please don't cry. I promise I will do what I can to try and make it happen."

Berel gave the king his parents' names and thanked him, unsure of what to expect.

A month later, there was a knock at the door of the orphanage. Berel's parents had arrived. Somehow, they were brought out of Germany and were reunited with their son.

Our sages teach us that in the days leading up to Rosh Hashanah, (Elul) the Almighty leaves His palace and roams throughout the villages and fields to be closer to His subjects. It is our chance to jump the barricade and come closer to the King. It's the time we can pour out our heart and ask Him for anything.

This Rosh Hashanah, take advantage of this special time to experience the Almighty's closeness. Clarify the goals you deeply yearn to accomplish this coming year, and beseech God to invest in you a year of tremendous blessings and joy.

Rabbi Y.Y. Jacobson

◆◆◆

The Real Key To Teshuvah

The story is told of a country boy who visited the big city. Suddenly, while walking around, he heard the sound of a bugle being blown from a high tower; a fire had been spotted! Immediately, a "bucket-brigade" was formed, water was passed from hand-to-hand, and soon the fire was put out.

The boy was greatly impressed, and he bought a bugle. He returned to his village and called all the people to come around him. He then threw a match onto the roof of one of the thatched houses. The people were aghast, but the foolish lad told the people not to worry. He took out his new bugle and began blowing and blowing, but the fire soon spread to the whole town!

It is the action we take during these days, and not a mere Shofar blast, that is the real key to Teshuvah.

◆◆◆

Where is God?

A man was going from village to village, from rabbi to rabbi, asking the same question: "Where can I find God?" he was never satisfied with the answers he received, so he would pack his bag and move on to the next village.

Some of the rabbis told him, "Pray, my son, and you'll find God." But the man had tried to pray and he could not.

And some replied, "Study, my child, and you shall find God." But the studies seemed dry and irrelevant. The more he read, the more confused hen became – and the further removed from God he seemed to be.

And some rabbis said, "Forget your quest, my child. God is within you." But the man had tried to find God within himself, and failed.

One day, the man arrived, weary and discouraged, at a very small village set in the middle of a forest. He went up to a woman who was minding some chickens. She asked whom he could be looking for in such an isolated place, but she did not seem surprised when he told her he was looking for God. She quickly finished her chores and escorted him to the rabbi's house.

When he went in, the rabbi was studying. The man waited a moment, but he was impatient to be off to the next village if he could not be satisfied. So, he interrupted: "Rabbi! How do I find God?"

The rabbi paused, and the man wondered which of the many answers he had already heard the rabbi would give. But the rabbi said simply, "You've come to the right place, my child. God is in this village. Why don't you stay for a few days? You might meet God." The man was puzzled. He did not understand what the rabbi could mean. But the answer was unusual. It intrigued him enough to stay.

For two or three days he explored every corner of the tiny village. He would ask the villagers where God was that day, but they would only smile and invite him to have a meal with them.

Gradually, he got to know them and even helped with some of the village work. Every now and then, by chance, he would see the rabbi, and the rabbi would ask him, "Have you met God yet, my son?" And the man would smile and sometimes he understood, and sometimes he did not understand.

For months he stayed in the village, and then for years. He became part of the village life and shared in all the activities. He went to the synagogue on Friday and prayed with the rest of the community, and sometimes he knew why he prayed and sometimes he did not. And sometimes he really said the prayers and sometimes only the words.

And he would join one of the families for a Friday night meal, and when they talked about God, he was always assured that God was in the village, though no one was quite sure where or when God could be found. Gradually, he, too, began to believe that God was in the village, though he wasn't quite sure where. He knew, though, that sometimes he had met God.

One day, for the first time, the rabbi sought him out, and said, "You have met God now, have you not?" And the man said, "Thank you, Rabbi, I think I have. But I'm not sure why I met God or how or when. And why is God only in this village?"

The rabbi replied: "God is not a person, my child, or a thing. You cannot meet God in that way. You were so caught up in the question that you could not hear the answers. Now that you can find God, you can return to your village, if you wish."

So the man went back to his town, and God went with him.

And the man prayed and studied, and knew that God was within him and within other people. And others sensed that, and sometimes they would ask him, "Where can we find God?" And the man would always answer, "You have come to the right spot. God is in this place."

A version of this Hasidic story appears in The Assembly of Rabbis of the Reform Synagogues of Great Britain, Forms of Prayers for Jewish Worship: High Holidays, by Jeffrey Newman as well as in *From Generation To Generation* by Debra Orenstein and Israel Mowshowitz.

◆◆◆

Heaven And Hell

Rabbi Bana'ah the son of Rabbi Ulla taught, Why does it not say "it was good" on the second day of Shabbat. Because on that day the light of hell was created. (Pesachim 54a)

There was a Buddhist monk who was considered the wisest man in the world. And there was a warrior who was considered the strongest man in the world. One day the wise monk met the vicious warrior on a narrow bridge.

The warrior saw the monk and became angry. "You think you are so wise. But I am far stronger than you. Tell me, what can you possibly teach me that I do not already know."

The monk answered, "I can show you the door to hell and the door to heaven."

The warrior was infuriated. He screamed, "How dare you! Get out of my way before I kill you."

The monk answered, "That is the door to hell."

Suddenly, the warrior felt bad and said, "I am so sorry. I guess I lost my temper."

The monk replied, "And that is the door to heaven."

This story is similar to another one often told, and encourages people to be kind to each other. A man asks an angel to show him heaven and hell. First, he is taken to hell. He sees a room full of people sitting at tables with delicious food. But everybody is crying. He notices that the people have no elbows; they cannot bend their arms. Then he is taken to heaven. Here too is a room full of people sitting at tables with delicious food. Here too the people have no elbows. But everybody is laughing and having a great time. He asks, "What is the difference?"

The angel answers, "In heaven they feed each other."

The theme of both of these stories is the same. Heaven and hell are something that we create in this world. My tradition is not about getting to heaven in the next world, but creating heaven in this world. Too often we miss that urgent point.

What about the next world? We Jews speak about *Gan Eden* (Garden of Eden), the place where righteous souls go in the next world. We speak about *Gehinom* (literally the valley of Hinom, a valley near Jerusalem where child sacrifice used to take place.) That is where sinners go in the next world. But even for sinners, the maximum punishment is for one year.

Rabbinic sources often wax poetic on what life is like in *Gan Eden*, and alternatively on the horrors of *Gehinom*. But the final description is kept deliberately vague.

Let me share my vision of what happens when we reach the next world. Imagine a child sent to the market with a grocery list and money, and he buys what he is supposed to buy. Now imagine that same child sent to the market, who buys candy and toys instead.

What would it be like when each child returns home and faces his or her parents? I imagine that we are like those children sent into this world with a job to do. Suppose we did our best to fulfill our mission and do the right thing on this earth. We can face our Creator with assurance of acceptance. That is heaven. Now suppose we wasted our life, pursued meaningless pleasure, acted cruelly towards others. We face our Creator with fear and trembling. That is hell.

My tradition believes in life after death. But the key question we each must face is – when we lived, did we create heaven on earth or did we create hell on earth?

Rabbi Michael Gold, A Rabbi's Guide to Being Human

◆◆◆

Fulfilling "Love Adonai Your God"

It happened on one occasion that a heavenly voice informed the Besht that a certain shepherd worshipped the Holy Blessed One even better than himself. He had a deep yearning to see this shepherd face to face. He had his horses tied up to his wagon, and he traveled there with his students.

He approached the foothills of a mountain on which a shepherd was sounding his horn to gather his sheep. When the sheep gathered, the shepherd brought them to a pond of water to have them drink, and at that moment he began to speak in a loud voice:

Master of the Universe, you created the heavens and the earth, this mountain and these sheep, the one who owns these sheep, as well as me and Your people Israel. You sustain all your creatures, and fulfill all my needs. I, who am a simple, ignorant man, do not know how to worship You, and how to praise Your name. With this horn in my hand, I will make a loud sound, as with a shofar, and I shall proclaim: "Adonai is God – Adonai Hu HaElohim."

The shepherd puffed with all his strength into the horn, and suddenly he fainted. When he awakened, he began to speak:

Master of the Universe, Who created heaven and earth, You provide for all creatures, You created both these sheep and me, and You have one nation, since You are one, a nation that studies Your Torah and prays to You. But I am but a simple shepherd, who does not know either Torah or prayer, since I have been an orphan since my youth, and I grew up among Gentiles, and all I can do is sing to You some of the songs of shepherds.

The simple shepherd began to sing with all his might, with great enthusiasm, until he fell to the ground, weak and pale. When his strength returned he began to speak:

Master of the Universe, I blew my horn, I sang songs to You, but are these are important in Your eyes, Master of the World, who brings food and sustenance to all?

What else can I do to worship You, our Father in Heaven? I am able to do one more thing, and I will do it for Your glory.

When he finished speaking, he stood on his head, feet up in the air, and waved his feet this way and that. Then, he stood again on his feet, and again stood on his head, feet in the air. He repeated this over and over until he fell to the ground. When his strength returned he concluded:

Master of the Universe, I sound my horn, I sang songs to You, I stood upside down for Your glory, but is this important to You, our Father in Heaven? What else can I do to worship You?

Last night the owner of the sheep made a feast for his servants, and gave each one a gift of a coin of silver. Me too he gave a silver coin, and this coin I contribute to You as my gift, O God.

The shepherd threw the silver coin up in the air, and the Besht saw a hand reach down from Heaven and accepted it.

The Besht said to his pupils: This shepherd fulfilled "And you shall love Adonai your God with all your heart, with all your might, and with all Your soul."

From "Hakh-may Lev," ed. Simcha Raz,
Translated by Rabbi Dov Peretz Elkins

◆◆◆

The Smart Woman

In his book, *Days of Awe*, Nobel Prize winner S.Y. Agnon tells the story of a woman so enamored with planning that her dreams, quite literally, broke apart.

There once was a poor countrywoman who had many hungry children whom she was unable to feed. One day she found an egg. Calling her children together the woman cried out, "We have nothing to worry about any more; I've found an egg.

And being a smart woman, we will not eat this egg. Instead, I will ask our neighbor permission to put it under her hen until a chick is hatched.

And being a smart woman, we will not eat the chicken but instead set her on her eggs until they hatch into chickens and produce many eggs of their own.

And being a smart woman we will not eat the chickens or the eggs but will sell them and buy a cow.

And we'll not eat the cow but wait until it calves and its calves calve.

And being a smart woman we will not eat any of the cows but rather buy a field. Then we will have fields and cows and calves and chickens and eggs and we won't need anything anymore!"

While the woman was speaking, the egg fell out of her pocket and broke.

Said Agnon, we are no different from this woman. "When the [High] Holy Days arrive, everyone resolves to do *teshuvah* (repentance), thinking in his heart: 'I'll do this and I'll do that.' But the days slip by in mere talk, and talk doesn't lead to action."

◆◆◆

Is it Okay to Have Doubts?

A bit of doubt is healthy. It can teach us some humility. But, can we doubt the existence of God? Perhaps the Hasidic story of the rebbe who lived many years ago in the old country, who told his followers that everything that exists, can teach us something.

One Hasid asks, "What can we learn from a train?"

The rebbe answers, "We learn about leadership. One car full of energy can pull a string of cars with no energy."

Another Hasid asks, "What can we learn from a telephone?" The rebbe answers, "We learn about gossip. What is said over here can be heard over there."

Finally, a third Hasid, hoping to get the best of the rebbe, asks, "What can we learn from atheism, doubting the existence of God?"

The rebbe answers, "Atheism teaches us the most important lesson of all. We should always think there is no God. When your fellow is in trouble, do not say God will provide. Perhaps there is no God, and you need to provide."

Even doubt about God serves a purpose. If there is no God, we must act in God's stead.

Rabbi Michael Gold

The Power Of Renewal

Reb Shlomo zt"l was once flying to upstate New York for a concert, and sitting next to him on the plane was a holy non-Jewish brother. Reb Shlomo got into a conversation with him, and he told Reb Shlomo that in his community, about 40 families had broken away from the church in order to form a community that was wanting to really pray, to really learn.

Reb Shlomo saw that this man was a very special holy soul. A few minutes before landing, Reb Shlomo felt that he wanted to share a holy Torah thought with this man. Reb Shlomo, who always had a *sefer*, (holy book) with him, simply opened the book on his lap, and started teaching from the first Torah lesson he saw on the page before him. And this is what he taught:

There is a question, Why does the holy Torah start with the word "*bereishis*", which is usually translated as "in the beginning"? Would we not otherwise have known when God created the universe? The Torah does not even have any superfluous letters, and certainly not any superfluous words! So then why does the Torah not start simply, "God created heaven and earth"? Should anyone ask you: "When did Hashem do this"?, you would certainly answer, "It was in the beginning."

There is an entire Kabbalah *sefer*, the *Tikkunei Zohar*, in which there are seventy different answers to this question alone. The Beis Yakov gives the following answer:

This is a teaching from a rabbi who lived about one hundred and fifty years ago, the holy Beis Yakov. The Beis Yakov says that the word *bereishis* – in the beginning, is not intended to tell us *when* God created the universe. Rather the Torah is teaching us – "*Bereishis*" – with the power of renewal, "*bara Elokim es hashomayim v'es ha'aretz* – God created heaven and earth. Meaning that God put the power of renewal into the creation.

Why is it that when you are feeling down, and you go for a walk in the forest, fifteen minutes later you find yourself feeling better? It is because of the power of renewal that Hashem put into the creation. Walking in the forest connects you with the power of renewal, that is what is refreshing you. At this point the plane landed, and Reb Shlomo and this young man parted in friendship and love.

About two or three years later, Reb Shlomo was once again in Poughkeepsie, New York. At his concert, Reb Shlomo noticed a very special couple with a young child, sitting in the front row. During intermission, the couple came over to greet Reb Shlomo. The woman said to Reb Shlomo, "I don't know if you remember my husband, but a couple of years ago, he was sitting next to you on a plane flying to Poughkeepsie and you taught him a teaching from a Rabbi who lived about 150 years ago?" Reb Shlomo immediately remembered the young man.

"You know, that teaching saved my husband's life! At the time you met my husband, he was a multi-millionaire. About six months later, something went wrong in his business and he lost all his money. It was very hard for him to live with his downfall and he decided to commit suicide. My husband is a very organized and methodical man. So he had everything planned out. He chose a date, and at 7:30 in the evening he was going to commit this final act. At 7:15 my husband sat down at his desk in the study, to write his last letter to us. He finished the letter five minutes before 7:30, signed it and put it in an envelope. My husband is a religious man, so he always kept a Bible on his desk. Since there were a couple of minutes left, he thought he would take one last look in the Bible. He flipped it open, and staring him in his face were the words, 'In the beginning, God created heaven and earth'. And he remembered you taught him, 'With the power of renewal, God created heaven and earth.' My husband closed the Bible and came up to my room. He said to me, 'remember a few years ago, I met a Rabbi on a plane, who taught me a lesson from a Rabbi who lived along time ago, about the power of renewal, about starting again. Will you please help me start again, my holy wife?' And so here we are. We thank God, and with all our hearts, we came to thank you."

Transcribed by R' Sholom Brodt

◆◆◆

Lost in the Forest

The Holy Rebbe of Tzanz used to tell parables during the third meal of Shabbos during the month of Elul which proceeds Rosh HaShanah. One of his parables was:

There were two people lost in a forest. One of them was going alone and he was lost for many days in the forest, and he had no idea of the right way to go to get out of the forest. Suddenly, he saw another person in the forest coming towards him. Great excitement rose in his heart that now, finally, there would be someone to show him the correct way out of the forest. When they came to each other, he asked him, "Brother, can you tell me the best way to go out of the forest? I have been lost in this forest for many days."

The second one answered him, "I cannot tell you what is the proper way. I have also been lost here for many days. However, there is one thing I can tell you. The way that I have been going you should not go. It is not the correct way. Come, let us together choose a new way."

When the Rebbe finished the story, there were tears in his eyes from emotion. Then he said, "I am not able to tell you anything except this. The way in which we have been going until now, we should no longer follow. This way is an error. Let us try for ourselves a new way."

Sefer Otzer HaChaim, Customs of the Holy Rebbe Chaim of Tzanz

◆◆◆

Fairy Tales, Treasure and Teshuvah

"The secret things belong to Hashem ... For this Mitzvah is not hidden from you, nor far away across the sea ... it is close to you, and you can perform it."

Once there was a boy who sat under a beautiful oak tree in his backyard, swinging upon a wooden swing. He had a dream. In his dream he saw a magnificent palace with tall stone walls around it. The walls had seven gates, and next to one of the gates was a statue of a lion. On the side of the lion, beneath the ground, was buried a huge treasure.

The boy woke up, but each day the dream came back to him. And so the boy finally decided that he must have this treasure. He packed his belongings and journeyed to that far-off land. He found the palace and approached it, circling the wall until he came to the Lion Gate. He took out a small shovel and was about to start digging when a burly guard approached him.

"No one digs here!" said the guard, "This is the king's property and no one else's!"

"But there is a treasure here. I dreamt of it and I must find it!" said the boy.

The guard laughed. "Silly boy, there is no treasure here! But it's a funny thing that you say you having been dreaming about the treasure. Because, for the last many nights, I myself have dreamt that there is a great treasure located far from here, hidden under a swing that is held by the branches of a large oak tree!"

Understanding that he could not finish his quest to dig on the king's property, the boy returned to his home.

Sitting in his backyard, the boy remembered the guard's dream and started to think about it. Sure enough, there was a treasure hidden under the swing, right where the guard had dreamed it was.

The treasure, THE unique Mitzva of which the Torah speaks, is none other than Teshuvah, the God-given ability to "re-boot," to go back, to take back the mistakes we've made and return *ourselves* to a more pristine condition.

Could there be a more precious gift than this, the opportunity to start over and get it right? It's something we can do right now, today, in our own home, in our own room – and it can – and will – change our lives for the better.

When Dorothy despairs of ever being able to go home, Glinda the Good Witch of the North points to Dorothy's ruby slippers and says, "You have had the power all along, my dear!" And so do we.

We have the power, anytime we choose, to come home, to return. Not to Kansas, but to Torah, to Israel, to Hashem. We just have to tap into our thoughts, and turn to Hashem, and He show us the proper path to return.

Rabbi Stewart Weiss

Jewish Survival

The dramatic announcement by scientists that, despite the Biblical promise, the entire world would be engulfed by a massive flood in just three days' time. The media then allowed several clergy to issue a global proclamation.

The priest addressed his congregants and told them that they should hurry and try to do all the things they longed to do in the short time still left to them.

The imam spoke to his flock and urged them to make amends over the next three days with anyone they may have wronged.

The rabbi then delivered his message to one and all: "People, we have exactly 72 hours to learn how to survive – underwater."

◆◆◆

Tzedakah

A very rich, but miserly man passed away and was standing in line waiting to hear his final judgment. As he watched the procedure with those in line before him, he became far less fearful. He noticed that reported acts of charity had tremendous influence on the Divine decree; gifts given during one's lifetime would outweigh many sins.

And so when it was this rich man's turn to stand before the heavenly judge, he said: "It's true, I may not have done all I should have while I was on earth, but permit me to take out my checkbook and write out very large donations for any worthy institutions you recommend."

To which the judge replied, "Here we do not accept checks. We only accept receipts."

◆◆◆

Bird of Good Fortune

In most kingdoms, when a king died, his son or daughter succeeded to the throne after him. Not so in this kingdom. When the king died, a special bird, called the "bird of good fortune" was released. This bird flew around, and the person upon whose head it finally landed became the next king. A curious custom indeed.

In this same kingdom, there was a slave who lived and worked in the king's palace. This slave was a musician, who entertained the king, his family, and guests by dressing in funny clothing – including a cap made of chicken feathers and a belt made from the hooves of sheep – and playing music on a drum.

It came to pass that the king died one day, and the "bird of fortune" was released. It circled in the sky some time, while the people of the kingdom watched in wonderment. Finally, it came to rest on the head of the slave, nesting itself in his hat of chicken feathers. Immediately, and to his surprise and consternation, he was declared king of the entire kingdom, and in an instant, the slave was transformed into a powerful sovereign.

The slave moved into the quarters of the king, donned his royal attire, and sat upon his throne. As his first royal decree, he had a shack built next to the palace and there he kept his chicken-feather hat, belt, and drum – the vestiges of his life as a slave. The only furnishing in the entire shack was a large mirror. Every day, the new king visited the little hut, disappearing behind the door for a short time. Then he would emerge, and lock the door behind him. His ministers and advisors thought this very peculiar behavior, but after all, he was the king now and who would question the king?

As the years went on, the new king passed many laws aimed at reducing slavery and suffering. The changes were made gradually, so gradually that no one noticed them. The king was known to all for his kindness and compassion, as well as his peculiar habit of visiting the odd little hut once a day.

One day, his closest advisor asked, "Your majesty, what is it that you keep in that hut of yours?"

"My most treasured possessions!" the king replied, and he led the advisor into the hut and showed him the chicken-feather hat, the belt, and the drum.

"But these are things of a slave!" the advisor replied in disgust. "These are not the possessions of a king, Your Majesty!"

"Ah, but they are," replied the king. "You see, once I was a slave and now I am free. When you made me your king, I promised myself and God that I would never forget that I was once a slave, lest I grow arrogant and haughty, and treat people as I was once treated. Every morning, I come here and dress as I was once forced to dress as a slave. I stare at myself in the mirror until tears come to my eyes, and only then am I prepared to leave this hut and rule as a good king should. It is this memory which makes me the king that I am. These are the most treasured possessions I have."

This week we begin the month of Elul and soon Tishrei and the High Holidays, when the gates of teshuvah (repentance) and forgiveness are open wide waiting for our souls' return. Elul is the month to look in the mirror, to remember who we once were and what we are capable of becoming. This past year, we have all had successes and failures, doors opened and others closed. We must learn from the past year, and seek out change, for we all have the capacity to transform and give ourselves second and third chances. The act of Teshuvah or Repentance means changing, turning our course around, seeking forgiveness and returning to a better, higher, more ascendant place.

The Hasidic Master the Maggid of Zlotchov taught, "Every person born into this world represents something new, something that never existed before, unique and original and is called upon to fulfill one's particular mission in this world." We don't forget ourselves and our past, when we seek to transform; we learn from our past – like the king who each day recalled his life as a slave to better serve his kingdom.

During the month of Elul, may we all change for the better, like the slave who became king. May the bird of good fortune land on our heads – or at least we can each seek to make our kingdom – our world, our community and family, more than a little better and prepare ourselves for the coming new year through repentance, tzedakah, and prayer.

♦♦♦

Taking Responsibility – the First Step to Change

In 1937, Frank Lloyd Wright built a home for a prestigious businessman. One rainy evening, as the businessman was entertaining colleagues, the roof began to leak directly over the businessman's chair at the head of the table. The man called Wright on the phone and said, "Frank, you built us a beautiful house, but the roof leaks. I'm entertaining a bunch of guests right now and the water is dripping directly on my head!"

Wright replied, "Well, then move your chair."

As it is with leaky roofs, so it is with our lives; if we don't take responsibility for our errors, we cannot fix them.

♦♦♦

Lost – And Found – In Israel

I thank and acknowledge You, O living and eternal King, for having compassionately returned my soul to me; great is Your faith (in me).

Prayer upon awakening, the "Modeh Ani"

On the day I arrived in Israel, a quarter of a century ago, my close friend who had already been living here for several years offered me a piece of wisdom that continues to support and strengthen my *Aliya*. He told me: "No doubt you will face a lot of challenges in the years ahead, and no lack of disappointments. There will be times when you will be so frustrated, so disenchanted with life in this country that you will even contemplate leaving. But then, something will happen, either to you personally or to the country as a whole, that will reaffirm your decision, and remind you what an amazing place this can be."

Not long ago, a relative of ours, we'll call her Kari, was visiting the Grand Canyon in Arizona. Stopping to take a picture at the magnificent Mooney Falls, she accidentally dropped her phone. It fell into a whirlpool below and vanished. Kari let out a scream, not only because a smart phone today is a compact library, symphony and lifeline all in one, but because she is a serial picture-taker and her precious phone contained thousands of photos and videos. She and her friends searched for hours, but couldn't find the phone; she even returned the next day and looked again, but to no avail. The phone had vanished.

Fast forward one month. A group of Israeli kids were rafting near the canyon – is there any place on Earth that Israelis AREN'T visiting?! – when one of them spotted the water-logged phone. He thought he would discard it, but another boy took it and said, "It's an important mitzvah to return a lost article; I'm going to somehow find the owner and get it back to him or her." So the young man removed the memory card, which was intact, and scrolled through the pictures until he came upon a screenshot of Kari's Facebook page. He looked up the names visible in the picture and then searched through all their friends until, lo and behold, he finally saw a name he recognized; it was that of my son, with whom he served in the army! So he took the phone back with him to Israel, and gave it to our family.

Some time later, Kari came on her first trip to Israel and was reunited with her precious phone/photo album. She called her rescuer and pleaded to send him a reward. He refused any compensation; "Mitzvot are their own reward," he told her.

"Well, let me at least come and thank you in person," she asked. "I'm studying in Yeshiva now," he replied, "so I don't have much free time. Just knowing you got back your phone is thanks enough."

This is one of those feel-good stories that help to restore our faith in the kindness of strangers and the goodness of others. But as I thought about the concept of Lost and Found, it struck me as being particularly relevant to the current month of Elul, and our fast-approaching New Year.

In a way, many of us also find ourselves "lost" at times. We wander dizzily and directionless through the days as they frantically speed by us, wondering where we are going with our lives and how we are spending the precious, finite minutes which our Creator has loaned to us. It is precisely that sentiment we express each morning when we open our eyes and recite the *Modeh Ani*, thanking God for returning to us our soul, which lay dormant throughout the night in a state of semi-death. And we are buoyed by the knowledge that if the Almighty, in His eternal wisdom, saw fit to give us another day of life, then He must surely believe in our ability to make good use of that life.

Though Elul is devoid of any Jewish holidays, it does contain the custom of sounding the Shofar each morning. That sound is meant to be a bell, a beacon to those struggling to find their way out, to find their way home. It is a call to lose our uncertainty, our self-doubt, our incitement and our in-fighting; and to find our common ground, our collective soul and the absolute confidence that we are not sacrifices to, but shapers of our own glorious future.

Rabbi Stewart Weiss

◆◆◆

Promises to God

A man was driving down the street frantically looking for a parking space. He had an important meeting and was running late. Not a space was in sight. In desperation, the man turned toward heaven and prayed:

"Hashem, if you find me a parking space, I promise to only eat kosher food, and stop speaking lashon hara."

Suddenly, the parking space in front of him opened up. The man looked back up and said, "Never mind, Hashem, I found one!"

This story drives home two points. First, it demonstrates our tendency to turn to God only in times of trouble and crisis. Secondly, this story points out that although we may make all kinds of changes and commitments to God during our time of need, we often forget about our promises when we no longer "need" Hashem's assistance.

◆◆◆

The Secret of the Shofar

Blessed are those who have learned to acclaim you, who walk in the light of your presence, Lord.

Psalm 89:15

Jews around the world are observing the most holy time on the Jewish calendar, the High Holy Days. Beginning with Rosh Hashanah, the Jewish New Year, and ending ten days later with Yom Kippur, the Day of Atonement, this season is marked by intense reflection and repentance. This is one of 18 devotions focused on this holy season, exploring its meaning and the many lessons we can learn from this biblically mandated observance.

My friend Jonathan had been pulled over by the police for talking on the phone and driving at the same time. The officer immediately started with his diatribe, scolding Jonathan and explaining to him that he had earned himself a sizable fine and points on his license. Jonathan's wife tried making excuses. The officer seemed to anticipate an argument and only got louder and stronger.

Finally, Jonathan said something that stopped the officer mid-sentence. He said, "You are right. Hand me the ticket." The officer's mouth hung open as if he had suddenly forgotten how to talk. He obviously didn't hear that too often!

Jonathan continued saying how wrong and dangerous it was to talk and drive at the same time and even thanked the officer for calling him on it. It was a lesson that he needed to learn. The officer walked away for a moment and when he came back, his demeanor had totally changed. He handed back Jonathan's license and registration with a smile and a kind warning – but no ticket.

Tradition teaches that when we blow the shofar on Rosh Hashanah, God our King, who is sitting on His throne of judgment, gets up and takes the seat of compassion. With just one piercing sound, the day is transformed from a day of stern judgment into a day of merciful compassion. Why?

These days, at the start of a trial, the judge bangs his gavel in order to bring the court to order. But in the olden days, a Jewish trial began with the sounding of the shofar. So when we blow the shofar, it is as though we are willingly starting our trial. We initiate the judgment. It is as if we are saying to God, "hand me the ticket – give me my penalty! I know that I am guilty."

We recognize that we have done things wrong and we accept our verdict, acknowledging that it is for our own good. In response, God switches his mode from judgment to one of compassion.

The psalmist writes: "Blessed are those who have learned to acclaim you ..." The Hebrew for "to acclaim you" in this verse is *teruah*. As you may recall, *teruah* is also the name of the nine-note shofar blast. So the Jewish sages interpret this verse to mean: "Blessed are those who know the secret of the shofar blast." The secret of the shofar blast is that it unleashes God's mercy.

Jewish tradition teaches "when there is judgment below, there is no need for judgment above." In other words, when we are able to take responsibility for our shortcomings on our own, God doesn't have to correct our behavior for us. Instead, He hands out His love and mercy.

Rabbi Yechiel Eckstein

♦♦♦

Israel's Hidden Heroes

Shortly after arriving in Israel from the Soviet Union, Natan Sharansky was asked how he felt going from a country with abundant natural resources – Russia is a leader in oil production, along with Saudi Arabia – to a country with almost no natural resources (this was before the discovery of substantial gas fields here). Sharansky replied that Israel's prime resource was ABOVE the ground, not below it – in the person of stellar, golden human beings who possess priceless qualities of intelligence, creativity and integrity.

We have an amazing propensity – despite our hard-shell exterior – for performing acts of kindness for others, for volunteering and for "filling in the gaps" that our government and social services may not always be able to provide. Israel is a rich country with poor people – or is it a poor country with rich people?! – that survives so well because so many everyday, simple, good people step up and decide to do something extra to make life more livable for those in need.

The extended Rachamim family lives a few blocks away from me. Their two adjoining homes are modest, with an expansive yard that takes up a half-block. The Rachamims have a "family business:" They distribute virtually every kind of item to the less fortunate. Clothes of all types, children's toys and games, used appliances, shoes, linens, pots, pans and dishes are stockpiled on their property. People from throughout the city drop off their used items, and others come by to browse and choose the things they need.

Three generations of the family lovingly help them – they have been doing this for more than a decade now, the parents and grandparents training their children to take part – and they ask for one or two shekels in payment. "To make the people feel that they are buying, getting a 'metzia,' rather than simply taking charity," explains grandmother Batsheva. The money collected is then given to the poor.

On Friday afternoon, the family goes to the various bakeries in town, who donate their challot that weren't sold that day, and then give them out to dozens of people who come by before Shabbat looking for the Shabbat bread.

I asked grandfather Shaul what inspires him to keep this project going, week after week; why he goes out of his way to help so many. He looks at me with a curious stare and simply says, "It's what we do."

Vici restaurant in Ra'anana does more than serve delicious food; it sponsors a unique program called Pay It Forward. Diners can purchase a voucher for soldiers to enjoy a free meal any time they like. They pin a note on the bulletin board with a message to the soldiers – "This is the least we can do for you, for keeping all of us safe," reads one note there – and soldiers come in, usually on Thursday and Friday, when they return home for Shabbat. Owner Idan Ianovici was once a lone soldier himself in the artillery corps, and fondly remembers the falafel shops and cafes that reached out to him when he was hungry and in uniform. After returning to the U.S. and working at various restaurants – including Katz's Deli in New York – he came back to Israel and opened his own place. "Life's not just about the money," he says, "you've got to give something back."

Speaking of lone soldiers ... Wendy Serlin and Gayle Shimoff moved to Ra'anana twenty years ago, and later became neighbors in Bet Shemesh. Both have children serving in the IDF. During Operation Protective Edge in 2014, as they worried about their own sons in combat units, they wondered how lone soldiers could better be provided for when far away from their families: Who would do their laundry, give them a home-cooked meal, where would they go when on leave?

And so they embarked on an ambitious project, to create a home-away-from-home for lone soldiers. They called a meeting of the community and began to fund-raise. They contacted the Michael Levin Center for Lone Soldiers and Bayit Shel Benji in Ra'anana for advice. They rented a home and furnished it with new beds, washing machines, dryers and other essential equipment. They collected donations from the community of furniture, pictures, a stereo and computers; all the things to make soldiers feel at home. And they hired a young couple as counselors.

Today, 12 soldiers live in the home, all from English-speaking countries. They no longer are without family; thanks to Wendy and Gayle – two energetic ladies who saw a need and filled it – they have been adopted by an entire community. (www.lonesoldiercenter. com)

The current Hebrew month of Elul is the gateway to the High Holidays of Tishrei when, on Rosh Hashanah and Yom Kippur, we join together with our congregations to offer communal prayers for repentance and God's blessing. But Elul is more about the individual mission to engage in introspection, to correct our misdeeds, and to somehow raise our personal level of goodness and holiness so that we might approach our Creator with confidence and strength. The symbol of this effort is the Shofar; it calls us to action as it is sounded each morning. The word "Shofar" comes from the Hebrew, "L'Hishtaper," to improve oneself. Each of us can certainly do something to better the lives of others and, in so doing, change our own lives.

Do not ask for whom the Shofar blows, it blows for thee.

Rabbi Stewart Weiss

How the Silver Torah Survived the Nazis

Our story takes us back 100 years to Dusseldorf, Germany. Shlomo Pfeiffer had recently been discharged from the Kaiser's army. Thank God, he had survived the heavy fighting of World War I, and was now back with his family.

Two years earlier, during the High Holiday season of 1916, just before going off to fight, he had made a vow in the presence of his wife and children: "If I come home safe and sound, I will donate a Sefer Torah of the highest quality to be used by our community."

Now alive and well, and full of gratitude to God, he turned to his friend Rabbi Dr. Emanuel Carlebach, who lived in the city of Cologne, and asked him to help arrange the procurement of the new Torah scroll from Poland.

A year later, the long-awaited scroll was welcomed to its new home. It was exceptionally beautiful, made of the best parchment with the clearest writing. The *atzei chayim* (handles) were made of pure silver. Indeed, the Torah was to become known to all as the "Silver Sefer Torah."

Housed in the Adas Israel synagogue in Dusseldorf, the Torah was treated with deference, and was read only on Shabbat and the holidays. During the week, other Torahs (four of which were donated by the Pfeiffers) were used.

A year after the Torah was donated, Shlomo's son, Julius (Yoel), had his bar mitzvah, and of course, read the entire portion from the Silver Torah.

Years passed, and the dark cloud of Nazism began descending on Europe. Although Julius had graduated from law school, and even ascended to the bench of the Superior Court in Dusseldorf, as a Jew in 1933 Germany he was forced to resign from his position.

Reading the writing on the wall, Julius left for Holland. Instead of being an established public servant in the city where his family had lived for generations, Julius found himself an unknown and penniless refugee.

In 1936, he married his life partner, Flora, who joined him in Holland, where they would have two sons.

In 1937, Julius could not fathom just how terrible it would be for Jews in Germany, but he was concerned for his parents' property. In his parents' home there was a safe filled with valuable gold coins. He sent a trusted courier to his parents with a note: "Give this man the most valuable items."

A few days passed, and the messenger returned with the Silver Torah. His parents' concept of what was valuable was visibly different from his own.

Then came November 9, 1938. Known as Kristallnacht, that night saw the destruction of Jewish businesses and places of worship all over Germany. The Adas Israel synagogue was destroyed, and the other Torah scrolls there were burned. Because of the misunderstood letter (or, better said, by Divine Providence), the Silver Torah was safe.

A few months later, Julius was joined by his parents and father-in-law (his mother-in-law was no longer alive). But their tranquility did not last long. On May 10, 1940, the Nazis invaded Holland. Julius escaped to England four days later, not expecting that his family would be trapped on the continent. His parents and in-laws were deported to unknown destinations. Considered an enemy prisoner of war, Julius was soon sent off to Canada with a group of Jewish men. He lost all communication with his wife and children.

Meanwhile, Flora hid her older son with non-Jews, and went into hiding with her baby. They were discovered and sent to Westerbork, and then to Bergen-Belsen. With God's help, they survived.

In Westerbork, Flora was once standing near the entrance of the camp and recognized Shlomo, her father-in-law, as he was being marched to his death. (Westerbork served as a way station for Jews being shipped to the death camps in Poland.) Seeing his daughter-in-law, Shlomo discreetly whispered, "The Torah is with a craftsman in South Amsterdam." Before he could share any more details, he was whisked away by a Nazi guard, and she never saw him again.

After liberation, Flora went to Amsterdam and was reunited with her son. She then set about searching for the Silver Torah. Days and weeks passed, and she trudged between shops in Southern Amsterdam. There was almost no craftsman in the vicinity she did not visit. But she could not find the Torah.

Ready to give up, she decided to give it one more day.

She knocked on the door of a skilled craftsman, hoping that he would be the one. A gentleman with graying hair greeted her. After she explained the reason for her visit, he became thoughtful, and then said, "I don't know if this is what you are looking for; however, a while back, a German Jew entrusted me with a 'Jewish Bible.'"

He left for a moment and returned with a large, wrapped package. She did not need to remove the wrapping to ascertain that this was the Sefer Torah.

When she joined her husband in Canada, Flora came with the precious Silver Torah.

It was with a mixture of joy and sadness that Julius Pfeiffer witnessed his grandsons read from the Silver Torah at their bar mitzvahs, as did his numerous great-grandchildren.

Julius passed away in 1997 and Flora passed away in 1998, but the scroll, which tells the story of a family's devotion to Torah, is still read on a regular basis in the Agudath Israel synagogue in Montreal.

The story was adapted from Julius's firsthand account as published in the Jewish Observer (Oct. 1976), as well as a telling in Sichat Hashavua (#409, 1996) with information submitted by Mrs. Leah Neubauer.

Elchonon Isaacs, www.chabad.org

So, Shimshon, did you see My Alps?

In his later years, the renowned Rabbi Samson Raphael Hirsch (1808-1888), suddenly announced that he was going to Switzerland before Rosh Hashanah to climb in the Alps.

"Why?" asked his astonished students.

"Because, when I come face to face with the Creator of the universe," mused Hirsch, "I know He will look down at me and say 'So, Shimshon, did you see My Alps?'"

Appreciating beauty is an act of devotion. That is why Judaism contains blessings for seeing beautiful mountains, the ocean, a rainbow, and other natural sights.

To sing to God, and not to see God's world, is a contradiction.

♦♦♦

The Whale

If this doesn't bring tears to your eyes and a tug in your heart, I'm not sure what will...

The Whale... There was a female humpback whale who had become entangled in a spider's web of crab traps and lines near San Francisco. She was weighed down by hundreds of pounds of traps that caused her to struggle to stay afloat. She also had hundreds of yards of line rope wrapped around her body, her tail, her torso, a line tugging in her mouth.

A fisherman spotted her just east of the Farallon Islands (outside the Golden Gate) and radioed an environmental group for help. Within a few hours, the rescue team arrived and determined that she was so badly off, the only way to save her was to dive in and untangle her. They worked for hours with curved knives and eventually freed her.

When she was free, the divers say she swam in what seemed like joyous circles. She then came back to each and every diver, one at a time, and nudged them, pushed them gently around as she was thanking them. Some said it was the most incredibly beautiful experience of their lives. The guy who cut the rope out of her mouth said her eyes were following him the whole time, and he will never be the same.

May you, and all those you love, be so blessed and fortunate to be surrounded by people who will help you get untangled from the things that are binding you. And, may you always know the joy of giving and receiving gratitude.

◆◆◆

Heaven – Or Higher?!

It was the first night of Selichot and the rabbi was in a rush to get to the shul on time. But just as he was about to leave the house, his wife asked him to help put the baby to bed.

"Of course," he said, and softly whispered the words of *Ashrei*, the opening psalm of Selichot. "*Karov Hashem l'chal kor'av*; God is close to all who call out to Him!"

On his way to the shul, the rabbi bumped into one of his congregants, who said he urgently needed to talk about the dire difficulties he was having with one of his children. The rabbi nervously glanced at his watch, but stopped to hear the man's tale and offer some wise advice.

Thought the rabbi: "He who sits in glory directs His attention *'lishmo'a el ha-rina v'el ha-t'fila*," to listen to the song and the prayer, as the key *piyut* of Selichot goes. "And is this man's 'song,' sad as it may be, not worth listening to?!"

Meanwhile, at the shul, the assembled were buzzing about the rabbi's absence. "How can he be late on such an important night, the 'opening' of the High Holiday season?!" said one.

"Maybe he's in Heaven, having a chat with the Almighty!" said another.

The Chazan carried on, hoping nothing serious had occurred.

As the rabbi now hurriedly ran to the service, he passed an elderly lady struggling with her packages, one of which had fallen to the ground.

"Should I stop to help her?" he said to himself. "But I'm so late already!" Shrugging his shoulders, he picked up the fallen package and walked the woman to her nearby house. On the way, he recited: "Please, God; do not cast us out in our old age," echoing the *Sh'ma Koleynu* prayer, "when our strength falters, do not forsake us!"

Now hopelessly late, the rabbi hoped that he would still be able to get to shul before the service was over, and that he would have a moment to offer words of inspiration to the community, words that would help to secure Hashem's positive response on Rosh Hashanah and Yom Kippur.

"Hashem, do it for Your glory," he prayed as he ran.

"Do it for Your honor; Your righteousness; do it for Your great kindness, for Your love, for the great ones who sacrificed everything for You. Do it – if not for me – then for You, so Your name will be sanctified and You will save us."

The rabbi entered the sanctuary just as the Chazan was saying the final Kaddish. Huffing and puffing, he tried to explain why he had come so late, and then he begged the crowd to be *dan l'kaf z'chut*, to give him the benefit of the doubt, just as they, too, would soon request the same of Hashem.

"I think the rabbi was late because he was in Heaven," repeated a man.

"Perhaps even higher," smiled his friend.

Rabbi Stewart Weiss

◆◆◆

Rosh Hashanah

The Shofar Of Bergen-Belsen

Rosh Hashanah has come and gone on the calendar, but it never really goes away. It always takes me back several decades to my birthplace, the Hungarian city of Szeged.

My father, HaRav HaGaon HaTzaddik Avraham HaLevi Jungreis, zt"l, was a visionary. Long before the ba'al teshuvah movement of recent times, he reached out to everyone. In Szeged he built a shul, a mikveh, and a school for children. With his beautiful long beard and rabbinic hat and coat, he was a strange sight in that secular city. But "strange" quickly gave way to beloved.

My saintly father became the much-loved spiritual leader of the Jewish community. He was blessed with the most magical voice. When he chanted the prayers, they penetrated the deepest crevices of one's heart. They made one's soul soar to the greatest heights. No one could daven like him. It was not only his voice but also the genuine tears flowing from his eyes that gave an added dimension to every prayer he chanted.

Every Rosh Hashanah I would arrive early to shul with my saintly mother, Rebbetzin Miriam Jungreis, a"h. But as early as we came, there were always some elderly ladies already there, weeping as they recited their tefillos. Nowadays, if you go to shul and see someone crying with such intensity and devotion you would be prompted to go over and ask, "Is everything okay? Is someone sick, God forbid?"

In my father's shul it never occurred to us to do that. Of course, the women were crying. It was Rosh Hashanah – how could a Jew not cry on such a sacred day when the life of every person hangs in the balance?

It's a different world today. Yes, we know it's Rosh Hashanah, we know it's the Days of Awe, we know it's Yom Kippur, but we do not feel it.

Our grandmothers may not have been learned or sophisticated but they genuinely feared God and their tears ascended to their Maker. My revered father was not a chazzan but his voice rang with love of Hashem. And he inspired those who heard him to love Hashem as well.

Memories, crossing oceans and continents, penetrating the darkness and yet basking in the sunshine of Torah. It's all part of my mind's journey at this time of year.

Darkness? How can Rosh Hashanah exist in darkness? Are not Rosh Hashanah and darkness contradictory terms?

Come with me to Bergen-Belsen. Allow me to introduce you to my father. It's Rosh Hashanah. But where is one to find a shofar in that satanic place? Over there, there were only demons. But the demons of Bergen-Belsen did not realize with whom they were contending. There is no power on earth that can silence our shofar or the hearts and souls of our people. Our shofar is the shofar of Torah, the shofar of faith, the shofar of Mashiach. Time and again throughout the long painful and bloody centuries our enemies tried to destroy us but we triumphed, our shofar in hand, awaiting that final call of Redemption. Even those who stood on the lines to the gas chambers sang *"Ani Maamin* – I believe in the coming of Mashiach and even if He may tarry I believe."

In that hellhole of Bergen-Belsen my father and the other rabbanim held a secret meeting and concluded that a shofar must be obtained. They were determined that Rosh Hashanah would not pass without the sound of the shofar.

There was a black market in the camp and things could be acquired for the right price, especially if those "things" were Jewish ritual items. They were all in the junk pile waiting to be destroyed.

So it was through the heroic efforts of our people that 300 cigarettes – powerful currency in the camps – were collected to buy a shofar and a machzor.

But there was another problem. One shofar could be heard by multitudes but surely one machzor would not suffice. So once again our rabbis designed a plan. Everyone would learn at least one prayer to be recited from memory. But which prayer, which Psalm, which brachah? Surely all the supplications, all the Psalms, all the blessings in the machzor are holy. So which one should it be?

The decision was made: "Bochen Levavos – let us pray to Him who searches and tests our hearts on that Day of Judgment." Yes, we invited God to come to Bergen-Belsen and examine our hearts in order to see for Himself that despite our pain and suffering, we had not faltered one bit in our faith and our love for Him.

Adjacent to our compound was a Polish camp (the Nazis often kept nationalities separate). Somehow, our Polish brethren got wind of our treasure. So when Rosh Hashanah came and the piercing cry of the shofar was sounded, they crept close to the barbed wire fence separating us to hear the ancient call. The Nazis also came running and beat us mercilessly. But even as the truncheons were falling on our heads, we cried out, "Blessed is the Lord our God who has commanded us to listen to the sound of the shofar."

Many years later I was lecturing in Israel in a village in Samaria called Neve Aliza. It was just before Rosh Hashanah, and I felt a need to tell the story of the shofar of Bergen-Belsen. When I finished, a woman in the audience got up.

"I know exactly what you are talking about," she said, "because my father was the rabbi in the Polish compound. You may not realize this, but your shofar was smuggled into our camp in the bottom of a large garbage can filled with soup and my father blew the shofar for us."

I looked at her, momentarily speechless.

"And that's not all," she went on to say. "I have the shofar in my house, here in Neve Aliza. When we were liberated, we blew the shofar again and my father took it with him. Today I have it here in Eretz Yisrael."

With that, she ran home and returned a few minutes later with the shofar in her hands. We wept and embraced. Here we were, two little girls from Bergen-Belsen holding that shofar in the hills of Israel.

The entire world had declared us dead. Millions of our people had been slaughtered but the shofar, the symbol of Jewish piety, triumphed over the flames. And God granted me the awesome privilege of rediscovering that shofar in the ancient hills of Samaria to which our people had returned after more than two thousand years of wandering, darkness, oppression, and Holocaust.

The call of the shofar is eternal. Its magnetic allurement cannot be explained. It is not musical. Those who lack understanding might describe its sound as primitive. But when the Jewish people hear the cry, it's familiar. It awakens us. We heard that cry before and we remember it. We heard it at Sinai when it entered our souls and it is forever embedded in our collective memory, in our inner hearts, in our very neshamahs.

Consider what we have been destined to hear with our own ears and see with our own eyes. We Jews have traversed the world, surviving long, tortuous centuries. Many of us have forgotten our past but even the most assimilated among us have never forgotten that shofar, that call that pierced the heavens and the earth.

Our generation has been blessed to behold that which our Zaidies and Bubbies could only dream of. We heard and saw the chief rabbi of the Israeli army, Rabbi Shlomo Goren, blow the shofar at the Kotel and in Hebron and Kever Rochel after long centuries of exile. Its sound remains as fresh and inspiring as it was at Sinai. From

Bergen-Belsen to Eretz Yisrael and back to Sinai; that would seem to be sufficient reason for every Jew to stand in awe and say, "Hineni, here I am, ready to serve my God."

May the sound of the shofar that will summon us to welcome Mashiach be heard speedily in our own days.

Esther Jungreis

♦♦♦

The Shofar of Auschwitz

In a Nazi labor camp, Jewish prisoners blew the shofar on Rosh Hashanah, 1944. A group of ragged Jewish prisoners assembled for yet another exhausting work detail. All around, Jews were starved, tortured and murdered. The slightest expression of Jewish faith was strictly forbidden, grounds for execution by Nazi guards.

Yet on that Rosh Hashanah, a group of courageous Jews managed to pray with a minyan. Miraculously, they even managed to blow a shofar and evade detection. Prof. Judy Tydor Schwartz, the Director of Holocaust research at Bar Ilan University in Israel, is the daughter of the man who facilitated that astounding feat. In an Aish.com exclusive interview, she described her remarkable father, Chaskel Tydor, and his shofar.

When World War II broke out, Chaskel was 36 and living in Frankfurt with his wife Bertha and young children. They managed to send a son and daughter to relative safety in Belgium on the Kindertransport, a scheme that allowed Jewish children to escape Nazi Germany in 1939.

Later that year Chaskel was arrested and sent to Buchenwald concentration camp; in 1942 he was sent to a forced labor camp near Auschwitz. There, he learned that Bertha and other relatives had been murdered in Auschwitz.

Though he briefly succumbed to despair, Chaskel soon found meaning in helping others. "He had done all he could to save lives and help as many as he could retain their spirits and religious beliefs," Prof. Tydor Schwartz said. "He sent friends *mishloach manot* (gifts of food) on Purim when it meant he went without food to do so. He secretly lit Chanukah candles. He taught *Pirkei Avot* (Ethics of the Fathers) secretly in Buchenwald and later in Auschwitz."

Chaskel was named block secretary and worked arranging labor details for his fellow Jews. He used that position to help others, sending groups of prisoners to faraway sites where they could pray together as a group. On Rosh Hashanah in 1944, he scheduled a group of over ten Jewish prisoners to work in a remote location. It was understood that they would pray at least part of the Rosh Hashanah service.

When the men returned, they told Chaskel an astonishing secret: one of them had managed to smuggle a shofar into their work detail and they'd listened to its blasts. The thought that Jews had managed to fulfill the mitzvah of blowing a shofar, which is meant to rouse us out of spiritual slumber with its piercing sound, seemed to almost defy belief. Yet the men had done it, hearing the Rosh Hashanah shofar in the very shadow of Auschwitz's crematoria.

Prof. Tydor Schwartz hypothesizes that the shofar might have been smuggled into the camp after mid-1944, when 440,000 Hungarian Jews were deported to Auschwitz. Their belongings were warehoused in a vast area known by the nickname "Canada" and some Jewish prisoners succeeded in smuggling objects from there into Auschwitz.

In her research, Prof. Tydor Schwartz has come across many other stories of Jews defying Nazi guards and performing Jewish *mitzvot* and prayers during the Holocaust.

"The mother of one of my dearest friends is a religious survivor of Auschwitz in her mid-90s. She and her sister worked in the 'Canada' storehouse barracks and would try to smuggle out things, including religious artifacts, to the camp. My father and friends of his told me of the shofar and a pair of tefillin in Auschwitz."

Prof. Tydor Schwartz has also gathered first-person accounts of Jews constructing a makeshift sukkah secretly in Auschwitz, made out of an empty barrel.

"Of course if caught, they would have been killed," she said. "Even to stand and pray for a moment was dangerous."

In the beginning of 1945, with Allied troops advancing, the Nazis began blowing up the Auschwitz death camp and satellite labor camps. Chaskel Tydor and about 60,000 other Jewish prisoners were sent on a death march to another camp thirty miles away. The night before they left, a fellow prisoner came up to him and handed him a bundle wrapped in dirty rags: the precious shofar they'd sounded on Rosh Hashanah.

The man told Chaskel that he didn't think he'd survive the march, so he wanted Chaskel to take it. If Chaskel survived, the man instructed, he should tell the world that Jews blew the shofar in Auschwitz. Chaskel survived the war and moved to the land of Israel, then under British rule. As his ship approached the coast of Haifa on Rosh Hashanah in 1945, Chaskel blew the Auschwitz shofar once again, celebrating the Jewish New Year within sight of the Israeli city of Haifa.

In later years, Chaskel worked in America, where he met his wife Shirley Kraus and where his daughter Prof. Tydor Schwartz was born. He worked in New York, Montana and South Dakota, and eventually moved back to Israel. Everywhere he went, he took his precious shofar.

"My father would blow the shofar at home for those who could not go to shul to hear it – women with small children, ill, elderly. He would blow it for my grandmother when she was unable to walk to shul, for me when I gave birth, and for all the women in our building with small children who could not go to shul," Dr. Tydor Schwartz recounted.

"My father was extremely courageous and had a strong belief in God. He always tried to help as many as he could, even at great personal cost. He was a tremendous mensch and so much more. He may have been five foot two, but he was a giant of a man."

On September 23, 2019, her father's precious Auschwitz shofar came to America where it will be displayed in the Museum of Jewish Heritage in New York. But first it will be blown in some New York City synagogues on Rosh Hashanah, letting Jews once again hear the sounds that helped sustain Jewish prisoners in Auschwitz a generation ago.

She hopes his legacy and the story of the shofar gives people hope and conveys the message that "we all have to look inside ourselves to find the inner strength to do good in this world, under all circumstances and conditions."

Dr. Yvette Alt Miller
Reprinted by permission, www.aish.com

◆◆◆

Blowing the Shofar at Risk of Death – in Auschwitz

Rabbi Tzvi Hirsch Meislish, a Holocaust survivor who eventually found his way to Chicago, where he became a prominent rabbi, tells his personal and fascinating story of blowing the shofar in Auschwitz.

One year on Rosh Hashanah, during the Holocaust, a group of fervently religious boys were told that they were about to be cremated alive.

The boys approached Rabbi Meislish, who was known to have successfully smuggled a shofar into Auschwitz and asked him to blow it for them so that they could perform one last mitzvah before they died.

Indeed, they begged Rabbi Meislish to come to their barracks and blow all 100 shofar blasts, as is ritually required on the Jewish New Year.

Rabbi Meislish didn't know what to do. If he agreed to their request, he would likely be caught and put to death. His own son was begging him not to blow the shofar, as he did not want to become an orphan. The son correctly explained that there was no requirement to put one's life in danger in order to fulfill the mitzvah of blowing the shofar.

Rabbi Meislish decided to blow the shofar. He argued that although his son was right in that there was no requirement to put one's life in danger in order to fulfill the mitzvah of shofar, he did not expect to live much longer in any case. He'd rather die for performing a mitzvah than just be thrown into the gas chamber in a random roll call. Thus the rabbi proceeded – shofar in hand – to the boys' barracks.

Just as he was about to blow the shofar, however, the boys asked him to hold off and first deliver an inspirational sermon!

Imagine – the boys were minutes away from death, but they wanted to feel Rosh Hashanah. They want to hear the shofar.

Rabbi Meislish complied. He began by quoting the verse in the Book of Psalms relevant to Rosh Hashanah: "Blow shofar on the new month, at the time of hiding on the day of our holiday" (Psalms 81:4).

Of course, the true meaning of "at the time of hiding" refers to the moon which is "hidden" on Rosh Hashanah, as the Holy Day takes place on the first day of the lunar month, when there is a new moon that cannot be seen.

Rabbi Meislish interpreted the verse as referring to their own situation, as it seemed that God Himself was hiding from them. He told the boys to have faith.

He then blew the shofar. One of the boys stated, "Let us all acknowledge the great self-sacrifice of the rabbi for coming here to blow the shofar for us. In the merit of this mitzvah, may he be spared and go on to have a long, good and healthy life."

Everyone then said "Amen."

And as you know from the beginning of the story, Rabbi Meislish survived and made his way to Chicago.

Rabbi Meislish writes that he recorded this story to show that young Jews in Auschwitz were so dedicated to the performance of *mitzvot* in general and the blowing of the shofar in particular.

Rabbi Ari Enkin, Rabbinic Director, United with Israel

Looking for Love and Forgiveness

There is a story from Spain about a father and son who had become estranged. The son ran away from home, and his father set out to find him. The father searched for months, but to no avail. As a last-ditch effort, the father took out a full-page ad in a Madrid newspaper. The ad read: "Dear Paco, meet me in front of the newspaper office at noon on Saturday. All is forgiven. I love you. Your father."

The next Saturday, 800 men named Paco showed up, all looking for love and forgiveness from their fathers!

How many people in life are walking around looking for love and forgiveness from their Father in heaven?

The Announcing Tool

A long time ago, when all the people lived in one place, getting the news was easy. They had yellers then who would walk around town and after a few minutes of yelling, everyone got the news. But when people began living all over the place, even the yellers couldn't yell loud enough to get the news around. Mostly people just didn't get the news. But some special times just had to be announced. And the arrival of the new year was one of those times.

So God asked Enoch to go find an announcing tool. The next day Enoch returned with two rocks. "Oh God, listen to my fine announcing tool," said Enoch, who banged the two rocks together making a loud, rock-banging sound.

God said to Enoch, "What kind of announcing tool is this to tell of the arrival of the new year? Rocks don't make music. They only make noise. The new year is a time for music and singing, not banging and yelling."

Enoch ran off to find another announcing tool. The next day Enoch returned with a gong. "Listen to this one!" shouted Enoch as he gonged the gong, making lots of gonging sounds until God said, "STOP! What kind of announcing tool is this to announce the arrival of the new year? The gong does make a strong sound. But the gong is made of iron and iron is used to make swords and spears and arrows and other weapons of war. The new year is a time of peace, not war."

So Enoch ran off to find a new announcing tool. The next day Enoch returned with a harp. "God, this one is a winner!" he said as he strummed some lovely harp sounds that filled the air. "Close," said God. "Very close, but not close enough. The harp is a lovely instrument. It is not noisy. It is not made of iron. But it is too soft and fine for an announcing tool. The new year is a time of loud rejoicing. We need an announcing tool that will carry the news from hilltop to hilltop around the world. Try again."

The next day Enoch returned with a golden trumpet in his hand and announced to God, "What you see here, God, is the perfect announcing tool! It makes music, not noise; it is not made of iron. And it is loud enough to carry the news of the new year from hilltop to hilltop!" Enoch then blew some fine notes on the golden trumpet. Then God said, "The golden trumpet is a good announcing tool."

Enoch jumped up and down with joy until God continued, "Good, but not good enough. The golden trumpet makes loud, beautiful music and is not made of iron. But it is made by somebody who pounded it and rolled it and shaped it. I want a natural announcing tool that is not shaped by people.

I want an announcing tool that is not made of gold. Prices are going up. Nobody could afford such an announcing tool." Enoch was getting depressed, but he ran off one more time to hunt down another announcing tool.

The next day Enoch was a little late in coming to God. When he did arrive, he was out of breath. "I am embarrassed, God, to show you my new announcing tool. It is only this ram's horn – not nearly as sweet as the harp or as beautiful as the golden trumpet. But it is not made of iron. And nobody pounded it or shaped it (except the ram). I even think it is loud enough to get the news from hilltop to hilltop. But I am not sure if it is a good enough announcing tool."

"Why are you not sure?" asked God.

Enoch replied, "Well, you see, Oh Holy One, Blessed be You, I have been practicing with this thing all morning and it is ever so hard to blow. Sometimes I blow and blow and all I get is a peep, or a pillt! or a skeek! and then maybe another pillt!"

God spoke to Enoch with great love: "Enoch, you have done well! The ram's horn is a perfect announcing tool. It is natural and loud and it can make beautiful sounds. I know it is hard to play, but that is just right.

The new year is hard too. It is a time for deciding to do good things and give up bad things. The new year is a time for apologizing to others for hurting them in any way. And all that is very very hard to do, even harder than blowing the ram's horn."

Then God sat Enoch down and taught him to blow the ram's horn for the big celebration of the new year that was soon to begin. By the end of one lesson from God, Enoch could blow the ram's horn without a peep! a pillt! or a skeek!

Mark Gellman

The Rabbi and the Thief

My great-uncle, Reb Mendel Futerfas, of blessed memory, was one of the outstanding heroes who survived Stalin's Gulags. After many years of forced labor as punishment for his "crime" of helping strengthen Jewish life in the Soviet Union, he was eventually able to leave Russia and reunite with his wife and children, who had escaped Russia years earlier and were living in London. He was later appointed by the Rebbe to serve as head *mashpia* (spiritual mentor) in the Lubavitcher yeshivah of Kfar Chabad, Israel.

Often he would sit with fellow Hasidim and students, and recall his prison experiences and the lessons that he learned from them.

I recently heard my father-in-law, Rabbi Hirsch Chitrik, retell the following anecdote that he heard from Reb Mendel.

One of the activities prohibited in the Gulag was card playing. It was considered a severe crime, and harsh punishment was imposed if one was caught violating this prison rule.

Somehow, the inmates managed to smuggle in a deck of cards, and would while away their free time with the forbidden game.

The guards were told about the breach, and came to inspect the prisoners' quarters. They found nothing.

Were these uncouth prisoners really outsmarting them? As weeks went by, and the games continued, the guards were baffled. Are these uncouth prisoners really outsmarting us? they wondered.

They finally decided to put an end to this affront to their authority and pride, and carried out a surprise inspection, checking every inch of the barracks as well as the bodies and clothes of the inmates.

They found nothing.

They came to the conclusion that the informer had lied to them, either to curry favor in their eyes or to make a joke out of them.

As soon as the inspectors left, the cards appeared and the games continued as usual.

Reb Mendel couldn't understand how it had happened: the inspectors had checked every possible hiding place.

Eventually, he was let in on the secret.

"You see," the head thief began, "we are professional pickpockets. As soon as the guards would enter the barracks, we would slip the cards into their pockets. Right before they would leave, we would slip them back out again. Obviously, it never occurred to the guards to check their own pockets . . ."

The lesson is clear. If you want to make an accurate assessment of reality, start your search by checking your own pockets.

Often, when we make our spiritual and personal inventory, we instinctively look to place blame on those around us. "My parents are responsible," "my wife is responsible," "my education is responsible," etc. Everyone is blamed except oneself. That is an easier and less painful way to do things, but it is not effective in the long run.

In order to really put your life into order, you must not overlook your own "pockets."

Remember: Every time you point a finger at someone else, you have three fingers pointing back at yourself!

Rabbi Eliezer Shemtov, Chabad-Lubavitch emissary in Montevideo, Uruguay, www.chabad.org.

◆◆◆

Wisdom from Dear Abby

The "Dear Abby" advice column was written by the late Abigail Van Buren, who was actually a Jewish woman named Pauline Phillips from Sioux City, IA.

The wisdom of her answer for the writer "Unfulfilled in Philly" speaks to new moments, of times like New Year's when we rethink our future.

"Unfulfilled in Philly" wrote that he would love to be a doctor, but if he were to go back to college and get his degree, then go to medical school, then do an internship, and finally practice medicine, it would take him seven years and he'd be 43 years old.

Dear Abby astutely asked: "How old will you be in seven years if you don't do all those things? It's better to fulfill our dreams later in life than never."

What dreams do you have that you can begin to fulfill now so you won't regret it seven (or seventy) years later?

◆◆◆

The Image of God

When God was creating the world, God shared a secret with the angels – human beings will be created in the image of God.

The angels were jealous and outraged. Why should humans be entrusted with such a precious gift when they are flawed mortals? Surely, if humans find out their true power, they will abuse it. If humans discover they are created in God's image, they will learn to surpass us!

So the angels decided to steal God's image. Now that the Divine image was in the angels' hands, they needed to pick a place to hide it so that man would never find it.

They held a meeting and brainstormed. The angel Gabriel suggested they hide God's image at the top of the highest mountain peak. The other angels, objected, "one day humans will learn to climb and they will find it there."

The angel Michael said, "let's hide it at the bottom of the sea."

"No," the other angels chimed in. "Humans will find a way to dive to the bottom of the sea and they'll find it there."

One by one, the angels suggested hiding places, but they were all rejected.

And then Uriel, the wisest angel of all, stepped forward and said. "I know a place where man will never look for it."

So the angels hid the precious holy image of God deep within the human soul. And to this day, God's image lies hidden in the very place we are least likely to search for it. Lying there, it is farthest away from you than you ever imagine. Lying there it is closer to you than you will ever know.

◆◆◆

Adam and Eve

Adam and Eve were exiled from the Garden of Eden. And they lived together, east of Eden, tilling the earth and raising children, and struggling to stay alive. After the years of struggle, when their children were grown, they decided to see the world. They journeyed from one corner of the world to the other. In the course of their journeys, wandering from place to place, they found the entrance to the Garden of Eden, now guarded by an angel with a flaming sword. They were frightened and they began to flee when

God spoke to them:

"Adam, you have lived in exile these many many years. The punishment is complete. You may return now to the Garden."

And suddenly the angel disappeared, and the way to the Garden opened. "Come in, Adam. Come in, Eve."

"Wait," Adam replied, "You know, it has been so many years. Remind me, what is it like in the Garden?"

"The Garden is paradise!" God responded. "In the Garden there is no work. You need never struggle or toil again. In the Garden there is no pain, no suffering. In the Garden there is no death. Day after day, life goes on forever. Come Adam, return to the Garden!"

Adam listened to God's words – no work, no struggle, no pain, no death. An endless life of ease. And then he turned and looked at Eve. He looked at the woman with whom he had struggled to make a life, to take bread from the earth, to raise children, to build a home. He thought of the tragedies they had overcome and they joys they cherished. And Adam shook his head, "No, thank you, that's not for me... Come on Eve, let's go home." And Adam and Eve turned their backs on Paradise and walked home.

◆◆◆

We Don't Have the Merits

There is a fellow who owns a jewelry store in Israel. One day a nine-year-old girl walked into the store and said, "I am here to buy a bracelet." She looked through the glass cases and pointed to a bracelet that was 10,000 shekels. The man behind the counter asked her, "You want to buy that bracelet?"

"Yes," she replied.

"Wow, you have very good taste. Who do you want to buy it for?"

"For my older sister."

"Oh that is so nice!" the storekeeper replied. "Why do you want to buy your older sister this bracelet?"

"Because I don't have a mother or father," the little girl said, "and my older sister takes care of us. So we want to buy her a present, and I'm willing to pay for it." She pulled out of her pocket a whole bunch of coins that totaled just under nine shekels, a little less than three dollars.

The fellow says, "Wow! That's exactly what the bracelet costs!" While wrapping up the bracelet, he said to the girl, "You write a card to your sister while I wrap the bracelet." He finished wrapping the bracelet, wiped away his tears, and handed the little girl the bracelet.

A few hours later the older sister entered the store. "I'm terribly embarrassed," she said. "My sister should not have come here. She shouldn't have taken it without paying."

"What are you talking about?" the storekeeper asked.

"What do you mean? This bracelet costs thousands of shekels. My little sister doesn't have thousands of shekels – she doesn't even have fifty shekels! Obviously, she didn't pay for it."

"You couldn't be more wrong," the storekeeper replied. "She paid me in full. She paid eight shekels, eighty agarot, and a broken heart. I want to tell you something. I am a widower. I lost my wife a number of years ago. People come into my store every single day. They come in and buy expensive pieces of jewelry, and all these people can afford it. My wife died a few years ago, but when your sister walked in, for the first time in so very long, I once again felt what love means."

He gave her the bracelet and wished her well....

During the High Holy Days, we come to the Almighty and we want to buy something very expensive. We want to pay for our life. But we cannot afford it. We don't have enough of the Almighty's currency to pay for it. We don't have the merits.

So we come to the Almighty and we empty out our pockets, giving him whatever merits we have plus promises for the future.

- I'll pick up the phone and call someone who is lonely,
- I will learn an extra five minutes of Torah,
- I will be kind and ...
- I will be scrupulous about not speaking lashon hara (gossip) for one hour a day.

The Almighty says, "You don't know how long it's been since I've felt what love means." He sees how much we love Him and how much we yearn to improve, and He says, "You know what? You have touched my heart. Here it is, paid in full."

The story was told over by Rabbi Go'el Elkarif who said he heard it from the person to whom it happened.

◆◆◆

Choose Life!

Here is a story that helps illustrate what it means to "choose life," assisting us to be more prepared for Rosh Hashanah.

There was once a king who had three sons. He wanted to give them all prestigious jobs. The law, however, was that before a person could be given such a job he had to prove his wisdom. Therefore, the king told his three sons to go travel the world to gain wisdom and life experience.

The brothers set off in a boat. As they were approaching an island, they saw in the distance a beautiful orchard. As soon as they docked they went to explore the orchard. When they got there, they saw three men at the entrance of the orchard. One was very old. One had terrible bodily afflictions. One was a very wise man.

Each of these men spoke to the three brothers and offered them advice.

The first one told them: "Remember: you cannot remain in the orchard forever."

The second one warned them: "You can eat whatever you want but do not take anything with you."

The third one said: "When you eat from the fruits, stay away from the bad fruits – only choose the good ones."

They then entered the orchard. They were blown away by its beauty, sights, and smells. They saw fountains and springs. It was clearly a well-planned out orchard built wisely. There were even gold and silver mines in the orchard.

The brothers explored the orchard together, enjoying its fruits and beauty. After a few days in the orchard, the brothers split up and went out on their own.

One brother spent his time eating and drinking as much as he could, one brother spent his time at the mines gathering gold and silver, and one brother simply spent his time contemplating the orchard. This third brother was mesmerized by the orchard.

He wanted to meet the wise man who designed it. He searched and searched for some information on who made the orchard. He even came across some texts written by the designer which further testified that the designer was a genius.

Eventually, a message reached the brothers that their father, the king, wanted them to return home. And so they did, or at least, tried.

The first brother had become so accustomed to the sweet pleasures of the orchard that he was unable to live without them. He never went back. The second brother tried to carry out all the gold and silver he amassed but was prevented from doing so and went back a broken man. The third brother was ecstatic. He couldn't wait to get back to his father and tell him all that he had learned while in the orchard.

When the two remaining brothers reached the palace, the guards recognized the "third" brother and welcomed him back royally. The "second" brother, however, was unrecognizable and was therefore not permitted to enter the palace. The king, therefore, sat with the only one of his sons that made it back to the palace, heard about his experiences, and gave him one of the most prestigious positions in the kingdom.

The Torah portion "Nitzavim" in Deuteronomy concludes with the following verse: "I have placed before you the choice of life and death...choose life!" – just 24 hours before Rosh Hashanah when God evaluates every single human being and decides, based on their merits, what kind of year they are going to have. This Torah portion is one last reminder to prepare for Rosh Hashanah – the day we all pray for life!

My dear friends, the three sons represent us and our mission in this world. Moses tells us: "choose life" on Rosh Hashanah, which we can do by focusing and committing ourselves to what's important in life. We take nothing with us into the next world ("fruits", "gold", "silver") – only our good deeds ("wisdom"). It doesn't matter what kind of person you have been until now, it matters what type of person you want to be. The orchard is this world, the designer is God Almighty.

Rabbi Ari Enkin, Rabbinic Director, United with Israel

The Shepherd's Prayer

Ashepherd once pastured his sheep in a field outside the city of Cordoba. He did not know how to read or write, nor could he say any prayers; no one had ever taught him. But that did not stop him from praying.

The shepherd so loved God that he simply made up his own prayers out of whatever thoughts came to mind. This is how he prayed: "God, if You had sheep, I would take care of them as if they were my own. And I would charge You only half what I charge everybody else for looking after them. And if You didn't have any money, I would take care of them for free. That's how much I love You."

And at other times he would pray: "God, if You were hungry and I had radishes, I would give You half my radishes. And if You were still hungry, I would give You all of them. That's how much I love You."

He would go on like that, day or night, shouting out prayers as his heart moved him. One day a famous scholar passed by the field on his way to attend the High Holiday service at the Cordoba synagogue and chanced to overhear the shepherd saying his prayers.

"God, if it was raining and You didn't have a hat, I'd lend You mine. And if my hat wasn't big enough to keep You dry, I'd lend You my cloak. And if that wasn't enough, I'd stand over You and let the rain fall on me. That's how much I love You."

"What nonsense is this!" the scholar scolded the shepherd. "Do you think that The One Who Made the heavens and the earth needs you to keep the rain off Him?"

The embarrassed shepherd did not know how to reply. "Forgive me, Rabbi. I meant no harm. I was only saying my prayers."

"You call that idiotic twaddle 'prayer'? Ignoramus! Has no one ever taught you how to pray?" The shepherd shook his head.

"Come over to the fence. I will teach you." The shepherd left his sheep and came over to where the scholar stood. The learned man then delivered a long lecture about the different prayers, their origin and meaning, and the prescribed order of the service. "From now on, either pray properly or don't pray at all!" he warned the shepherd. Then he continued on his way to the city.

The shepherd now faced a terrible dilemma. He had not understood a word of the scholar's lecture. Nor could he remember any of the prayers the scholar tried to teach him. Yet he was ashamed to go back to his own way of praying because he thought it was wrong. The shepherd did not know what to do, so, bewildered, he stopped praying entirely.

God's Throne stands on the highest pinnacle of heaven. Yet if a single downy feather falls from the breast of the smallest bird, God is aware of it. God hears spiders spinning their webs in dark corners, listens to bees buzzing among summer flowers and hears the gnat's whine at evening – the sounds of the world form a vast symphony whose every note God hears. Thus God knew immediately that something was missing. The shepherd who pastured his sheep outside the city of Cordoba had ceased to pray.

God summoned an angel. "My beloved servant, the shepherd of Cordoba, no longer says his beautiful prayers. He has lost his way. Go down and help him."

The angel went down and found the shepherd in the field, sitting sadly among his sheep.

"Shepherd," the angel said, "The Holy One no longer hears your voice. Why do you no longer pray?"

The shepherd lowered his eyes. "My prayers are no good."

"Who told you that?"

"A learned rabbi. He called them 'idiotic twaddle.'"

"He is wrong. He does not know. He has never heard the Hosts of Heaven."

"How do they pray?" the shepherd asked.

"I'll show you," the angel said. Enfolded in the angel's wings, the shepherd rose into the air. High above the clouds he flew, past the moon and stars, until he came before the Eternal Throne where choirs of angels – Ophanim, Seraphim, Cherubim – poured out choruses of prayer like waves of silver light.

"If You had sheep," sang the Cherubim.

"If You were hungry," the Ophanim replied.

And the Seraphim answered, "I'd stand over You and let the rain fall on me."

The shepherd listened, astonished. "The Hosts of Heaven pray just like me!" he exclaimed.

"That is because, like you, they pray with a pure heart. That is the way you should pray. Always." The angel carried the shepherd back to his pasture.

Once more the shepherd lifted his voice in joyous prayer: "God, if You were hungry and I had radishes, I would give You all of them."

And the Hosts of Heaven answered, "That's how much I love you."

Anonymous

♦♦♦

A Rosh Hashanah Riddle

It's five days before Rosh Hashanah and Yonatan runs in from school, shouting: "Aba! Aba! Wanna to hear a Rosh Hashanah riddle?" I look at him, kipa hanging on the side of his head, nose running, shoes untied, knees dirty, looking like a typical third grader.

"Sure, Yonatan, tell me your Rosh Hashanah riddle."

So he asks me, "What do a sheep, a man on a tightrope, and a soldier have in common?"

Now with a third grader, you just can't say, "I don't know...you tell me!"

The way it works is: you have to guess.

To be perfectly honest, I had no idea (and not much interest) in what a sheep, a man on a tightrope and a soldier have in common, and I was hoping that an ice cream bribe would get me off the hook.

"Yonatan, sweetheart, I give up. I have absolutely no idea. Please tell me the answer and we'll have some chocolate-chip-fudge-ripple."

Slightly mollified, Yonatan agrees. "Okay Aba," he says, "I'll tell you the answer, but next time you have to guess!"

I humbly accept his scolding and then Yonatan explains:

On Rosh Hashanah, we act like *all* these things –

- We pray like sheep...
- Like a man on a tightrope, we try not to make any mistakes...
- And we fight like a soldier, against the bad in us.

Extremely pleased with himself, Yonatan took his ice cream cone and ran off to play soccer with his friends.

Yet his answer left me intrigued.

I had never heard of a Rosh Hashanah riddle before. Yet I do know that Yonatan's answer sounded very familiar. I went to the shelf, pulled out the section of the Oral Tradition which deals with Rosh Hashanah and began to skim the pages until I finally found it.

The Gemara asks (Rosh Hashanah 18a):

"What are the three ways one should approach God on Rosh Hashanah?" And it answers: "Like a sheep, like a man walking on a very narrow descent and like King David's warriors."

What does this mean? I will share two explanations with you, and perhaps you will share with me your own.

One: The intense self-evaluation process of Rosh Hashanah humbles us like sheep, for we become aware that we are to be judged by the King of all Kings.

In addition, we become acutely aware of how much power we have to either hurt or heal another's feelings, of how at each moment we can either act correctly or incorrectly with ourselves and with others. We must make each choice in life so carefully, like someone making a very narrow descent or walking a tightrope.

Finally, we come to realize that God expects us to be like soldiers, who battle evil and fight to make the world a better place.

Two: The Rebbe of Sochochov understood that this Gemara is discussing the three areas in which we need to improve ourselves for the coming year: physically, emotionally and spiritually.

The sheep represents our physical, animalistic needs. When we focus on taking care of our body: eating, sleeping or engaging in sexual activity, we are likely to become narcissistic and think only of our own needs.

And so this Gemara advises us to use humility when dealing with our physical needs. We should "sheepishly" ask ourselves: "Do I really need this ice cream, cigarette, Rolex, Jacuzzi, _____ (you fill-in-the-blank), or am I just being self-indulgent?"

A man walking on a very narrow ridge is symbolic of emotional growth. We all know how cutting words can be and how vital are words of encouragement. The Sages are showing us that the way to become emotionally sensitive to the impact we make is by considering our every word as if we were making a very narrow descent or considering our next step on a tightrope. Just as carefully as we would consider where we place each step, that's how carefully we should consider each word before we speak and each act before we do it.

Finally the Sages teach that as we approach Rosh Hashanah, we need to look at our spiritual side and ask ourselves: "What have we fought for during this past year?"

Did we wage our battles on the highway or on issues of social injustice? What kind of soldier were we this past year?

Yonatan's clever teacher wanted to convey the Gemara's beautiful teaching in a way a third grader could relate to. As a Rosh Hashanah riddle...

Rabbi Yehoshua Rubin

◆◆◆

The Master Key

One year, Rabbi Israel Baal Shem Tov said to Rabbi Ze'ev Kitzes, one of his senior disciples: "You will blow the shofar for us this Rosh Hashanah. I want you to study all the kavanot (Kabbalistic meditations) that pertain to the shofar, so that you should meditate upon them when you do the blowing."

Rabbi Ze'ev applied himself to the task with joy and trepidation: joy over the great privilege that had been accorded him, and trepidation over the immensity of the responsibility. He studied the Kabbalistic writings that discuss the multifaceted significance of the shofar and what its sounds achieve on the various levels of reality and in the various chambers of the soul. He also prepared a sheet of paper on which he noted the main points of each kavanah, so that he could refer to them when he blew the shofar.

Finally, the great moment arrived. It was the morning of Rosh Hashanah, and Rabbi Ze'ev stood on the reading platform in the center of the Baal Shem Tov's synagogue amidst the Torah scrolls, surrounded by a sea of tallit-draped bodies. At his table in the southeast corner of the room stood his master, the Baal Shem Tov, his face aflame. An awed silence filled the room in anticipation of the climax of the day – the piercing blasts and sobs of the shofar.

Rabbi Ze'ev reached into his pocket, and his heart froze: the paper had disappeared! He distinctly remembered placing it there that morning, but now it was gone. Furiously, he searched his memory for what he had learned, but his distress over the lost notes seemed to have incapacitated his brain: his mind was a total blank. Tears of frustration filled his eyes. He had disappointed his master, who had entrusted him with this most sacred task. Now he must blow the shofar like a simple horn, without any kavanot. With a despairing heart, Rabbi Ze'ev blew the litany of sounds required by law and, avoiding his master's eye, resumed his place.

At the conclusion of the day's prayers, the Baal Shem Tov made his way to the corner where Rabbi Ze'ev sat sobbing under his tallit.

"Gut Yom Tov, Reb Ze'ev!" he called. "That was a most extraordinary shofar-blowing we heard today!"

"But Rebbe . . . I . . ."

"In the king's palace," said the Baal Shem Tov, "there are many gates and doors, leading to many halls and chambers. The palace-keepers have great rings holding many keys, each of which opens a different door. But there is one key that fits all the locks, a master key that opens all the doors.

"The kavanot are keys, each unlocking another door in our souls, each accessing another chamber in the supernal worlds. But there is one key that unlocks all doors, that opens up for us the innermost chambers of the Divine palace. That master key is a broken heart."

Rabbi Shlomo Yosef Zevin, www.chabad.org

♦♦♦

Rav Kook: The Modern Prophet of Redemption

The name of the righteous is invoked in blessing, But the fame of the wicked rots.

Proverbs 10:7

Judaism has clear traditions of mourning, but when a *tzaddik* (righteous man) dies, the anniversary of their passing becomes a day of celebration. The Zohar teaches, "A *tzaddik* who passes away is present in all worlds even more than during his lifetime." This transcendence in the afterlife gives the righteous even greater energy to affect this world, and so their passing is celebrated.

Rabbi Abraham Isaac Kook, the first Ashkenazi Chief Rabbi of British Mandatory Palestine, passed away on the third day of Elul, 5695 (September 1, 1935). A brilliant scholar, he was also considered to be one of the fathers of religious Zionism, a revolutionary movement in the Orthodox world. He also founded the Mercaz HaRav Yeshiva, an institution for high-level Torah learning in Jerusalem.

Like most great men, his real greatness is revealed in the true-life stories of his righteous character, his great love for every Jew, and his passion for the land of Israel.

Most rabbis connect with the members of their community. Rabbi Kook not only saw all of Israel as his congregation, but as members of his extended family. He loved each and every Jew and treated all human beings with respect and sensitivity.

One year, on Rosh Hashanah, a group of non-religious Jewish workers was doing construction in a building in Jerusalem. Their activity was absolutely forbidden by Jewish law. The neighbors, aghast at this public transgression on such a holy day, contacted Rabbi Kook.

The rabbi immediately sent a messenger to the site. But rather than rebuke the workers, he greeted them with the traditional holiday greeting. He then told them that Rabbi Kook had sent him to blow the shofar for them, one of the commandments of the day. The workers took a break from their labors and gathered around the rabbi's emissary as he recited the blessings and began to blow.

The workers were deeply touched as the sound of the shofar took them back to their childhood. They began to tell each other and Rabbi Kook's messenger about the sweet memories they had of the shofar and of the holiday. After discussing what had happened, they unanimously agreed to cease working on the holiday. They all went home, changed into holiday clothes, and went to pray in synagogue.

Another anecdote illustrates how Rabbi Kook constantly envisioned the imminent Messianic era, as well as his acceptance of all Jews. Rabbi Kook's passing was announced at the 19th Zionist Congress in Switzerland. Menachem Ussishkin, a respected Zionist leader and the president of the JNF, addressed the gathering to speak about Rabbi Kook. After acknowledging the rabbi's great scholarship, Ussishkin described his first meeting with Rabbi Kook. He noted Rabbi Kook's strong connection with non-religious youth, a trait that was uncharacteristic of most Orthodox rabbis.

"His admiration for youth in general, and particularly the youth living in *Eretz Yisrael* – youth thousands of miles away from his own worldview – was like a father's understanding of his son, a father who wishes to instruct his son and draw him close with insight and love," Ussishkin said.

When he was questioned about this approach in his lifetime, Rabbi Kook responded:

"The Holy Temple had separate courtyards. Some areas were only for priests; others were for Levites, or regular Israelites, or women. And there was one special place called the *Kodesh HaKodashim,* the Holy of Holies. There, only the High Priest was allowed to enter, and only once a year, on the holiest day of the year.

"All this was true when the Temple was standing. Then there were separate areas for each sector of the nation, and each person knew where he was allowed and where he was not allowed to enter.

"However," Rabbi Kook said, "what do you think it was like while they were constructing the Temple? Then there were certainly no barriers. The workers went to any area that required their skills. Even into the Holy of Holies."

"Nowadays, the Rabbi concluded, we are building "the Third

Temple." We are in the process of building. There are no – and there must not be any – barriers between the young generation and us, between the religious and the secular. We are all busy with one project; we are all working toward one goal. First, let us build this Temple. Afterwards we may discuss our differences...."

Rabbi Kook's all-abiding love for his fellow Jew was powerfully illustrated in the following incident. A group of ultra-Orthodox Jews in Jerusalem were vocal critics of Rabbi Kook, criticizing him for his connection with secular Jews. They posted these criticisms in the streets and in the newspapers, defaming him and discrediting his authority.

One day, Rabbi Kook was walking home from a *brit milah* (circumcision ceremony) in the Old City of Jerusalem, accompanied by several of his students. Suddenly, a small group of his detractors accosted him, throwing waste water at the rabbi and soaking him in filth.

News of the attack spread throughout the city and several prominent men came to express their anger at the assailants. One of the visitors, the legal counsel of British Mandate, suggested that Rabbi Kook press charges against his assailants, assuring the rabbi that if he did, his opponents would be deported.

Rabbi Kook rejected this suggestion.

"I have no interest in court cases," replied the rabbi. "Despite what they did to me, I love them. I am ready to kiss them, so great is my love! I burn with love for every Jew."

Sinat chinam, causeless hatred, is the sin that led to the destruction of the Second Temple. Often people say that the way to rebuild the Temple is through *ahavat chinam,* groundless love. Though Rabbi Kook burned with love for each and every Jew, he took exception to this term:

"There is no such thing as *Ahavat Chinam* – groundless love. Why groundless? He is a Jew, and I am obligated to love and respect him. There is only *Sinat Chinam* – hate without reason. But *Ahavat Chinam*? Never!"*

Perhaps the greatest impact of Rabbi Kook was his framing of modern Israel in terms of the Messianic era. In Jewish tradition, the Messiah is a two stage process. The Messiah from the House of

---

* Adapted from *Orot HaKodesh* vol. III, pp. 324–334; *Malachim K'vnei Adam,* pp. 262, 483–485.)

Joseph comes first, returning the exiles and the building up the land of Israel. He is followed by the miraculous Messiah from the House of David. Rabbi Kook saw the manifestation of the Messiah from the House of Joseph in the secular Zionists bringing the desert back to life. This vision earned him the title of "The Modern Prophet of Redemption".

Adam Eliyahu Berkowitz, ISRAEL365

◆◆◆

The Value of Each Day

In Thornton Wilder's play *Our Town*, the character Emily dies as a young woman. As she joins those who have preceded her in death, she begins to adjust to her new circumstances. She says to her late mother-in-law, "But, Mother Gibbs, one can go back; one can go back there again...into living. I feel it. I know it." Mother Gibbs tells her that she can go back, but then cautions her not to do it (as does another character).

Nevertheless, Emily chooses to go back. She chooses to return to her twelfth birthday, but she is cautioned that she will not only be there but that she will observe herself being there. "And as you watch it, you see the things that they – down there – never know. You see the future. You know what's going to happen afterwards."

Emily does return, but her experience is unexpectedly difficult for her. She finds it painful. She says, "I can't. I can't go on. It goes so fast. We don't have time to look at one another... I didn't realize. So all that was going on and we never noticed. Take me back... Goodbye, Goodbye, world. Goodbye Grover's Corners... Mama and Papa. Goodbye to clocks ticking... and Mama's sunflowers. And food and coffee. And new-ironed dresses and hot baths... and sleeping and waking up. Oh, earth, you're too wonderful for anybody to realize you."

She then asks the Stage Manager (one of the characters) "Do any human beings ever realize life while they live it? – every, every minute?"

The Stage Manager replies, "No" and then pauses and adds "The saints and poets, maybe they do some."

This scene from *Our Town* reminds us of the teaching of an ancient poet, the author of Psalm 90, who would have understood the import of the scene. The psalmist wrote, "*Limnot yameinu ken hoda, v'navi l'vav chokhmah* – Teach us to number our days, that we might attain a heart of wisdom." The psalm teaches us that every day of our lives is important, that every day that passes is a day that has the potential to be used wisely. We know, however, that we are not always wise, that we tend to let too many of our days go by all too easily. Once in a while we suddenly become aware of the passage of time, and we wonder how we have spent the time since last we noticed that time was passing.

Rosh HaShanah and Yom Kippur are upon us, bringing us a heightened awareness of the passage of time. One of the most revered portions of the Rosh HaShanah and Yom Kippur liturgy is the prayer *Unetaneh Tokef*, the prayer that includes the text that so many find disturbing: "On Rosh HaShanah it is written, and on Yom Kippur it is sealed, how many shall pass away and how many shall be born; who shall live and who shall die..." It is important for us to read this prayer as I believe that it was intended, as a prayer asking us to awaken to the beauty and transient nature of life. As we hear the prayer chanted we are conscious of the absence of some who used to be there with us but who no longer dwell in the land of the living – and we are aware that we do not know on that day who will return the next year. We need to awaken to life's gifts and brevity at all times, not just at the high and low points of our lives, at weddings, births, graduations, illnesses, and deaths.

Life is filled with days, but the number of our days is limited. How do we live each day? Hillel once taught: "If I am not for myself, who will be for me? If I am only for myself, what am I? And if not now, *eimatai*, when?"

Our good intentions in life are often relegated to the bottom of our "to do" list while we are busy with other things. Do we take care of ourselves? Do we ignore others? How do we balance the competing demands on our time? If we are not aware of how we live each day, we tend to let things slide. Later, we find ourselves asking "Who knows where the time goes?"

The Psalmist knew this and thus prayed *"Limnot yameinu ken hoda, v'navi l'vav chokhma."* Hillel knew this and asked *"Eimatai?"* The author of *Unetaneh Tokef* understood this and pointed out that our days are "like a passing shadow, like a vanishing cloud, and like a dream that flies away." The endless days of childhood yield to weeks and months and years that speed by.

Let us learn to count our days, to take note of them, to hold each one carefully in our thoughts. Let us use our days mindfully and wisely. Let us learn from Emily's question, "Do any human beings ever realize life while they live it? – every, every minute?"

Rabbi Stephan O. Parnes

♦♦♦

The Call of the Shofar

Once upon a time there lived a poor orphan, who had neither father nor mother. His name was Moshe, but because he was a small boy and an orphan, everybody called him "Moshele." As long as he was still a little boy he went to cheder where he learned chumash and gemara together with the other children, but when he grew a little older he had to go out and earn his livelihood. So a collection was made to provide him with a basket full of merchandise, such as needles, buttons and other trinkets, and Moshele set out to sell them to the peasants and farmers in the villages and hamlets that surrounded his native town.

It was a very hard job, of course. In the summer the heat was unbearable, and in the winter the snow and icy winds often made his teeth chatter. But Moshele did not mind. His only regret was that he could not go to the yeshivah, for he wanted to become a scholar.

One wintry day Moshele was trudging along on the snow-covered road, with his basket of merchandise under his arm. He knew some Psalms by heart and he recited them cheerily as he walked. Snow kept on falling from the gray skies, and soon he found himself plodding ankle deep in snow. It was getting difficult to walk, and it was even more difficult to follow the road, which was now completely covered with snow, as far as the eye could see.

Unwittingly, he strayed off the road and presently found himself in a small forest. Moshele felt very tired and decided to have a little rest. He noticed a big stump and sat down on it, placing his basket down on the snow.

"No, you must not fall asleep" he kept on telling himself, "it is very dangerous; you might freeze to death!" So he sat there huddled up and shivering, trying in vain to keep himself warm, and his eyes open.

Suddenly, he felt a breath of warmth through his body. He found himself sitting by a nice, cozy fire, and stretched out his hands and feet towards it. He felt as if sharp needles were pricking his fingertips, but that stopped soon as the flames blazed stronger.

A peasant passing on the road on his sledge noticed the huddled figure of a lad almost fully covered with snow. He stopped his horse and ran to the body. Brushing the snow off, he found that the body was almost frozen stiff, with no sign of life.

Without losing time, the peasant set to work. He pulled out his knife and cut up the clothing around the still body. Then he started to rub it briskly with snow. After half an hour's work, the blood began to flow in the young body again, and the boy stirred. The peasant then carried the lad to his sledge, covered him up, and drove his horse as fast as he could to his home in the nearby village. There he again rubbed the body of the lad with snow, until his skin began to glow, and finally poured some hot brandy down the lad's throat. Moshele opened his eyes and closed them again. Thereupon the peasant carried him onto the oven and covered him up snugly. Moshele fell asleep.

The crowing of the cock woke him up very early the next morning. Moshele opened his eyes and looked around. He could not understand where he was, and why so many pins and needles were pricking him all over his body.

The farmer's wife was up and came up to see him. "How do you feel?" she asked him in Russian, for she was a Russian peasant-woman.

"All right," Moshele said, still wondering what had happened to him. The woman boiled up some tea for him, and he drank it gratefully.

"What is your name?" she asked him.

Moshele tried to think hard, but could not remember. "I don't know," he said, thinking how strange it was that he could not remember his own name.

"Never mind," said the peasant woman, "we'll call you Peter."

Thus Moshele, or Peter as he was now called by all, remained in the peasant's home, little knowing that he was a Jewish boy and did not belong there at all.

When summer came, Peter helped the farmer in all the work in the field: plowing, sowing and reaping. Peter was an industrious, capable lad, and the farmer was very pleased with him.

The summer passed by and autumn came. One day the farmer said to Peter: "Tomorrow we shall drive to town and take some of our products to the market."

Peter was very glad, and looked forward to seeing the town. When they finally got there the next day, the marketplace and all the streets were deserted. When they passed by the synagogue, they saw it was crowded with worshipers, and the peasant realized that it was a Jewish holiday. There was nothing to do but to drive back home. But Peter was fascinated by the quaint synagogue and begged the peasant to stay in town a while.

"Very good then," said the peasant, "you will meet me in the public house," and he went to have a drink, while Peter felt an irresistible desire to look into the synagogue.

Peter came in quietly and stood by the door. The worshipers wrapped in praying-shawls seemed very intent on their prayers; many of them were weeping. No one paid any attention to him. Peter looked closely around him. His heart began to beat faster. Somehow, the scene was familiar to him. Had he ever been here before? Slowly his memory returned to him, as everything in the synagogue brought new memories into his conscience. The tune and melodies of the cantor were familiar to him. The scrolls of the Torah that had just been brought out of the Ark were familiar too. As if glued to his place, Peter stood motionless and stared...

Peter did not know how long he stood there, but presently he noticed a little excitement among the worshipers. The very air appeared to become tense with sacred animation, as if angels were fluttering in the air. Peter was transfixed with awe.

The silence was broken by the shaking voice of the aged cantor, and immediately the entire community joined in fervent prayer. For some time the roar of the whole community praying seemed to shake the very walls of the synagogue, and then it began to subside gradually, until a solemn silence fell again. In the stillness of the air, the sobbing of the cantor became clearly audible, and Peter found himself weeping too.

Suddenly, he heard – *tekiah* – and the blast of the ram's horn pierced the air. *Shevarim – teruah* – and again the broken sound of the shofar seemed to stab Peter's heart. *Tekiah* – the shofar called again.

"Moshele, you are a Jew," the shofar called. "Moshele, you are a Jew! Hurry ... Now is the time to return to God. *Tekiah – Teruah* ....

Everything now became very clear to Moshele....

"Dear God, forgive me," Moshele cried, and fainted.

Kehot Publication Society, www.chabad.org

♦♦♦

Yom Kippur

Teach Us How To Atone

It was a few days before Yom Kippur, and the students of Rabbi Zusha of Hanipol came to him with a burning question.

"Rabbi," they pleaded, "the day of atonement is almost upon us. Could you kindly teach us how to atone?"

To their surprise, the rabbi refused.

"Zusha doesn't know how to atone," said the Hasidic master, who always spoke of himself in the third person, believing that "I" was a pronoun reserved only for God. "But Moishele the shoemaker knows. Go and ask him."

The students were shocked. Moishele was a crass man who hadn't studied Torah a day in his life; what could he possibly know that the righteous sage didn't? Still, intrigued, the students decided to head out to Moishele's house.

Arriving at the humble home, the students hid in the bushes and peered in. They were just in time: Having just finished his simple supper, Moishele commanded his daughters to bring him the books, and the girls returned a moment later with two volumes: one large and bound in fine leather, the other small and tattered, no bigger than a notebook. Moishele took the small one in his hands and opened it.

"God," he said, "I will now read to you an account of my sins." And so he did: that time he overcharged for a pair of shoes, that time he lost his temper with his children – mostly the mundane stuff of everyday life. When he was done, he put the notebook down and picked up the larger, fancier book.

"And now, God," he added, "I will read to you an account of your sins." These were much graver: the family that perished from hunger in the next village over, the plague that killed scores in the nearest town, the war raging across the border that had claimed the lives of thousands.

"I'll make you a deal," Moishele said to the Almighty, looking heavenward. "If you forgive me my sins, I'll forgive you yours."

Touched by the shoemaker's wisdom, the students rushed back to see their rabbi, and, excitedly, told him everything they'd seen. When they were done, Zusha started weeping bitterly.

Confounded, the students stood there for a few moments, until one of them finally gathered up the courage to ask the rabbi what was wrong.

"Don't you see?" Zusha wailed. "Moishele had God in the palm of his hand. He could've brought him to justice, but instead, he let him go."

That is the true power of prayer. It's not a plaintive plea, like a child begging a parent for a doodad or a treat. Instead, it's a conversation, at the heart of which is a deeply complex idea: that God and Man are intertwined, each having the power to foil the other's plans, each needing the other's faith for life to go on. This is what the Mishnah meant when it taught us that "everything is foreseen and permission is granted:" God, knowing and seeing all, nevertheless leaves us room to exercise our free will, and by doing so we have the power to bring His Divine plan to fruition or lay it to waste. This is why prayer is so powerful. It's a conversation between two unequals who are trying to work together and bring solace and joy to a world in dire need of both.

◆◆◆

Forgiveness is my Teacher

On a chilly day in February several years ago, I drove my mother to the hospital to visit her only sister, Emily. My mother was, as always, anxious about seeing her. Not just because of her condition, which was bordering on terminal, but because of their relationship, defined by years of unspoken hurt and unfinished conversations.

We both fidgeted in the elevator as we approached the room to say what we anticipated were our final goodbyes. No matter how hard you try, there is no way to prepare for a moment like this. You can intellectually comfort yourself with thoughts like "She's so sick, it's for the best," or "She's lived a good life and now it's her time." But as we entered the room I was struck by the realization that the cadaverous shell of a woman lying in bed, the same woman who had caused my mother so much grief and pain in her youth, might never be able to speak again. And there was still so much left to say.

Her daughter greeted us at the door.

"She's been calling for you for days," she said softly, looking at my mother.

My mother's discomfort permeated the room. Unclear how to act and unsure of what to say, she tried at first to be upbeat and optimistic, brightly suggesting that perhaps more time and a new medication might make a difference. But her sister's unfocused gaze and low, continuous moans punctuated each word and soon my mother stopped talking.

Something inside me knew that Emily recognized that Mom had come, so I bent over my mother and whispered in her ear.

"Hold her hand, Mom, and stroke it so she knows you are here. Tell her you love her, comfort her and tell her you love her and that it's okay."

Which is exactly what she did. When she began stroking Emily's forehead with her own tired hand, Emily looked up and SAW. She SAW and she KNEW, clear as I knew, that it was my mother. A smile spread slowly across her face and for a few moments, her weary eyes were young again.

My mother kept repeating softly, "I love you Emily. I really love you." And Emily, who had been unable to talk for days, uttered the words which have helped to heal my mother's pain and teach her how to forgive: "I love you too, Elise. I have always loved you."

Granting forgiveness to those who have hurt us is one of the most difficult things to do: it doesn't come easily or naturally for most of us. When a person is wronged, the natural tendency is to withdraw or become hostile or even vindictive, all of which can lead to increased strain in a relationship. The emotional, psychological and spiritual strength that it takes to forgive someone who owes us love and affection but instead hurts, abandons or betrays us challenges the capacity of the average person.

There is profound wisdom in the Jewish tradition about the human capacity to forgive. We are taught that we can't seek forgiveness from God for a wrong we have committed to others. For those acts, we must ask forgiveness directly from the person we have offended and, if we still are not forgiven after three attempts, our obligation is satisfied.

When we are wronged, the Torah counsels us not to take vengeance or to bear a grudge. (Leviticus 19:18). We are inspired by our Talmudic sages who taught that when we forgive the sins of others, we will likewise be forgiven for our own sins. (Megillah 28a)

There is a lovely prayer called the Bedtime *Shema* which is traditionally recited before retiring each evening. In it, we explicitly forgive anyone who angered, antagonized or hurt us that day whether by speech, deed or thought – regardless of whether it was accidental and careless or willful and purposeful. Each night we are reminded that to be human is to err, but to forgive brings us closer to the Divine.

I think of the years of hurt that my mother endured and of how she longed for her sister to acknowledge and apologize for the wrongs she had done, or at least to talk about them. She will never have that conversation now, but what she does have is almost as good. She was able to put her own anger aside long enough to have a final, connecting moment where the bond of two sisters prevailed. And in doing so, she found a path to her own forgiveness and way to remember her sister with love.

Amy Hirshberg Lederman

◆◆◆

Caring For Others Precedes Everything

One year on Yom Kippur, the first Chabad Rebbe, Rabbi Shneur Zalman of Liadi, was late coming to synagogue. The entire congregation was waiting, and as time passed, they sought him throughout the village. Eventually, they discovered that he had gone to the home of a poor woman who had recently given birth and had nothing to eat. He cooked for her and fed her (her condition was such that it was permissible to cook for her and for her to eat on Yom Kippur).

The Hasidim learned that caring for others precedes everything.

◆◆◆

I've Changed Since Then

There is a story of the late Professor Mordecai Kaplan, the founder of Reconstructionist Judaism. Kaplan taught homiletics (the art of sermons) at the Jewish Theological Seminary.

One day a young rabbinical student delivered a sermon to the class, and Kaplan said, "Very nice." The student was relieved until he came back to class a week later. Kaplan harshly criticized the sermon. "But last week you liked it," said the student. Kaplan replied, "I've changed since then."

◆◆◆

The Last Song

I've been keeping this story to myself for almost twenty years. Well, not entirely to myself – I did share it with people close to me, but this is the first time I'm passing it along to someone who will make it so well known.

It has a historical dimension, and it will answer questions that have been hanging silently in the air for the past twenty years or more. It may also raise some new questions.

It was the month of Cheshvan in the year 5755 (October 1994). I was in New York at the time on business, staying at the Avenue Plaza Hotel in Brooklyn. I ate lunch each day with a different businessman, and we negotiated our deals over a pleasant meal.

On 16 Cheshvan 5755, I was sitting over a business lunch with a man by the name of Yossel W. Yossel did, and still does, business on a broad scale and with considerable success. He is also a sincerely religious man, meticulous about Halachah and strict with himself about all religious matters. Just as he did not tolerate laxness in himself, he had little tolerance for it in others, either.

As we sat there eating our meal and discussing business, suddenly someone walked into the restaurant, a man whose face was familiar to everyone sitting there. In fact, his face was known to every religious Jew in the world.

His name was Reb Shlomo Carlebach. His guitar was slung over his back. He started going from table to table, greeting everyone warmly and shaking their hands. Some of the diners starting talking with him, and he lingered at their tables for a few moments of conversation, so it took about twenty minutes before he got to our table, which was in the middle of the restaurant.

He extended his hand to me, and I gave him a friendly handshake. He extended his hand to my colleague, and his hand was left dangling in midair.

"Reb Yossel," I said, thinking he hadn't noticed. "What?" Yossel asked me, as if he had no idea what I wanted from him.

"This is Reb Shlomo Carlebach," I said. "I know it's Reb Shlomo Carlebach," he answered.

"I'd like to shake hands with you," said Reb Shlomo.

"Very nice that you want to shake hands," said Yossel in a loud voice. "But I don't want to!"

A few forks fell from people's hands, and the waiters stood frozen. Reb Shlomo looked very embarrassed. "Reb Yid, he said in his soft voice, "All I want to do is shake your hand. Why do you refuse me?"

"Because I'm opposed to you and your *derech*. I don't want to be in your *dalet amos*!" Yossel shouted.

The restaurant was packed with people, and there was nobody there who wasn't aware of the drama they were witnessing. No one was eating; the waiters stopped serving. Everyone was just watching. I was more embarrassed than I've ever been in my life. This situation was just impossible for me.

"I don't ask you to agree with me, and I'm even willing to listen to your views," said Reb Shlomo, "but Reb Yid, I'm just asking you to take my hand. I'm not asking, I'm begging you."

Surely, after words like those, anyone would relent, but Reb Yossel was adamant. "I don't give my hand to *posh'im*," he said.

I was afraid there was going to be a big fight, but Reb Shlomo looked at him gently and said, "You know, Reb Yid, when we daven Neilah we say, 'You give Your hand to rebellious sinners.' What will be next year on Yom Kippur? Maybe you won't be comfortable asking Hashem to give you His hand?"

That was a brilliant answer, but Yossel had a comeback: "You're quoting only part of it. It goes on to say, 'Only if a person does *teshuvah* is Hashem willing to stretch His hand out to him' not to a person who is stubbornly rebellious."

By this time, half the people in the restaurant had gathered around our table. Reb Shlomo listened, thought a bit, and said, "So what will it take to get you to shake hands with me?"

"When you do *teshuvah*, then I'll shake your hand!"

"And suppose I promise to do *teshuvah*? "

Now Reb Yossel was losing ground, but he recovered his position quickly. "What good is a promise? Who will guarantee that you'll keep your promise?"

Reb Shlomo thought that over. He looked very serious. Then he took his guitar case off his shoulder, took the instrument out, and started strumming it in his typical way while speaking to Reb Yossel:

"A Yid wants others to shake his hand, even if he's not a tzaddik, even if he's strayed far, and even if he's got a lot of *klippos*... he still wants Hashem to stretch His hand out to him." And then he sang in an improvised melody.

Again, he spoke to Reb Yossel: "It's so hard to do *teshuvah*. How can a Yid who has sinned do *teshuvah sheleimah*? The solution is found in the same line from Neilah."

And he sang, "And you have taught us, Hashem our God, to confess all our sins before You, so that our hands might cease from abuse..."

"*Ribono shel Olam*," said Reb Shlomo, "all my life I went down into the mud, into the garbage piles, to collect gems for you, to shake hands with pure, good *neshamos* who only wanted simple, genuine love, who only wanted to be judged favorably, and I found many, many gems for You, but I got soiled with mud... and now I meet a clean, righteous Yid who lives in a higher sphere, and he's willing to shake my hand, he just wants me to clean up first. And I, who got dirty in order to shake hands with Yidden, will I not get washed in order to shake hands with Yidden? So, I tell You now, *Ribono shel Olam*, that just as I got dirty, so will I now accept upon myself to do complete *teshuvah*, just as it says in *Neilah*, "to confess before you all our iniquities."

Reb Shlomo then began reciting the *Vidui*, word by word, including *Al Cheit*, and many of the onlookers joined him, some of them crying openly. The atmosphere in the restaurant was like *Neilah* on Yom Kippur, and as the *Vidui* ended, Reb Yossel put his head in his hands and cried harder than anyone.

The moment Reb Shlomo finished, Reb Yossel got up and embraced him. They hugged each other for a long moment, and there wasn't a dry eye in the place.

Reb Shlomo glanced at his watch and said he was late for his flight. He began making his way to the exit, but not before shaking hands with all the men in the restaurant. Some of them hugged him warmly, and then he left without having eaten, pensive and alone with his guitar.

If I ended the story right here, it would still be one of the most touching stories you've heard. But the story doesn't end here.

Three hours later, I phoned Reb Yossel and said, "Did you hear the news?"

"No, what news?" he asked.

"Reb Shlomo Carlebach left the restaurant, caught his flight, and just when they were landing, he had a heart attack and passed away!"

"What?!!" I heard Reb Yossel yell in alarm. He said nothing more, he just cried bitter, desperate sobs. I'd never heard anyone so shocked and upset, and really, I'd never heard of such a tragic sequence of events before.

Of all the many people who were touched by Reb Shlomo's passing, perhaps only Reb Yossel never got over the trauma. He went and poured out his heart to rabbanim about it, and they all tried to reassure him that rather than feel guilty, he should feel privileged that he was the *shaliach* who brought Reb Shlomo to do *teshuvah sheleimah* just hours before his death and to leave this world pure as an angel.

According to Rav Yisrael Meir Lau, who traveled on the same flight as Reb Shlomo, the last song Carlebach played in his life was the pasuk from Eichah, "*Chasdei Hashem ki lo tamu, ki lo chalu rachamav* – For Hashem's kindnesses never cease, for His mercies never end."

Apparently, Reb Shlomo was a Jew with a special neshamah, and the fact that he was given the opportunity to do *teshuvah sheleimah* with *Vidui* shortly before his sudden death is proof of that.

David Mescheloff

♦♦♦

Reb Zusha and the Tormentors

Something was terribly wrong with the city of Bar in central Ukraine. Instead of spending days and nights in yeshiva, the youth now trifled their time in the streets, sneering at religion. They embraced every opportunity to ridicule Hasidic rabbis and their simple faith, but Rabbi Zusha of Anipoli, who journeyed from town to town looking for Jewish souls he could help, bore the brunt of their scorn, enduring malice every time he visited the city.

Rabbi Zusha secured his few worldly possessions on the wagon's bed and climbed into the passenger seat. Before the driver could direct the horses forward, Rabbi Zusha held out a few kopeks.

"I'm aware that the road goes through Bar," he said, "but I ask you not to enter the town. I know it is quicker to go through the city, so here is payment for the additional distance. Please, whatever you do, don't enter the city!"

The wagon began to move, and before long the rhythmic swaying lulled Rabbi Zusha to sleep. As the town of Bar appeared on the horizon beneath the darkening sky, a carriage sidled close to the wagon and Rabbi Moshe of Pshevorsk – a renowned scribe and a student of Rabbi Zusha's brother, Rabbi Elimelech – poked his head out from one of its windows. The wagon driver slowed to a stop.

"Who's riding with you?" Rabbi Moshe asked, motioning to the sleeping bundle.

"Rabbi Zusha of Anipoli."

"Are you traveling through Bar?"

"Oh no," the driver shook his head. "Rabbi Zusha gave me specific instructions not to go there."

"Well then," Rabbi Moshe went on, "I advise you to redirect the wagon to Bar. Nothing will happen to you. I promise. But if you decide not to go, it might not end well."

Rabbi Moshe signaled to his driver and they rode off. The carriage's rattling slowly faded, leaving the wagon driver quietly weighing his options.

Should he obey Rabbi Zusha or Rabbi Moshe?

He picked up the reins and urged the old horse into action, heading directly towards Bar. Circumventing the town would make the journey much longer, and besides, the wagon driver had Rabbi Moshe's assurance that nothing would happen to them.

As the horse slowed, Rabbi Zusha awoke, sat up, looked around at the familiar streets, and realized where he was.

"Zusha! You wicked person," he moaned. "How dare you travel through such an impure city?"

Although the rabbi's reproach was self-directed, the wagon driver knew Rabbi Zusha had a peculiar way of censuring others. He quickly tried to placate him by offering, "I'm sorry, it was a mistake. If you want, we can retrace our steps and go around."

But it was too late. The sun had already dipped beyond the horizon and Rabbi Zusha was particular not to travel at night. Seeing no alternative, he requested a room at an out-of-the-way inn, selected specifically so that no one would learn of his presence. But every inn was full and he was left with no choice but to ask his wagon driver to take him to the community hostel, the *hekdesh*, where all travelers were welcome to rest free of charge. Quietly, he spread his bedding in a corner and turned his face towards the wall.

Word of his presence soon spread and a crowd gathered around the sleeping rabbi. Cheering noisily, they began playing cards, peppering their conversations with inventive profanities. The ruffians glanced over at Rabbi Zusha frequently, waiting to see how he would react to their provocation.

Finally, Rabbi Zusha could take it no more. He sat up and said to himself loudly, "You wicked person, Zusha, oh you wicked person! Remember the time you sinned? Do you recall the despicable acts you did in that place? You did this particular sin. And in the other place, you committed this and this sin...?"

Hardly believing their ears, the young men lowered their cards and watched the old man in the corner. Rabbi Zusha was still going at it, listing sins they themselves had committed as though reading them off a piece of paper.

"And what are you going to claim on Judgment Day, eh, Zusha? Your soul will know no peace when that time comes!"

Rabbi Zusha's words had their desired effect. The young men dropped their cards and covered their faces, deeply ashamed. Some sobbed while others were stunned into silence.

After some time the erstwhile tormentors approached Rabbi Zusha with a collective request for help. Rabbi Zusha saw their honest expressions and downcast eyes and created a personalized path of repentance for each one.

By morning, word of the night's wondrous events had spread through the town, and everyone else wanted to ask the saintly visitor to help them too. Many, however, were ashamed to approach him, fearing he would see their sordid secrets.

This was Rabbi Moshe's cue. He had arrived in Bar to greet Rabbi Zusha and couldn't help but beam delightedly when he found a sizable group of desperate young people wanting to repent. Rabbi Moshe explained the situation to Rabbi Zusha, who approached each one individually and helped them amend their wayward behavior.

From that time forward, Rabbi Zusha was never again bothered in Bar. On the contrary, whenever he passed through the city, he was greeted warmly and exuberantly, and kept busy advising and encouraging the now good-hearted townsfolk.

Asharon Baltazar, www.chabad.org

♦♦♦

Giving to Charity

Reb Shlomo died penniless, because he gave all his money to charity. His followers had to collect donations to take care of the funeral arrangements. He is buried on Har HaMenuchos, but his singing still echoes in the heart of every Jew around the world.

David Mescheloff

♦♦♦

But He Had No Tears In His Eyes

There is a famous story about a *shohet* (ritual slaughterer) who came to a new town and wanted to be employed by the community. As was the custom, he came to the town's rabbi and sought approval. The rabbi asked the *shohet* to demonstrate how he prepared the knife for the slaughter of animals. The *shohet* showed how he sharpened the knife; and he ran his thumb up and down the blade checking for any possible nicks. When he completed the demonstration, he looked to the rabbi for validation.

The rabbi asked: "From whom did you learn to be a *shohet*?"

The *shohet* answered: "I learned from the illustrious Rabbi Israel Baal Shem Tov."

The rabbi replied: "Yes, you have performed the task of sharpening and checking the knife very well. However, you did not do so in the manner of the Baal Shem Tov.

Yes, the *shohet* had learned the technical skills of his trade – but he did not plumb the depths of his work. He had not internalized the emotional, psychological and spiritual elements that were the hallmark of his teacher. He was technically proficient – but he had no tears in his eyes.

Religious life (and life in general!) can sometimes be technically correct; but at the same time it might be missing the inner spiritual content, the tears in the eyes. A synagogue service might be conducted with great accuracy, and yet fail to produce a real religious experience. A person might fast and pray all day on Yom Kippur, but still be exactly the same person at the end of the day as he/she was at the beginning of the day.

Rabbi Marc D. Angel

Testament of a Jew in Saragossa

Elie Wiesel recounts an experience he once had on his visit to Spain years ago. In "Testament of a Jew in Saragossa" the title of his story, Wiesel tells of being approached by a man who offers to provide him with some guiding around the Spanish city. When the discussion turned personal, the Spanish guide discovered that Wiesel knew many languages and he begged him to come to his apartment to decode a parchment document that had been handed down, father to son, for generations. This devout Catholic family believed that the document protected them from evil. Yet no one in the family understood its contents.

Wiesel immediately recognized the script as Hebrew, and with trembling hands and heart, he translated slowly:

"I, Moses, son of Abraham, forced to break all ties with my people and my faith, leave these lines to the children of my children and to theirs, in order that on the day when Israel will be able to walk again, its head high under the sun, without fear and without remorse, my descendants will know where their roots lie. Written at Saragossa, this ninth day of the month of Av, in the year of punishment and exile."

It had taken four centuries, since the days of the Spanish Inquisition, for this family testament to fulfill its objective. But now, this Catholic Spaniard knew that he was descended from Jews. Of course, the date of the testament's writing, the 9th of Av, is the same date as the destruction of both the first and second Temples of Jerusalem, a day that has also marked an uncanny number of tragedies throughout Jewish history – expulsions, massacres, discriminatory regulations and the like. It is a day that observant Jews mark with fasting, recalling how much the Jew has been victimized through history as guests in foreign lands. It is also a day that reminds us how important it is for Jews to have a homeland in which they can control their own destiny and how fortunate American Jews are to live in a land that protects minority rights and honors religious pluralism.

The Elie Wiesel story ends with Wiesel jumping forward ten years past his encounter with the lost Jew of Saragossa. He was walking on King George Street in Jerusalem when a stranger grabs his elbow and whispers in his ear: "Saragossa". Wiesel can hardly believe the coincidence. The man takes him to his apartment where he shows him the old parchment that Wiesel first decoded for him. It was now framed prominently on the wall of his apartment ... next to the mezuzah. "And my name now," continued the man to Wiesel, "is Moshe ben Avraham", the name of the last person in my family to live as a Jew in the 15th century.

One final thought...

On this Yom Kippur there will be many opportunities in the service when we reflect on the past – we reflect on our own lives, we remember our parents, we recall ancient Israel's Temple Service, we are saddened by the Martyrology. It is appropriate that we also consider the mystical tenacity of the heritage, faith, and people of Israel. How blessed we are to be alive and witness the recreation of modern Israel when Israel is able to walk again with "its head high under the sun", *She'heheyanu.*

◆◆◆

Let Us Make Up

Dr. Louis Finkelstein was one of the greatest Judaic scholars of the 20th century and was the Chancellor of the Jewish Theological Seminary from the 1940s to the 1970s.
This is a story about Dr. Finkelstein's father, who was the rabbi of a synagogue in the Brownsville section of Brooklyn.

It happened that in that congregation, as it sometimes does, (may God protect us from it ever happening here) that the rabbi and the cantor quarreled.

The congregation took sides, and the quarrel escalated until finally the congregation decided that both of them, the rabbi and the cantor, had to leave.

Years later, Rabbi Finkelstein's father found himself the rabbi of another congregation, and much to his surprise, he found that that cantor was now a member of the same synagogue.

For years, the rabbi would walk from his seat to the middle of the room where the speaker's stand was in order to give his sermon every week. On the way he would have to pass the seat of the former cantor, and the two of them would ignore each other. Not a single word of greeting passed their lips for years.

And then the rabbi's wife died. The children worried about how their father would survive the enormous loss. During *shiva*, the house was full and his mind was occupied, but they worried about how he would manage after *shiva*. One day, soon after the completion of the *shiva*, they came to see him and they found him, much to their surprise, all excited.

"Do you know who came to see me today?" he asked. "It was the cantor." The children were surprised that after so many years of stony silence, the two men would have made up, and they asked their father: "What did he say?"

"He said to me, Reb Shimon, *mir halten shoin baide bai neilah; lomir zich iberbeten.*" (We are both already at the *neilah* stage in our lives. We are both closer to the end than to the beginning, so let us make up.)

And they did. And from that day on till the day that the rabbi died, the two of them played chess together every single afternoon.

Let that story be a lesson to all of us. We are all one year older than we were at this moment a year ago. We are all a year closer to the *neilah* stage in our lives. Let us make up.

◆◆◆

The Hands Of The Clock Stopped Moving

R' Hanoch Henich, the son-in-law of R' Shalom Rokeach, the founder of the Belz Hasidic dynasty, once extended the Yom Kippur Musaf prayer far beyond the normal time. Before Mincha, he told the anxious daveners exactly when he would finish Neilah, the closing prayer. But here too he was running late, only about half-way through by the time he had announced. At that moment the people noticed something very strange – the hands of the clock stopped moving and stood still until R' Hanoch finished Neilah.

Rabbi Daniel Goldfarb

◆◆◆

Cry Over Every Stitch

Sometimes we feel so old and so much not alive that we don't even have the capacity for newness anymore. But really, when we look at it, we don't need to do anything to start anew! Because beginnings are the gift from Heaven. The middle is in our hands, but beginnings are only in God's hands. It's up to me what I do with it after the beginning. So how do we begin the New Year?

Sadly enough, a lot of people think Rosh Hashanah and Yom Kippur is a time to regret what we did wrong and to promise God that we'll be better. It is all good and well, but don't waste your time with that.

Reb Shlomo always said that Rosh Hashanah is not about cleaning, it is about beginning, taking things apart and putting them together anew, it's about a new chance.

There is a story he told about the Porisover Rebbe who had a Hasid, a tailor who made just enough for bread and herring.

A nobleman came to his shop, took a liking to him, and appointed him his tailor. Now, when you are the tailor of the nobleman, you don't need a Rebbe, and you don't eat bread and herring anymore. He kept away from Jews, kept his nose in the air, and was a very outstanding tailor. One day, the nobleman came with material from Paris, and he said to the tailor, "This is the best material I ever bought, and I want you to make me a suit like you never made before."

The tailor thought, "I am the best tailor in the world. I once was a Hasidisher Yid; all I had was bread and herring, and now, thank God, I have bagels and lox." He made the suit, and it really was beautiful. He brought it to the nobleman, who put it on and couldn't get it off fast enough. He yelled at the tailor, "This is the most terrible suit I ever wore." Cursing him, he took out his pistol and said, "If I ever see you again, I'm going to kill you." Then he took the suit and threw it out of the window. The tailor ran out of the room and recovered the suit, and then ran for his life.

He also remembered his Rebbe because he couldn't understand anything any more. He said to the Porisover Rebbe, "Believe me, it's a beautiful suit. What did I do wrong?"

The Rebbe replied, "I'll tell you what. Undo the suit, and then put it together the same way. Just put it together, and tomorrow night take it to the nobleman, and God be with you."

The tailor was up all night, crying over every stitch. The next day, he brought it to the nobleman and said, "Please give me just one more chance."

The nobleman put it on and said, "This is the masterpiece of the world. I never had such a suit. You outdid yourself."

The tailor went back to the Rebbe. "Rebbe, what's going on?"

The Rebbe said, "I want you to know, arrogance smells so bad. For the nobleman, the smell was so bad he couldn't stand it. There was no other way; you had to start all over again, even with the same fabric. Only this time, when you put the suit together, you cried over every stitch, all your arrogance was gone and you pleaded:

"Master of the World, have compassion on me. I have a wife and children. Please God, let the suit be beautiful."

And anything you do with great humility, with tears and with prayers, is so beautiful, so good.

Once a year God tells us, take everything apart, and put it together again. When we do teshuvah, we take everything apart. And then we go back on Yom Kippur and knock on the door of God.

Miriam Rubinoff

◆◆◆

Don't Miss Opportunities

In 1491, the Jews of Spain had a big convention.

They said, "We can get together and buy the Land of Israel. The king of Turkey is willing to sell it for a certain price and we have enough money." They were really getting ready to go to Israel and build the Holy Temple. The Kohanim and Levites were already learning the laws pertaining to the Holy Temple.

Then, unfortunately, one old man got up and said, "How do we know that we have the right to do this. We need a sign from Heaven."

The people answered, "The king of Turkey is ready to sell us the Land of Israel and we have the money! Do we need a bigger sign from Heaven than that?"

They started debating, and finally decided, "Let's wait one year and then we will have another convention." This was in 1491. In 1492, the Jews were expelled from Spain.

We have opportunities, openings when we could do so much, and the saddest thing is that we wait and wait.

The night after Yom Kippur, approximately seven years after Rebbe Shlomo Carlebach went to Heaven, I had a dream. In the dream I heard him retelling this story to me. I awoke at three in the morning hearing the words – "We have opportunities, openings when we could do so much, and the saddest thing is that we wait and wait and wait."

Zivi Ritchie
Reb Shlomo Carlebach, Ecstasy for the Soul
(The Rabbi Shlomo Carlebach Center, Kiryat Arba, Israel)

♦♦♦

Sand and Stone

O nce two friends were traveling together in the desert. At some point in the trip, the two began to argue. Then the first friend slapped his partner. The victim did not defend himself, but instead wrote in the sand: "Today my best friend gave me a slap."

The days passed and the two friends continued on their journey. They came to an oasis and decided to bathe in the spring. The man who had been slapped began to drown, but his friend threw himself into the water and rescued him. The man was grateful, and he took his knife and began to carve into a stone, "today, my best friend saved my life."

Now the first friend was really intrigued, so he asked his friend, "Why did you write in the sand when I slapped you, but now that I rescued you, you carved it into a stone?"

The second friend answered with a smile, "When someone offends me, I try to write it in the sand, where the marks are easily erased by the winds of forgiveness. When someone does something good for me, I prefer to leave it engraved in stone so that I never forget, so the memory will remind me that I should be grateful."

♦♦♦

Such Unheard of Honesty

A great scholar lived in Jerusalem many years ago. His name was Rabbi Shimon ben Shetah. He was a God-fearing man and spent all his time in the study of the Torah. Rabbi Shimon ben Shetah had many disciples and students, but he never accepted any fees from them. He earned his meager livelihood by making ink. Early in the morning Rabbi Shimon ben Shetah would go to the woods and gather a sack-full of chestnuts and carry it home on his shoulders. Out of these nuts he would make ink and sell it.

Rabbi Shimon ben Shetah was very poor, but he had no regrets except one – that too much time was wasted on carrying the loads of nuts on his bare shoulders. How he wished he could spend this time in the company of his students and teach them more and more of the Divine wisdom of the Torah. Finally, he decided to buy a mule. He sold the chattels of his home and bought a mule.

When he brought the mule from the market, his students went out to see it. They stroked it and petted it and admired it, and then they suddenly discovered a precious stone hanging down from its neck, hidden in a little bag. The students rushed into the house. "God's name be praised!" they exclaimed. "God has rewarded your piety. You are a wealthy man now! Our dear master shall know no more want!"

They showed him the precious diamond which they had discovered on the mule. But Rabbi Shimon ben Shetah did not share their excitement.

"God forbid, that I take this diamond," he said. "I only bought a mule from that Ishmaelite, and this diamond does not belong to me. Do you think that Shimon ben Shetah is a barbarian?"

Whereupon Rabbi Shimon ben Shetah ran to the market in search of the man who had sold him the mule. He found the Ishmaelite and returned to him the precious stone. The Ishmaelite was amazed at such unheard of honesty.

"Blessed be the God of Rabbi Shimon ben Shetah!" he exclaimed, and never became tired of repeating it over and over again.

Jerusalem Talmud, Bava Metzia 2:5

The Real Jew

Mendele Sokolover grew up in Kotzk, where he learned what a real Jew could do. He traveled around the Pale of Settlement, from shtetl to shtetl trying to find a real Jew in his day. He found observant Jews, studious Jews, kind Jews, yet none measured up to his image of a real Jew, until he met Moshele the water carrier, and this is the story he tells about Moshele:

I was passing a dilapidated hut one night. I happened to peer through the window and saw a man clutching a worn volume of Psalms praying fervently. I didn't want to disturb him, so I watched for a long time. He never raised his eyes from the page nor did his lips ever stop moving. I kept returning and seeing the same thing. Finally, I hesitantly knocked on the door to see if he had the spark of holiness for which I was searching. He opened the door. I asked his name. "My name is Moshele the water carrier." I tried to draw him into conversation, but he just shook his head from side to side. When I asked him how he was, he answered, "Good, thank God." I couldn't get him to answer any other question or to say anything else.

Many years passed, and I became the Rebbe of Sokolov. One night as I walked, I saw Moshele was not reciting his Psalms. There was a party in his hut. The shoemakers, tailors, and water carriers were there dancing around Moshele. It seemed like God's presence radiated from his face. I walked in, wanting to know why everyone was celebrating. Moshele was the first to notice. "Rebbe, what are you doing here?"

I told him I was walking by and saw that he was having a party and wanted to know why everyone was celebrating. For a while, Moshele wouldn't answer. I kept persisting.

Finally he said:

"I was orphaned at a young age. I don't remember either my mother or father. I grew up on the streets here and had no education. An old man took a liking to me and taught me to recite Psalms. I married a most beautiful girl, but she's no longer beautiful. We have seven children. They were born angels, but all they do is cry, and we can't bear to hear them cry. But it's impossible to make ends meet as a water carrier, so most of the time we go to sleep hungry. I can't sleep when I'm hungry, so I spend the night reciting Psalms, the only prayers I know.

"A week ago, I ran to the shul in the middle of the night. I couldn't bear my wife and children crying anymore. I stood before the Holy Ark and pleaded from the depths of my soul, 'Master of the Universe, I can't stand it anymore to see my wife and children suffering so much. Please help me. Give some money to ease their pain.'

"Two days ago, I was delivering water along my usual route. I carry two buckets full of water on a pole across my shoulders. Since it's heavy, I'm stooped and my eyes look at the ground. As I passed the shul, I saw one thousand rubles lying on the ground. I picked up the money and thanked God for answering my prayer.

"I vowed to keep my fortune secret for two days. When I returned home after I finished my route, I noticed that my wife appeared as beautiful as she was on the day we married. My children seemed to be angels again. I was bursting with joy. That evening, when I went to the shul to pray, I saw Channale, the widow of one of the other water carriers crying bitterly because she lost the thousand rubles that the other water carriers raised for her. I didn't enter the shul. I ran, and shouted at God, 'Why did You have to give me Channale's rubles. Couldn't you find one thousand rubles someplace else? What kind of compassionate God are You?!'

"I ran home sullenly. I hated the world. I was angry at God. I lay on my bed for a whole day. I cried and cursed. I ranted and raged. I was brokenhearted and distraught. Suddenly, I was in touch with my soul. My soul asked, 'What happened to you? All of your life you prayed. Why did you stop praying now?'

"I swear Rabbi, my soul talked to me. It continued, 'The soul that stood on Mount Sinai, the soul that swore we will do and we will listen, this soul is incapable of keeping the widow's money. Return the money to Channale.'

"I ran out of my hut and found Channale still crying, sitting at a broken table in her dilapidated hut. I put the money on the table. She looked up and smiled weakly. She couldn't believe that someone had returned one thousand rubles. Her smile returned until it was like the smile of Heaven. I felt so good at that moment. I realized that my life would never change. My children would always wear used clothes. We would never have enough food on the table. But I know how good it is to be a Jew. My friends are making this party in my honor. They too are celebrating how good it feels to listen to God's voice."

Rebbe Mendele Sokolover joined the party of shoemakers, tailors, and water carriers in celebration. He had found his real Jew. Each year on the yahrzeit of Moshele's death, he told the story of Moshele the water carrier, the real Jew.

Annette and Eugene Labovitz
tell this story about the Real Jew.

♦♦♦

Eating by Example

It once appeared in an Israeli newspaper and had the elements of a good story: An epidemic. A famous rabbi. Public eating on Yom Kippur to prove a point.

The epidemic took place somewhere in Europe, sometime in the 19th century.

The protagonist was Rabbi Meir Leibush ben Yehiel Michel Wisser, better known as "The Malbim", the scholar, biblical commentator and crusader against non-traditional Judaism who was once imprisoned and exiled from Romania following particularly heated ideological disagreements with his co-religionists. Formerly chief rabbi of Bucharest, the aged scholar spent much of the end of his life on the road, including stops in Istanbul, Paris, Prussia and the Russian Empire.

According to the story, this staunch advocate of Orthodoxy commanded the normally forbidden act of eating on the holiest day of the year due to the dangers posed by an epidemic. The preservation of life, after all, supersedes virtually all other considerations and rules according to Jewish law.

When he realized that those attending synagogue had not listened to his instructions and were clearly fasting in any event, he had a bowl of grits and peas brought up to him. He made a blessing over his food and finished off the portion in front of his congregation, declaring:

"I said there is no obligation to fast at this time. 'Preserving your lives' overrides many commandments in the Torah, but I was nonetheless concerned that you would close your hearts and put your lives at risk, and so I had to serve as an example so that you would see me and do so yourselves..."

The problem? The story doesn't seem to have been about the Malbim at all.

While a number of epidemics plagued Europe during his lifetime, a survey of works ranging from children's stories about him to doctoral theses and scholarly books revealed no clear mention of this perhaps apocryphal story.

A nearly identical – and better documented – tale is told of another famous rabbi of the period, Yisrael ben Ze'ev Wolf Lipkin, better known as Israel Salanter, the father of the modern Mussar Movement, which emphasizes the centrality of ethics and personal morality and growth to Jewish practice.

Zack Rothbart

The Shepherd and His Flute

Long ago, in a small shtetl in what is now Ukraine, where the famous Rabbi, the Baal Shem Tov lived, also lived a family of scholars. The father of the family, Moshe, was the son and grandson of very respected rabbis, and he himself was a well-respected teacher of Torah and Talmud. And the mother, Rachel, was the daughter and granddaughter of very respected rabbis. Though many women of her time did not know how to read Hebrew or study the Torah, Rachel did, and she would read and study along with her husband at home. Their home was always full of joy, full of learning, full of conversation, full of exploration, full of consideration of life and how best to live it.

Moshe and Rachel were blessed with five sons, and together they taught their sons the treasures of Torah. When their eldest, Meir, was six years old, it was time to go to Cheder, to learn to read and write. He said goodbye to his parents and his younger brothers, and he excitedly went off to school, eager to learn. It was obvious right from the first day that he too would be a brilliant scholar. He was a quick learner, and soon was able to assist the Rabbi in teaching the other boys.

Next came time for the second son, Menachem, to join his older brother in Cheder. He too said goodbye to his parents and younger brothers, and happily joined his older brother in Cheder. Sure enough, just as everyone expected, he was just as sharp a student as his older brother and his parents and grandparents and great grandparents.

Soon, the third son, Shmuel, was old enough to join his brothers in the Cheder. Shmuel was a wonderful, sweet boy. But his parents had a suspicion that he would not have the same experience in Cheder that his older brothers did. And sure enough, as obvious as it had been that Meir and Menachem were going to grow to be brilliant scholars, it was quickly clear that Shmuel would not. He wasn't like his brothers: he couldn't sit, he couldn't learn his letters, he didn't seem to be paying attention the way the other boys did, and he often would get up and walk over to the window, staring longingly outside at the trees and the fields and the clouds.

So Moshe and Rachel and the Cheder's teacher realized that Cheder was not the place for Shmuel to learn and thrive and grow. They didn't know what to do, because all of the boys of the shtetl went to Cheder, and everyone in their family had always gone to Cheder.

But the solution came clear very quickly: early in the morning, every day, the shtetl shepherd would come by to collect the community's sheep and goats and cattle to take them out to the meadows and pastures around the village for the day, and then bring them back every evening. Though Moshe and Rachel had never noticed before, Shmuel had a special friendship with the shepherd, and used to rise early every morning just to greet the man, and walk with him a bit. Moshe and Rachel asked the shepherd if Shmuel could be his apprentice, and the shepherd was thrilled to have the young boy's company and help. And so, unlike his brothers and his cousins and everyone else in his family, Shmuel did not go to Cheder. Instead, he spent every day in the fields and meadows learning how to be a shepherd. Shmuel was thrilled. He loved the animals, he loved being outdoors, he loved being with the shepherd, and he loved learning how to play the flute, which the shepherd taught him as they sat for many hours every day with the flocks of animals. Shmuel always felt that he was praying as he played his flute.

In time, the two youngest brothers, Simcha and Yitzchak, were also old enough to go to Cheder, and they joined their oldest brothers, and showed that they too would soon be star scholars. Moshe and Rachel were proud of all of their sons in Cheder, and of course loved Shmuel dearly, but worried about him in a way that they did not worry about the other four boys.

As each of the boys grew, they reached Bar Mitzvah age, and Meir, Menachem, Simcha and Yitzchak all led the prayers of the congregation on their respective Bar Mitzvahs beautifully. Shmuel did not, but instead quietly celebrated his Bar Mitzvah playing his flute in the fields. For him, playing the flute was praying. He always felt that he was talking with God as he played his quiet tunes.

When Shmuel was about fourteen, the old shepherd decided that it was time for him to stop going to the fields with the flocks, and Shmuel became the official shepherd for the village. It was bitter-sweet of course for Moshe and Rachel, they were proud of their son, but it was never what they would have dreamed for one of their children.

Now, all of these years, there were two days every year when Shmuel would not take the flocks to the fields, on Rosh HaShanah and Yom Kippur. On those days, he would join his grandfathers, his father and his brothers in the synagogue, where everyone would gather to join the Baal Shem Tov in the holiday prayers. Every year Shmuel sat quietly, unable to speak the words of the prayers, unable to read. He loved the melodies of the community praying around him, but as the years passed, he felt sad that he couldn't join in.

One year on Rosh HaShanah, Shmuel was sitting with his family as usual, in the midst of the prayers, and he happened to look up at the Baal Shem Tov. As the prayers were being sung all around him, Shmuel again longed to join in. He noticed that the Baal Shem Tov seemed to look concerned. Shmuel sat and wondered what he could do to add his voice to the prayers of the community. His hand went to his flute in his pocket, and at once it was obvious how he could join in. He pulled out his flute and began to play a beautiful melody that wove harmoniously with the prayers of the congregation. He played with all of his heart and all of his soul, so happy to finally have found a way to participate in the community.

But the community stopped their praying, and a sound of shock and horror went through the room. Suddenly, men were shouting at Shmuel to stop, shouting at Moshe, Shmuel's father to stop him, shouting at the Baal Shem Tov to stop him. Moshe rose to reach out and grab Shmuel's flute, but the Baal Shem Tov reached them first, and, putting his hands on both Moshe and Shmuel's shoulders, the Baal Shem Tov said, "Finally, our prayers will truly reach Heaven as a full community, because Shmuel has joined us with his pure love, joy and devotion. We needed his voice in order for God to hear all of us. This is how he prays, and though it is different than our prayers, it is wonderful."

A tale of the Baal Shem Tov, retold by Joanie Calem, an autism parent, teacher, songwriter, performer and disability awareness advocate.

This centuries-old story reminds us that there have always been those amongst us who could not worship in exactly the way that a community might expect.

◆◆◆

Blessed is the Match

The soul of man is the candle of God.

Proverbs 20:27

Blessed is the match consumed in kindling flame.

Hannah Senesh

In Yugoslavia in 1944, a paratrooper named Reuven Dafni escorted a compatriot of his, one Hannah Senesh, to the Hungarian border. They had both trained with the British in Mandate Palestine and then parachuted into Eastern Europe with the mission of joining the partisans and saving Jews.

As Senesh prepared to enter Hungary, the land of her birth, she turned to Dafni and held out a piece of paper containing a poem she had just composed. "If I don't come back, please bring this to the *chaveirim* in Sdot Yam," she said, referring to the members of her kibbutz.

Decades later, in a documentary interview, Dafni described his state of mind: "I was nervous like hell, and I was tense. What is she doing? In this situation, she writes me some poems?"

After Senesh left, he angrily threw the piece of paper into the bushes and headed back to base. But halfway there, something within him made him stop and turn around. Even with German patrols everywhere, he searched for the poem: "It took me about an hour to find this piece of paper." In the end, he discovered the small scrap that contained what would become one of the most famous poems in the Hebrew language.

Blessed is the match consumed in kindling flame.
Blessed is the flame that burns in the secret fastness of the heart.
Blessed is the heart with strength
        to stop its beating for honor's sake.
Blessed is the match consumed in kindling flame.

Hannah Senesh, whose centenary birthday was marked in 2021, is a famous figure in the story of Israel and Zionism, her diary and poems read by Israelis for decades. Her life had eerie parallels to Theodor Herzl's. Born and raised in assimilation, comfort, and culture, the daughter of an acclaimed playwright, Senesh had a sudden exposure to anti-Semitism that led her to embrace the Zionist movement and emigrate to Israel. Like Herzl, she joined literary gifts with Zionism, and like Herzl, her brief life inspired others far beyond its duration. The poignancy of her story lies in her connection to the Land of Israel, but also to the mother in Budapest that she had left. As she confided to a colleague, using a Hebrew pun, her two great loves were "*ami v'imi*" – my people and my mother.

It was this familial link that drew her back to Hungary, and to her mission. Caught with a radio while crossing the border, Senesh refused, under terrible torture, to reveal the transmitter codes, and she continued to do so even when the Gestapo brought her mother to the very same prison to threaten the life of the woman she had come to save. Senesh was, by all accounts, a beacon of inspiration to other Jewish prisoners, sustaining them with tales of the Holy Land and famously drawing a Jewish star on the window of her cell. She was executed by firing squad soon before the Allies conquered Hungary. Though her mission was a failure, nevertheless, as Martin Gilbert and Adam Kirsch have noted, she took part in the only Jewish military attempt to save Jews from the Holocaust – and thereby died for the Zionist principle that Jews should fight to defend Jews.

What is the meaning of "Blessed Is the Match," of the few lines salvaged in the forests of Yugoslavia? The Bible in Proverbs tells us that *ner Hashem nishmat Adam*; the soul of man is a candle, or lamp, of God. It is a powerful and enduring image: The human soul is akin to a candle lit by the Creator, and even a small flame contains an extraordinary amount of power. The verse describes the luminous courage of the human spirit, bringing to mind how Churchill described Harry Hopkins, a sickly and infirm man who did so much to bring America to support Britain during this terrible time. Hopkins, he said, was "a soul that flamed out of a frail and failing body. He was a crumbling lighthouse from which there shone the beams that led great fleets to harbor."

This is the biblical metaphor: the human being as a candle. But Senesh gives us a more modern image, seizing on an invention that did not exist in the biblical era: the match. Lamps and candles are infused with fuel so that their flames sustain themselves, but a match brings forth a fiery force from within that is gone within seconds. Yet if the match successfully kindles another flame, even as it is consumed it still lives on, and its apparently transient life endowed with endurance, continuity. In Senesh's words, the match is *nisraf*, burned up, consumed, but it can ignite others in its few moments in existence. And so we can pronounce *ashrei hagafrur*, fortunate is the match.

Did Senesh write these words because she had a sense of her coming death? We cannot know, but she certainly knew how dangerous her mission was, and this poem eerily captures her own life, one all too short but that nonetheless kindled and inspired others throughout Israel and the Jewish world. This past July, on the week of Senesh's birthday, more than 100 Israeli paratroopers, along with members of European militaries, re-created Senesh's jump. Their commander explained that they sought to perpetuate her memory in the land of her birth and "strengthen the sense of mission and the memory of heroism."

Was Senesh, who had asked for a Hebrew Bible while in prison, inspired by the verse in Proverbs that tells us the soul of man is the candle of God? Again, we do not know, but Senesh had certainly thought about her soul. Soon after her 15th birthday, she reflected in her diary: "I would rather be an unusual person than just average. When I think of an above-average man I don't necessarily think of a famous man, but of a great soul ... a great human being. And I would like to be a great soul. If God will permit."

At this point, Senesh had not even embraced Zionism, and certainly could never have conceived of the horror that would descend on her home in Hungary. But she did become a great soul, not a candle but a match. It is overwhelming to think of a young woman who suffered in prison and was murdered for trying to save Jews being remembered on the very same soil by so many, and by soldiers of a Jewish state of which she had dreamed but did not live to see.

In the hours before Yom Kippur, Jews light memorial candles for those who have passed away, a ritual inspired by the biblical proverb that the soul of man is the candle of God. I do not know whether this year, in some homes in Israel, a candle was lit for Hannah Senesh; but the truth is that perhaps in this case a candle is unnecessary. I will wager that there are Jews around the world who, whenever candles are kindled on Shabbat eve, on Hanukkah, or before Yom Kippur, see a match struck right before the candle is lit and think of Hannah. I know I do.

Meir Y. Soloveichik

♦♦♦

Promoting Torah Education

It was just a few months after the Yom Kippur war of 1973, when this Israeli professor of literature walked into the office of a Jewish in-reach organization in Tel Aviv and said, "Rabbi I came to tell you that I am ready and desiring to dedicate all my talents toward promoting Torah education."

The Rabbi was stunned to hear this because this professor had written and published some very stinging and confrontational articles against traditional Jewish education. He frequently used to confront and criticize the Rabbi, claiming that we would all be better off without religion. When he regained his composure, the Rabbi asked him, "what brought about this great change?" And here is the story.

The professor was a reservist medic in the Israeli army and there were many casualties in this war. One day he was in a jeep with two other soldiers when they were hit by an enemy shell. His two comrades died and he was seriously wounded. They were all alone somewhere in the Sinai desert. Being a medic, he could tell from his wounds that unless help would arrive soon, he would be dead within two hours. Thinking that these might be the last two hours of his life he wondered what would be the best way to spend them. He had dedicated his life to literature, the finest of world literature, much of which he knew by heart. So he began to recite his favorite poems and sonnets, but he felt empty. So he tried another author and another and he still felt empty.

This disturbed him greatly. Could it be that all the literature and scholarship that he had dedicated his life to, could not offer him solace in these last few minutes of his life? He began to cry like a child.

"Was there nothing meaningful enough in my life, to be with me now?" He cried and cried. Suddenly in the midst of his tears, a childhood memory appeared. He was six years old and his grandfather had taken him to shul. It was Simchat Torah and there was much joy in the air. A kind man gave all the children flags crowned with apples. The people were dancing with the Torah and his grandfather picked him up, put him on his shoulders and danced with him. They were singing happy songs and everyone was kissing the Torah scrolls as they came around again and again.

After a few moments of remembering all this, even though he was in much pain, the professor found himself happy and comforted. Strange, how strange it is that this is the only comforting memory of my life. I never thought about this, I didn't ever remember it until now. Dancing with the Torah with a flag in my hand on grandfather's shoulders – this was the most meaningful moment of my life!?

The pain from the wound was getting stronger and he was feeling weaker, but this beautiful memory would not leave him. Was he beginning to hallucinate from pain? No! This is real! This is real; this is the deepest moment of my life! And he cried out, "Hashem, my God, if You save me, I will dedicate my life to Your Torah and to promoting traditional Jewish education."

It took two more days until he regained consciousness. They had found him and he underwent a few surgeries. Slowly, as he was coming out of his anesthesia, he opened his eyes and saw his wife and children and he began to cry; he cried like a little child, like a little child; he had regained his purest childhood moment and he was never going to let go of it again.

Reb Shlomo Carlebach

Clinging to Observance

From a Soviet labor camp to an ISIS prison, here are five true stories of people who clung to observing Yom Kippur despite the odds, great and small.

Steven Sotloff: Facing Jerusalem

In the middle of terrorist-controlled Syria, surrounded by murderous thugs dedicated to the eradication of Jews and the Jewish state, one Jewish, Israeli man was unbowed, observing Yom Kippur under the very noses of his captors. After the Islamic terrorists brutally murdered American-Israeli journalist Steven Sotloff, his story of enormous courage and faith has emerged.

An American-born Jew reporting from the Muslim world, Steven downplayed his religion and the fact that he was an Israeli citizen. When he was captured by terrorists in Syria in 2013, he did all he could to hide his Judaism from his captors. Steven's family, terrified that if his captors knew Steven was Jewish, they would do more to harm him, laid low, erasing all trace of their connection to their son from the Internet and refraining from making public appeals for his release.

Yet, despite the grave danger he was in, on Yom Kippur, Steven Sotloff managed to outwit his captors, fasting and even praying in the direction of Jerusalem on this holy day. A former prisoner who was held with Sotloff recalls: "He told them he was sick and doesn't want to eat, even though we were served eggs that day. He used to pray secretly in the direction of Jerusalem. He would see in which direction (his Muslim captors) were praying, and then adjust the angle."

The Soviet Guard

For years, Mendel Futerfas defied the Soviet Union. Studying Torah was strictly forbidden by the Soviet authorities – even possessing Jewish books was grounds for imprisonment – but Mendel risked his life day in and day out, educating his fellow Soviet Jews in secret. Finally, one day, he was discovered by the authorities and sentenced to forced labor in one of the USSR's feared labor camps in Siberia.

There, Mendel tried to keep as many of the mitzvot as possible, but it wasn't easy. One Yom Kippur, he felt particularly low. Without a machzor, the Yom Kippur prayer book, he was only able to recite a few prayers from memory. One was *V'chol Ma'aminim* – "We all Believe". But this Yom Kippur, Mendel had a difficult time believing the words. In such a dark place, he wondered, was it really possible to have such faith?

Just then, Mendel noticed one of the prison guards – a rough-looking man with a big scar across his face – staring at him. Frightened, Mendel tried to look as if he wasn't fasting and praying, but the guard came towards him.

Speaking quietly, the guard said, "I see you praying today. I know you are fasting today. I want you to know I am fasting as well. I know it's Yom Kippur today, yet I don't know a single thing about Judaism, except a prayer my grandmother taught me when I was a child called 'Modeh Ani'. I have been repeating this prayer all day, and I want you to know you are not the only one celebrating Yom Kippur."

After 14 long years, Mendel was able to escape from his gulag and make his way to Israel, where he dedicated his life to teaching Torah. It is not known what happened to the Jewish guard.

Rabbi Shlomo Zarchi transcribed this oral history.

Arrested for Blowing the Shofar

Under Turkish and then British rule, Jewish activity at the Western Wall – the last remaining remnant of the ancient Jewish Temple in Jerusalem and the holiest site of the Jewish people – was severely constrained. British law codified the restrictions on Jews who wanted to pray at the Wall: Jews were not allowed to recite prayers loudly, they could not bring a Torah to the Wall, and they were forbidden from sounding the Shofar.

On Yom Kippur, 1930, at the conclusion of the final Neila service, recited just before sundown, a sound rang out that had not been heard at the Western Wall in generations: the ringing blast of a Shofar. A young rabbi, Moshe Segal, had smuggled a Shofar to the Western Wall, and blew it at its traditional place at the end of the Yom Kippur service.

Rabbi Segal was soon arrested, but in the intervening years, other Jewish boys – all in their teens – took his place. Each year from 1930 to 1947, Jewish teenagers smuggled Shofars to the Wall, concealing them under their clothing, and blew them at the end of Yom Kippur. The boys worked in teams of three, aiming to blow the Shofar at each end of the Wall and in the middle. Abraham Caspi, who was 16 when he blew the Shofar at the Western Wall in 1947, remembers being told, "You'll be the first, and if you don't succeed or are caught, someone else will do it."

British soldiers arrested the boys who blew the Shofar. Each one was tried and sentenced to prison for terms of up to six months. Still, the volunteers were undeterred. "We swore to give our lives for the resurrection of the Jewish people," explains Jacob Sika Aharoni, who blew the Shofar at the Wall at age 16 in 1936.

When Jordan captured the Old City of Jerusalem, they forbade any Jew from setting foot near the Western Wall for 19 years. In 1967, Israel liberated the Wall, allowing all people – Jews, Muslims, and others, access – and the Shofar once again rang out. Abraham Elkayam, who was 13 when he blew the Shofar at the Western Wall in 1947, was fighting in the area, and quickly made his way to the Wall. An Israeli soldier was standing by the Wall, blowing a Shofar, and Abraham asked him if might have a turn as well. Abraham blew the Shofar, and a nearby soldier asked him why it was so important for him to sound this Shofar.

Abraham Elkayam explained he was one of the last people to sound the Shofar at the Western Wall, in 1947. The soldier then introduced himself, telling him that he was the first one to blow the Shofar. It was Rabbi Segal who started the yearly tradition back in 1930.

Sandy Koufax's Most Famous Game

In 1965, Los Angeles Dodgers pitcher Sandy Koufax was at the top of his game. Nicknamed "the Man with the Golden Arm," his skill had helped propel the Dodgers to the World Series. The Dodgers faced the Minnesota Twins. The opening game was scheduled for Metropolitan Stadium in the Twin Cities, on October 6 – a date that happened to be Yom Kippur.

Although he didn't consider himself particularly religious, Sandy Koufax didn't have to think twice. "There was never any decision to make," Koufax later recalled, "because there was never any possibility that I would pitch. Yom Kippur is the holiest day of the

Jewish religion. The club knows I don't work that day." Koufax sat out the game, and became best known, not for his amazing skill on the field, but for his principled stand.

The Dodgers lost that game without Koufax, but with his help in the rest of the World Series, they won the 1965 Pennant. Koufax was named Most Valuable Player of the season. He was induced into the Baseball Hall of Fame in 1972.

In the Polish Trenches

One of the most unusual Yom Kippur services didn't take place in a synagogue. The year was 1939. World War Two had just been declared, and Hitler's forces were battling in Poland, struggling for control of that country. Warsaw, the Polish capital, was under direct attack.

Augmenting the Polish army's efforts to repel the Nazi invaders, the Jews of Warsaw rallied to dig protective trenches around their city. Yom Kippur 1939 dawned on a city under siege. Homes and synagogues had been destroyed in German raids; Warsaw, battered daily from the Luftwaffe, was bracing for a ground assault.

Poland's army excused the Jewish residents of Warsaw from helping prepare defensive reinforcements on Yom Kippur, recognizing that it was a holy Jewish day. Yet, newspapers at the time reported that many of Warsaw's Jews had no place to go – their homes and synagogues lay in rubble – and instead they rallied at the city's barricades and desperately helped dig defensive trenches. Fighting-age men were in the army; those who remained were old men and children. Together, they worked feverishly, all the while reciting the Yom Kippur service.

The Jews – many of them elderly rabbis – recited Psalms and Vidui, the Yom Kippur confessional prayer while they dug the defenses. Under constant air attack, the elderly men and children together met each exploding bomb with a loud shout of "Shema Yisrael!"

Five True Stories for Yom Kippur, Dr. Yvette Alt Miller,
Reprinted by permission, www.aish.com

◆◆◆

Shabbat

Enter the Beloved

The Hasidic masters tell us that the name "Elul" (the month before the High Holidays) is an acronym for *ani l'dodi v'dodi li* – "I am my beloved's, and my beloved is mine." When the month of Elul approaches, its beautiful name always reminds me of how I would hear that verse from *Song of Songs* sung on Friday evenings at the Kol Shadai synagogue on Shimshon Street in Jerusalem. For many years before I married, I would go to this little Moroccan shul to welcome the Shabbat.

Feeling a little like Alice in Wonderland, with legs too long and hair too blond, I would come in time for the afternoon prayer, so that I could hear all of the *Song of Songs* sung during the pause before ushering in the Shabbat with the evening prayer. Although all Sephardi congregations chant *Song of Songs* on Friday evenings, this particular shul was blessed with wonderful voices. The little boys belted out, but didn't yell. Their fathers had young deep bass resonating voices, and their grandfathers, mature sweet lilting voices. Usually Moroccans sing out their prayers in unison, but here, *Song of Songs* and *Lechah Dodi* on Friday evening were multiple solo performances. Whoever jumped in first sang a few lines, until someone else glided in.

For me, coming from Washington, DC, where the synagogue members paid their cantor to allow their prayer to be as passive as possible, the spontaneity was wonderful. I felt I was wandering in the Sinai, with the voices of Kol Shadai blending with the minor keys of the wind and the desert.

The women's gallery was an impromptu arrangement of simple old wooden benches lining the walls of a narrow room adjacent to the men's section. We entered through a dark hallway with a few surprise stone steps. Nobody in Washington would accept such conditions, but here, old women who could hardly walk breezed their way in and out. The short older women who sat on long wooden benches with their hands cupped up to Heaven did not know how to read, but they knew the liturgy by heart. They were empowered to direct the music. When one of the men got carried away with his solo, trilling or holding a note too long, the women would laugh, Opera singer! pushing him off the stage.

I never learned the women's names, but there were two whom I especially liked. One was salty, with diamond-cut eyes and gaunt cheeks. The other had high cheeks, like apples, gracing soft sweet eyes. When we rose to greet and bow to the Sabbath Queen at the end of *Lechah Dodi*, she would walk to the open doorway, bow with outstretched arms, and kiss the mezuzah. As the Divine Presence lingered, all worry and weekday strife would vanish.

Now that I am married, I bring in Shabbat at home. When I reach the last verse of *Lechah Dodi*, I open the door and kiss the mezuzah. It is a moment of love and peace.

God is always with us, but we are not always with Him. A special day of the week, a special month of the year, enables us to come closer and to welcome in the Divine. No matter the worry or strife, if we open the door, the Beloved will enter.

Ilana Attia, www.chabad.org

♦♦♦

To Sign All Of Israel Into The Book Of Life!

Rabbi Levi Yitzhak of Berditchev was known as the "senigor" or defense attorney of the Jews, on a year when Rosh HaShanah begins on Shabbat.

Reb Levi Yitzhak informed God that this year God had no choice but to write the Jews into the book of life.

Why?

Well, writing is forbidden on Shabbat, so God certainly may not inscribe anyone for death. But saving a life – *pikuah nefesh* – overrides Shabbat, so God is "allowed" to sign all of Israel into the Book of Life!

♦♦♦

Challot in the Holy Ark

In the year 1502, a man named Jacobo, and his wife Esperanza, came to settle in the city of Tzfat, high on a mountain, in the holy land of Israel. Jacobo and Esperanza had been born in Spain, but in 1492, Spain expelled all her Jews. Jacobo and Esperanza, then young and strong, traveled from Spain to Salonika in Greece, where they lived for several years. There they heard of the great rabbi, Isaac Luria, who was known as the Ari, who led the Jews of Tzfat, a community steeped in kabbalah, the mystical teachings. Rabbi Luria taught that God is hidden and mysterious, but can be seen in the actions of those on earth who acknowledge God's creative power and seek to obey God's will. And so, in Salonika, Esperanza and Jacobo boarded a ship and sailed for Eretz Yisrael.

In Tzfat, they found a community of Jews dedicated to serving God, but struggling to feed themselves. One Shabbat, the rabbi, an elderly man, taught the congregation that when the Holy Temple stood in Jerusalem, before it was destroyed by the Romans, God was offered 12 loaves of bread each week just prior to Shabbat. Jacobo was a simple man, whose honesty, integrity, and kindness far exceeded his learning. He did not understand much of what the rabbi had said, but did remember about the loaves, so when he arrived home, he told Esperanza, "Next Friday morning, let us bake 12 loaves of challah. The rabbi taught this morning that God loves challah for Shabbat. I will bring them to the synagogue and give them to God."

Now Esperanza was a wonderful baker, and Jacobo was filled with joy at the thought that he and his wife would be able to please God in this manner. That week, they baked the finest 12 loaves of challah they had ever made. They kneaded the dough with love, expressing their awe of God and their love of mitzvot through their efforts.

When the loaves came out of the oven and had cooled, Jacobo carefully packed them in a burlap sack, hoisted them onto his shoulder, and headed for the synagogue. When he arrived in the synagogue, he looked around to be certain that no one saw him, then tiptoed to the Holy Ark. Opening the Ark doors and placing the loaves of challah in the Holy Ark, Jacobo whispered, "Senor Dios, I have brought You the challah You love so much. My Esperanza and I made it just for You. Tomorrow, on Shabbat morning, when they open the Ark to take out the Sefer Torah, I am going to look to see if they are gone – every crumb – so we will know that You like our gift." With that, Jacobo closed the Ark, drew the curtain closed across it, and tiptoed out of the synagogue.

No sooner had he left, than the shammes entered the room to sweep the floor and prepare the synagogue for Shabbat. When his eye caught sight of the Holy Ark, he put down his broom and approached it. "Lord," he prayed, "I don't ask for much. You know I am not paid for being the shammes of the synagogue. I do this job out of love for You and the Holy Torah. But my children are hungry. I need food for them. Even if the people of Tzfat cannot pay me, perhaps You can feed my children, Lord." It was then that the shammes noticed the enticing aroma of warm bread emanating from the Ark. Impulsively, he took a step forward and opened it. Gasping, he exclaimed, "My Lord, a miracle! I knew You would feed my children, just as we pray *ha-maycheen mazon le-chol b'riotav*. Oh, thank you, Lord, thank you so much!"

The shammes gathered the challot and ran home to his wife, who was overjoyed to see the food for their children. They decided to eat two challot that evening for their Erev Shabbat meal, two challot for lunch after they davened the next morning, two more for later in the afternoon at *Se'udah Shlishi*, and save one for each day of the coming week. "Next week, we shall see what happens," the shammes's wife told him, for her faith was strong.

The next morning, the congregation assembled in the synagogue to celebrate Shabbat. Jacobo waited eagerly for the Ark to be opened. He grew more and more anxious. Would the challot still be there? Had God accepted their gift? Had God enjoyed the challot? When Rabbi Luria opened the Ark, Jacobo's prayer was answered. There was not a crumb in the Ark! "Baruch Hashem! Thank God!" he prayed, and smiled at Esperanza.

As soon as three stars appeared in the sky, Esperanza and Jacobo made Havdalah to end Shabbat and set about discussing their plans to bake challot for God every Friday morning. The following Friday, they removed 12 beautiful challot from their oven, wrapped them in burlap, and took them quietly to the synagogue. Jacobo checked that no one was about before placing them lovingly in the Holy Ark. A short time later, the shammes came to clean the synagogue and, approaching the Ark, found his challah waiting for him, still warm from the oven.

This scene repeated itself each week, just before Shabbat, for thirty years.

One Friday morning, as Jacobo was placing the challah in the Ark, as he had done every week for three decades, he felt a hand on his shoulder. He turned to see the rabbi, now a very old man. "What are you doing?" the rabbi shouted at him angrily. "What do you mean by putting bread in the Holy Ark?"

"I bring these challot to God every week," Jacobo stammered. "I have been doing this for 30 years."

"You have been bringing bread to God each week for 30 years?" the rabbi asked in amazement. "Whatever for?"

"Because of what you taught," replied Jacobo, and he recounted what he remembered of the rabbi's sermon about the loaves of bread in the Holy Temple in Jerusalem.

"You fool! God doesn't eat food like people!" said the rabbi.

"Ah, you are learned and wise," said Jacobo, "but you don't know everything. You see, every week God accepts our gift of challah. For 30 years, there hasn't been a crumb left in the Ark come Shabbat morning."

Now the rabbi was curious, so he said, "Jacobo, let us hide in the back of the synagogue and see just what happens to your challot." So the two men hid behind the last row of benches and waited patiently. They didn't have long to wait.

Several minutes later, the shammes entered the room and immediately approached the ark. Opening the door, he prayer, "Lord, for 30 years you have fed my family and sustained us in good times and bad. We give you thanks."

The rabbi jumped up and screamed, "You, too, are a fool! Do you think that God bakes bread and leaves the loaves in the Ark?"

The shammes hung his head in shame and began sobbing. "I don't get paid for cleaning the synagogue, Rabbi. I thought this was God's way of repaying me for my work."

At just that moment, Rabbi Isaac Luria, the Ari, walked into the synagogue and, hearing the loud and angry voice of the rabbi and the sobbing of the shammes, asked what was happening. The shammes was miserable because he knew he would never find challah in the ark again. Jacobo was miserable because he had simply wanted to please God and now he could no longer do this. When the entire story had been explained to him, Rabbi Luria smiled and turned first to the rabbi. "Rabbi, never since the Destruction of the Temple, has God had such pleasure as from watching what has gone on in your synagogue each week. Thirty years ago, you were an old, sick man and God had decreed that you would soon die. But since your teaching resulted in so much righteousness on the part of these people, God wanted you to live." Then the Ari turned to Jacobo and the shammes. "Now that you know who is eating the challot, it will be more difficult to continue as you have for 30 years. But I want you to continue as you have, and believe with perfect faith that if you, Jacobo, bring your challot directly to the shammes, God will be pleased no less than before, for it is through acts of love and kindness that we serve God and repair the world. And you," the great Ari turned to the shammes, "know that these challot were baked by Jacobo and Esperanza, but they come from God, as well, because Jews are commanded to do the work of God in this world, feeding the hungry and binding the wounds of those who suffer."

From that day on, Esperanza and Jacobo baked a dozen loaves of challah each Friday, as they had for three decades, and brought it to the home of the shammes, who gratefully accepted the loaves.

Special thanks to Rabbi Fred Davidow for his generous help in writing this very classic Jewish folktale. Rabbi Davidow is a talented storyteller in his own right.

♦♦♦

Ribono shel Olam, Please Bless Your Children

The Juneliger Reb Levi Yitzhak of Berditchev gave notice to the whole city of Berditchev that he wants everyone to come Friday afternoon, before Shabbat, and receive his blessings – but that it would cost one ruble. Everybody came. One way or another, they either had a ruble, or they borrowed a ruble, but everybody came.

It was getting later and later, and Rebbe Yitzhak was not going to shul yet. People were saying, it's late, it's late, but obviously he was waiting for somebody.

Very late, very late – and all of us are so late. The secret of life is to know it's never too late, but *gevalt*, are we late?

Finally, a very poor woman came. And she said to him, "*Heileger* (Holy) Rebbe, here is my ruble, please bless me."

And Rebbe Yitzhak blessed her and she went on to say, "Rebbe, believe me, it was so hard for me to get this ruble. But here is my little girl with me. I don't have a ruble for her. Could you please bless her for free?"

So Reb Levi Yitzhak said, "I'm sorry, the price is one ruble. What can I do? If you don't have a ruble, I can't bless your daughter."

The woman burst out crying and said, "Rebbe, I have only one ruble. Take away the blessing you gave me. I don't care what happens to me, but please bless my child, *heilege* Rebbe, bless my child."

Rebbe Levi Yitzhak couldn't control himself any more. He got up and ran to shul. He opened up the Holy Ark and said, "Ribono shel Olam, Master of the Universe. Did you hear what this woman said? 'I don't care what happens to me, but please bless my child.' Ribono shel Olam, how can You not do the same? I don't care what happens to me, but please bless your children."

◆◆◆

The Right Kind Of Silence

The Talmud tells the story of Rav Safra, who was offered a price for some goods but could not respond as he was in the middle of prayers. The buyer kept upping the price. When Rav Safra concluded, he told the buyer he would accept the initial offer since his silence was misinterpreted, and he would have accepted the initial offer had he not been in the middle of prayer.

Rabbi Leo Jung told the story of the once formidable company Beer, Sondheimer and Co. In 1870, just before the Franco-German war, Mr. Beer left his office for the Sabbath. His company had the copper and other metals the war ministry required and they sent a series of telegrams offering him more and more for his material, none of them answered because of the Sabbath.

On Sunday morning, Mr. Beer returned to the office and said, recalling the precedent of Rav Safra, that he would accept the initial offer because they misinterpreted his silence.

The ministry was so impressed by his scrupulousness that they made his company the main supplier and so "established its global significance."

Sometimes doing the right thing turns out to be the right thing.

Rabbi David Wolpe

◆◆◆

What Will You Build?

Rabbi Joseph Horowitz, the Alter of Nowogrodek, at the urging of his teacher the Alter of Kelme, Rabbi Simhah Zissel Broida, tried to found yeshivot (schools) and discussion groups. It did not go well. At a low point he went back to Kelme to spend Shabbat with his teacher. Saturday night, the Alter of Kelme usually spoke for hours. That night, he stood mute, and finally cried out, "It is enough for a person to be alive!" He repeated it over and over with more passion and ended the Sabbath. This reminded Rabbi Horowitz of the verse in Hallel, "I shall not die, but I shall live to tell the deeds of the Lord," and it lifted him out of his depression. He went on to be successful after this.

Viktor Frankl learned from the Holocaust that one needs a purpose to life in order to survive, but the Alter of Nowogrodek reminds us that one also needs faith. Rabbi Max Arzt taught that worry and anxiety are "borrowing trouble from the future to use in the present", but faith is "borrowing hope from the future to use in the present". The true miracle takes place in our personality and psyche, our heart and soul. Only then can the human spirit work wonders. The Alter of Nowogrodek built a world of yeshivot.

What world will you build?

◆◆◆

Apikoros

This is the apikoros* from Brod story. In short, a Jew who fashions himself as an apikoros decides to travel to Brod to visit the famous apikoros of Brod. He is invited to spend Shabbat with him, and marvels at how he goes to shul, prays, has the three celebratory meals with Kiddush and Benching, divrei Torah, and then studies Torah.

At the end of Shabbat, after the Havdalah blessings, he approaches the apikoros of Brod and asks how he could be doing all these things.

"Don't you?" asks the Brod apikoros.

Not at all, and he describes his secular lifestyle.

The apikoros of Brod says to him, "Well then, you're no apikoros, you're a goy!"

---

* A non-believing Jewish person, especially one with knowledge of the laws of Judaism.

Another version:

A Jew visits Vilna and he hears a tale of the great apikoros of Vilna. He is having doubts himself about all the Jewish laws, and decides to go visit the apikoros before Shabbat. He goes to his house, and asks if he can come in for dinner.

The apikoros says yes.

He goes in and he sees that the apikoros has candles out to light, wine and challot. He sees the Shabbat meal set on the table. He is shocked.

"I was told you are the great apikoros," he exclaims.

His host says, "I am a great apikoros, there is no God, but I am not an *am ha-aretz*** like you."

A variation I heard from a member of the Talmud faculty years back. Wish I could remember who.

A young scholar decides he wants to become an apikoros. Naturally, he figures the way to do this is to go learn with the greatest apikoros in the world.

He travels to his city. When he finds his home, the young man knocks on the door. He is told that the man is in shul. So he goes to the shul and sees everyone in tallit and tefillin.

When the davening ends, he inquires and is pointed to the apikoros.

"Are you an apikoros?" the young scholar asks.

"Yes," he answers.

"If you are an apikoros, why are you in shul wearing a tallit and tefillin?"

"I'm an apikoros, but not a goy!"

Another variation:

After meeting each other, the apikoros asks the young man, "Which Mishnah are you learning now?"

** In rabbinic literature, this is a negative phrase, which refers to someone who is ignorant or is seriously lacking in the spiritual realm.

No answer from the young man.

Then the apikoros asks, "What is your favorite dvar Torah?"

Again, no answer.

"So, surely you can explain this week's parasha," the apikoros says.

No answer from the young man.

Finally, and a bit frustrated, the apikoros tells the young wanna be apikoros, "You cannot be an apikoros; you're an am haaretz."

Howard Hoffman

♦♦♦

And Even A Little Higher

There is a Jewish folktale set in the early 19th century in Eastern Europe about a Hasidic rabbi and his dedication to charity. One day a skeptic arrived in the rabbi's city to see for himself this rabbi and what the fuss was all about.

Every Friday morning, the rabbi would simply disappear. He wasn't in the synagogue or his home. The skeptic asked the rabbi's followers where their leader went. They replied, "Where else but to heaven? The people of the town need peace, sustenance, and health. Surely our rabbi is in heaven pleading our cause."

The skeptic decided to find out for himself. One Thursday night he hid himself in the rabbi's house. Before dawn, he heard the rabbi emerge from his bedroom, dressed as a peasant. Then the rabbi pulled out an axe and began to chop wood outside in the darkness. The rabbi brought the wood to a run-down cottage, not knowing anyone was following him.

When he got to the door of the house, the rabbi knocked on the door. An old, poor, and ill woman opened the door. The disguised rabbi explained that he had cheap wood to sell her so that she would be warm for the winter.

"But I have no money," the woman replied.

"I will give it to you on credit," the rabbi said.

"But how will I repay you?" the woman wondered.

"God will find a way to see that I am repaid," answered the rabbi.

"But who will light the fire; I am too sick," the woman protested.

"I will," said the rabbi, and he did.

Before the rabbi left the old woman, he wished her "Shabbat Shalom."

With a glowing, wide smile, she also said, "Shabbat Shalom."

After witnessing all this, the skeptical man decided to become a disciple of this particular rabbi. When he would hear other followers explain that their rabbi went to heaven on Friday mornings, he would add "and even a little higher."

The story teaches us the importance of giving charity and its centrality in the Jewish tradition. In Proverbs we read:

"Whoever is kind to the poor lends to the Lord, and he will reward them for what they have done."

Giving charity is tantamount to lending to God. God gives us the opportunity to do *Him* a favor! Of course, God could supply everyone with all their needs on His own, but He allows us to help Him in helping others and rewards us for our kindness as well.

◆◆◆

Middah Keneged Middah

Rav Eliezer Ginsburg recently related an amazing *middah keneged middah* story that reveals the incredible salvation that a father in Lakewood merited because of his special concern for the welfare of another boy.

Five American *bochurim* (yeshiva students) drove from their yeshiva in Yerushalayim early Friday morning to Netanya with the intention of spending Shabbos there. Before Shabbos, they hoped to have a chance to go to a deserted beach and enjoy a refreshing swim in the Mediterranean.

Unfortunately, when they got to the beach, they found it crowded, and since there was no separation between the genders, they quickly left and hailed a taxi to drive them down the coast in hopes of finding an isolated beach. After a ten-minute drive, the taxi driver left them off at a perfectly deserted, isolated beach.

After quickly putting on their swimming suits, the five boys went into the water. Then, without any warning, one of the boys was swept 400 feet into the ocean by a dangerous riptide. The other four boys were helpless to rescue their friend, and the *bochur* himself, despite making a valiant effort to swim back to shore, was unable to do so. With his strength used up, the young man cried out to

Hashem, "Only You can help me. There is so much more I want to do to serve You."

At that very moment, the boy saw a not-so-young man, perhaps 65 years old, with a long gray beard, on a surfboard, gliding towards him in the choppy waters. The man instructed the *bochur* to grab part of the board. He then guided the boy safely back to shore.

Wanting to express his *hakoras hatov* (gratitude) to his rescuer, the *bochur* asked, "Who are you? What's your name?"

The man simply replied, "Thank the *Borei Olam* (Creator of the World – Hashem)." With that, he disappeared back into the water.

Grateful for his new lease on life, the boy waited a few hours for his father to wake up back in Lakewood in order to tell him of his *neis* (miracle). He related the frightening story and how Hashem saved him through the messenger of that elderly surfboarder.

Excited by what his son was telling him, the father at that very moment received a message on his phone. It said: "You are a lifesaver!"

Earlier that week, on Monday morning, after davening, the father entered a local shul in Lakewood and noticed a teenage boy looking at the table in front of him. The man asked with concern, "What are you doing here? Why aren't you learning in yeshiva?"

The boy answered, "No yeshiva wants to take me in and I have nothing else to do."

"I'll get you into a good yeshiva," the man answered. "I have connections with the Waterbury Yeshiva in Connecticut."

He used his cell phone to call someone at the yeshiva. Based on his plea, they agreed to accept the boy, who thanked the stranger for his intervention.

On Wednesday, two days later, the father entered the shul and was surprised to see that the same teenager was there, doing nothing.

"I thought you were going to the yeshiva in Waterbury. Why are you still here?"

"I have no way to get there," said the boy.

"If that is the problem," the man said, "I'll take you. Go home and pack your stuff. I'll pick you up."

When the man returned home, he told his wife where he was going.

"What are you doing?" she asked incredulously. "The journey to Waterbury from Lakewood and back is at least six hours. You are 65 years old. You can't do it. It's too much physical exertion for you. Pay someone to drive the boy."

The father agreed, and he asked his son-in-law to find someone to drive the teenager. He found a person who agreed to drive the young man for $200. That same day, the boy began learning in Waterbury.

It was that same boy who, two days later, when his benefactor was talking to his son in Netanya, sent the following message: "I am having a great time learning in Waterbury. You are a lifesaver!"

Rav Ginsburg related that this was clearly a case of *middah keneged middah*. That father had made an extra special effort to save a *bochur* by getting him accepted into a yeshiva. And the result? Two days later, his own son was saved by Hashem from being buried in the water in Netanya.

Daniel Keren, www.matzav.com

♦♦♦

The Jews of Belmonte, Portugal

The holiday of Hanukkah is all about the light of truth. One of the darkest periods of Jewish history took place in 16th century Portugal. Despite the horrors of the Portuguese Inquisition, a small band of Jews remained loyal to Judaism until they were finally freed in the late 20th century. At the door to one of Belmonte's synagogues reads the following plaque that teaches us a great deal about the light of freedom. It reads:

"Here in this place, the chain of our tradition has not been severed. As a result of government decrees, the Jewish residents of this village, like other Jews throughout Spain and Portugal, were forced to publicly deny their Jewish religion. But they maintained their Judaism in their homes. Here the candle of Jewish light was never extinguished. For a period of 500 years, from 1492 [when the one synagogue in Belmonte was destroyed] until 2002 [when it was reopened], in the homes of this village the Jewish commandments were secretly performed, the tradition was transmitted from parent to child in hushed tones, the Sabbath was sanctified in hiding while Sunday was celebrated before the eyes of the neighbors. They made blessings over the Challah (fogaça) and the wine and mumbled words of

Hebrew prayers in the darkness. Here the Jewish soul was never lost. Here the Jewish soul remains forever. From the midst of the past will rise the future. From the bleak darkness of the Middle Ages shall emerge the light of this synagogue."

Today, as thousands of Portuguese citizens re-encounter their Jewish roots, we remember the brave people of Portugal who withstood the onslaught of prejudice and kept the lights of Hanukkah burning in the darkness of intolerance and fear.

◆◆◆

The Singing Heart

The Baal Shem Tov displayed a remarkable affection for simple, pious folk. This approach was widely known, and was a major reason for the tremendous number of simple Jews who became his devotees in a short while, as many accounts attest.

However, his greatest disciples, who were *tzadikim* (righteous and saintly) and *gaonim* (Torah geniuses), could not accept this approach. True, the Baal Shem Tov frequently sent them to learn traits like sincerity, trust, simple faith, faith in sages, faith in *tzadikim*, love of Israel and the like from simple Jews. Still, they could not appreciate the Baal Shem Tov's regard for ordinary people, and certainly could not emulate him in this.

It was the practice that guests ate two of the Shabbat meals at the Baal Shem Tov's table, but one meal – the second, noontime meal – was reserved for the inner circle of disciples, the "sacred fellowship," while guests were not admitted, even to observe from a distance. One summer Shabbat, between 1753 and 1755 – when the circle of disciples included brilliant and renowned men like the Mezeritcher Maggid and the Rav of Polnoah – an incident occurred that thoroughly perplexed and confused the disciples.

A large number of guests came for that Shabbat, including many undistinguished people like farmers, artisans, cobblers, tailors, vintners, gardeners, stockmen, poultrymen and small merchants. At the Friday evening meal, the Baal Shem Tov showed extraordinary affection for these people. He poured of the remains of his kiddush wine into the cup of one; to another he gave his own kiddush cup to recite the kiddush; he gave pieces of the loaves of his hamotzi to several; to others he gave of the meat and fish of his portion. He showed other gestures of friendship and regard for these guests, leaving his disciples not a little perplexed.

The guests knew that they could not attend the second Shabbat meal, which was reserved for the inner group of disciples, so after their repast they assembled in the Baal Shem Tov's shul, and – being totally uneducated, barely able to go beyond simply reading *Chumash* and *Tehillim* (Psalms) – they all started chanting *Tehillim*.

When the Baal Shem Tov sat at the table for the second meal, he arranged the disciples in a deliberate order, characteristic of the meticulous system governing everything he did. In a short while he started to hold forth, "saying Torah," and all of the disciples felt a tremendous Godly delight in their master's teaching. It was customary that they sang at the table, and when they saw the obvious cheery mood of the Baal Shem Tov, they were even more pleased, filled with a sense of gratitude and happiness for God's favor to them, granting them the privilege of being among the disciples of the saintly Baal Shem Tov.

It occurred to several of them that now it is so delightful, without the crowd of simple people who have no idea what their master is saying. Why, they thought, does he display such affection for these people, pouring from his cup into theirs, even giving his cup to one of them?

These thoughts still flitted through their minds, and the Baal Shem Tov's expression changed. He became serious, immersed in his thoughts (*devekut*), and without a shift in this mood he began to speak.

"Peace, peace, to the far and the near," he quoted. Our sages observe that "where the penitent stands, the perfect saints cannot," stressing perfect saints. He explained that there are two paths in God's service – the saint's and the penitent's. The service of simple people is similar to the penitent's, the simple person's humility of an order with the penitent's remorse and resolve.

When the Baal Shem Tov concluded, they resumed singing. Those disciples who had been questioning their master's open affection for simple people realized that he was aware of their thoughts. His exposition of the qualities of the simple, equating them with the superiority of the penitent over the saint, was obviously addressed to them.

During the songs he was still in his deep *devekut*, and when they finished singing, he opened his eyes, intently examining each disciple. Then, he told them to each place his right hand on the shoulder of his neighbor, so that the disciples sitting around the table would be joined. The Baal Shem Tov sat at the head of the table.

He told them to sing certain melodies while in this position of union, and after the songs he told them to shut their eyes and not open them until he tells them to. Then, he placed his right hand on the shoulder of the disciple to his right, and his left on the disciple sitting there. The circle was closed.

Suddenly, the disciples heard songs, melodies, interlaced with moving pleas, touching the very soul.

One voice sang, "O, *Ribbono shel Olam* (Master of the Universe)," and launched into a verse of *Tehillim*, "The sayings of God are pure sayings..."

Another sang, "*Ai, Ribbono shel Olam*," and another verse, "Test me, God, prove me, purify my heart."

A third introduced his verse with a spontaneous cry in Yiddish – "*Tatte hartziger* (heartful father)...Be gracious to me; I trust in You and I shelter in the shadow of Your wings."

A fourth voice: "*Ai gevald, zisser foter in himel* (sweet father in heaven), Let God arise; His foes will scatter; His enemies will flee."

Another voice was anguished. "*Tyerer tatte* (precious father), A bird has a home; a swallow a nest."

Still another pleaded, "*Lieber foter, derbarmdiger tatte* (dear father, merciful father), Bring us back, God who helps, erase Your anger against us."

The disciples, hearing these songs of *Tehillim*, trembled. Their eyes were still shut, but tears coursed down their cheeks. Their hearts were shattered by the songs. Each of the disciples fervently wished that God help him to serve Him in this manner.

The Baal Shem Tov removed his hands from the shoulders of the two disciples, and the group no longer heard the songs and *Tehillim*. Then, he told them to open their eyes and to sing a number of designated songs.

"When I heard the song of *Tehillim*," the Maggid later told Rabbi Shneur Zalman of Liadi, "my soul just spilled forth. I felt such a longing, such blissful love (*ahavah b'taanugim*), that I had never yet been privileged to feel. My boots were soaked with the perspiration and tears of *teshuvah* from the inwardness and depths of the heart."

When the Baal Shem Tov stopped singing, an instantaneous hush fell over the group. He sat in deep *devekut* for a prolonged time, then looked up and said, "The songs you heard were the songs of the simple Jews saying *Tehillim* with sincerity, from the recesses of the heart and with simple faith.

"Now, my pupils, think carefully on this. We are only the 'edge of truth' (*sefat emet*), for the body is not truth and only the soul is truth, and it is only part of the essence, and so is called the 'edge of truth.' Still we do recognize truth, and feel truth and are affected by truth, affected deeply. Consider, then, how God, who is perfect Truth, regards the Tehillim of these simple people..."

From the writings of Rabbi Yosef Yitzchak Schneersohn (1880-1950); translation by Zalman Posner, www.chabad.org

◆◆◆

Days of Faith

God's Faith In Us

Professor Reuven Feuerstein, who died aged 92 in April 2014, was one of the great child psychologists of the world, a man who transformed lives and led severely brain-damaged children to achievements no one else thought possible. I knew him and admired him, and I was recording a tribute to him when his son told me a wonderful story.

Feuerstein had been working with a group of Native American Indians and they wanted to show their gratitude. So they invited him and his wife to their reservation. They were brought into the Indian chief's wigwam where the leaders of the tribe were sitting in a circle in full headdress.

As the traditional welcome ceremony began, the professor, an orthodox Jew from Jerusalem, was overwhelmed by the incongruity. He turned to his wife and said to her in Yiddish, "What would my mother say if she could see me now?!" To his amazement, the Indian chief turned to him and replied in Yiddish: "And what would she say if she knew I understood what you just said!"

The Yiddish-speaking Indian chief told Feuerstein his story. He had grown up in Europe as a religious Jew, but having survived the horrors of the Holocaust, he decided that he wanted to spend the rest of his life as far away as he could from Western civilization, so he joined the Indians and became their doctor. Feuerstein was the first Jew he had met in his self-imposed exile.

There are certain people around to whom strange things happen and Reuven Feuerstein was one. Born in Romania, he studied psychology in Bucharest, but was forced to flee by the Nazi invasion. He settled in Israel after the war, and began by treating traumatized child survivors of the Holocaust. Returning to Europe he completed his education at Geneva and the Sorbonne. Later he returned to Israel where he established the Institute for the Enhancement of Learning Potential.

He dedicated his life to children with disadvantages, some physical – autistic, brain-damaged and Down Syndrome children – and others cultural or social. His methods have been adopted in more than 80 countries. He was a genius, a magician, a small, slight man with twinkling eyes. Children opened up to him like flowers in the sun.

I tell his story because he was a deeply spiritual Jew. His methods were elaborate and his theories complex, but seeing him at work you knew that there were three reasons he achieved miracles. First, the basis of his work was love. He loved the children and they loved him. Second, he had transformative faith. Under him, children developed skills no one thought they could because he believed they could. He had more faith in them than anyone else.

Third, he refused to write anyone off. He insisted that children with disabilities should be included in society like every other child. They too were in the image of God. They too had a right to respect. They too could lead a full and meaningful life.

I learned from Professor Feuerstein that faith really does change lives. The one thing that can rescue us from despair and failure to fulfill our potential is the knowledge that someone believes in us more than we believe in ourselves.

That is what God does. He believes in us more than we believe in ourselves. However many times we fail, He forgives us. However many times we fall, He lifts us. And He never gives up. As we say in *Le-David Hashem ori ve-yishi*: "My father and mother might abandon me, but God will gather me in." (Psalm 27: 10).

At the heart of Judaism is one utterly transformative belief: our faith in God's faith in us. That, as Reuven Feuerstein, showed can lead us to a greatness we never knew we had.

Rabbi Jonathan Sacks

♦♦♦

A Cracked Pot!

Once upon a time there was a water-bearer whose tools were two large pots suspended by a very long pole which he balanced across his shoulders each day. One of these pots had a crack – and although the man would fill both upon reaching the river near his village, he would always arrive home with one pot filled and the other half-empty. Years passed and eventually the cracked pot mustered up the courage to speak to her master.

"I'm so sorry," said the pot. "Over the years that I've helped you carry water, I've never been able to bring back a full load. Because of me, your efforts have never been completely rewarded and it is all my fault!"

Hearing this, the water-bearer felt sad and instructed the pot to keep her eyes open the next day as they traveled to the river, rather than worrying so much about the water that she was leaking. As the pot looked out, she saw a beautiful field filled with colorful blossoms.

"Do you see those flowers?" asked the water-bearer. "And do you notice that they are only on your side of the path? Without your glorious leak, the seeds I planted would not have had enough water to grow. So thank you, my friend. Thank you for being a cracked pot!"

I share this story in honor of Jewish Disabilities Awareness, Acceptance, and Inclusion Month (JDAIM) which is February. We are all, each and every one of us, imperfect vessels – abled and disabled in our own unique ways – and the various challenges with which we contend are not only liabilities but often sources of tremendous productivity, beauty, and blessing as well. This month, in particular, we celebrate the many different kinds of individuals who make up our congregational family and recommit ourselves to fostering within our synagogue a radically welcoming environment for all. During this week when we read the Ten Commandments, laws brought down the mountain to us by a man whose speech impediment almost prevented him from serving as our people's greatest leader, we are reminded of how very much the human spirit can accomplish and how much poorer our communities would be if we did not make room for individuals in all of their fullness.

Rabbi Annie Tucker

The Fearless Israelis

So the story goes like this: The President of Iran was sitting in his office when his telephone rang.

"Salaam! Mr. President," a heavily accented voice said. "This is Moshe from a small town in Israel. I am ringing to inform you that our morning minyan is officially declaring war on you!"

"Well, Moshe," the Iranian President replied, "This is indeed important news! Tell me, how big is your army?" "

At this moment in time," said Moshe after a moment's calculation, "there is myself, my cousin Shlomy, my next door neighbor Yossi, and the entire 6:00 AM morning minyan – that makes 18!"

The President sighed. "I must tell you Moshe that I have one million men in my army waiting to move on my command. If you attack, you'll be dead the moment your foot touches Iranian territory."

"Oy vay!" Moshe responded. "I'll have to ring you back!" Sure enough, the next day Moshe rang back. "All right Mr. President, the war is still on! We have managed to acquire some equipment!"

"And what equipment would that be, Moshe?" The President asked.

"Well, at the kibbutz we have two combine harvesters that we can use as tanks, a bulldozer and Yossi's tractor."

Once more the President sighed. "I must tell you, Moshe, that the army of the Islamic Republic has sixteen thousand tanks, fourteen thousand armored personnel carriers, and my army has increased to one and a half million since we last spoke."

"Really?!" said Moshe "I'll have to ring you back!" Sure enough, Moshe rang again the next day. "Hello Mr. President, the war is still on! We have managed to get ourselves airborne! We've modified Shimon's crop duster with a couple of rifles in the cockpit and the 8:00 AM minyan has joined us as well!"

The President was silent for a minute, then sighed. "I must tell you Moshe that the Iranian air force has ten thousand bombers and twenty thousand MiG 19 attack planes. My military complex is surrounded by laser-guided surface-to-air missile sites, and since we last spoke, my army has increased to two million. And in case you haven't been following the news, we're gonna have a nuclear bomb in like ten days."

"Oo lah lah!" said Moshe, "I'll have to ring you back. "Sure enough, Moshe called again the next day. "Mr. President, I am sorry to tell you that we have had to call off the war."

"I'm sorry to hear that," said the President. "Why the sudden change of heart?"

"Well," said Moshe. "We've all had a chat, and there's no way we can feed two million prisoners.

◆◆◆

Gross-Rosen Slave-Labor Camp

My beloved teacher, Rabbi David Weiss Halivni z"l, in his autobiography, describes his life-threatening forced labor in the Gross-Rosen slave-labor camp. On rare Sundays off, he describes how he and his fellow slave-laborers studied the Talmudic Tractate Shabbat from memory. He was the one who recited the text, and others discussed its meaning. He describes how, in the course of his labors, he would pass by a guard who would be eating a sandwich.

This time, [he writes] our meeting was different. His sandwich was wrapped in a page of *Orach Chaim*, a volume of the Shulchan Aruch, Pesil Balaban's edition. Pesil's edition of the Shulchan Aruch was the best; it had all the commentaries, including that of Rabbi Shloma Kluger.

As a child of a poor but scholarly home, I had always wanted to have her edition. We had a Shulchan Aruch, but it wasn't Pesil's. Ours was also old and torn. It was my ambition as a child to own a *Vilner Shas*, Pesil's *Shulchan Aruch*, and a set of "Rambams," a complete set of Maimonides' major legal writings. Here, of all places, in the shadows of [darkness], under the threatening gaze of the German, a page of the *Shulchan Aruch*, with fatty spots all over it, met my eyes. The page was from the laws of Passover. The question on the page deals with whether an agent can nullify the leavened bread of a household before Passover, which is the subject of a disagreement....

Upon seeing this wrapper, I instinctively fell at the feet of the guard, without even realizing why; the mere letters propelled me. With tears in my eyes, I implored him to give me this *bletl*, this page. For a while he didn't know what was happening; he thought I was suffering from epilepsy. He immediately put his hand to his revolver, the usual reaction to an unknown situation. But then he understood. This was, I explained to him, a page from a book I had studied at home. Please, I sobbed, give it to me, as a souvenir. He gave me the *bletl* and I took it back to the camp. On the Sundays we had off, we now had not only Oral Torah but Written Torah as well. The *bletl* became a visible symbol of a connection between the camp and the activities of Jews throughout history. It was not important what the topic was. The *bletl* became a rallying point. We looked forward to studying it whenever we had free time.... It was the *bletl*, parts of which had to be deciphered because the grease made some letters illegible, that summoned our attention. Most of those who came to listen didn't understand the subject matter, but that was irrelevant. They all perceived the symbolic significance of the *bletl*.

Rabbi David Weiss Halivni z"l

Rabbi Halivni notes how the *bletl*, how this page of *Shulchan Oruch* was entrusted to a particular Jew for several months, a Jew who carried the page with him into the crematorium on the last day of Pesah, 1945.

◆◆◆

Train-ride to Auschwitz

In 1985, my teacher, Rabbi David Weiss Halivni, was awarded Israel's coveted Bialik Prize. Accepting the award, he spoke of his train-ride to Auschwitz forty years earlier. He described the horrors of that journey into hell. The train reached its destination. They were ordered off the train at Auschwitz. The teenage boy David, in the midst of the nightmare, as he was being separated from his family forever, heard his Aunt Ethel, a young woman in her twenties, call out to him:

"The Torah, over which you have labored so diligently, it shall protect you."

"I am that boy," Rabbi Halivni recalled. "And it was the Torah that watched over me from one death camp to another. It is that Torah that still watches over me today."

David Weiss Halivni had much about which to question God; the loss of his entire family, the loss of his childhood.

He wrote as an introduction to *Sources and Traditions*, his multi-volume Talmud commentary, "I survived alone to tell, to remind and to demand answers." These very words are reproduced near the entrance to Yad Vashem in Jerusalem. Rabbi Halivni had much about which to demand answers. But he also had Torah. God's gift to Israel. The key, in very specific ways, to his survival. The reason, when all else would have suggested giving up, to persevere."

Our loss is great, a true *Gadol B'Yisrael*.

Rabbi Philip Scheim

◆◆◆

Sharansky's Little Book of Psalms

During the darkest period of his eventful life, a small black book gave light to the imprisoned Natan Sharansky, symbolizing his connection with his wife and with the Land of Israel

"On January 20th, 1980, my birthday, I was impatiently waiting for a congratulatory telegram from home… The next day I received an unexpected surprise – a real birthday gift! – The official in charge of storing the prisoners' belongings brought me a tiny book with a black binding, my Book of Psalms!"

(Fear No Evil, Natan Sharansky, translated by Stefani Hoffman, Random House New York, 1988)

Natan Sharansky's Book of Psalms accompanied him during his most difficult years in prison. In his autobiography, Sharansky tells of how the book, given to him by his wife Avital on the eve of his arrest, was confiscated. As a religious book printed outside the Soviet Union, it wasn't exactly recommended reading material in the Soviet prison system. At one point, when Sharansky was being transferred from one prison to another, the book was temporarily returned to his possession. The prisoner took advantage of this opportunity and tore out the page which indicated the book had been printed in Israel. When asked about it later, Sharansky described it as a "book of folklore". It was only thanks to this that the prison authorities finally agreed to return the book to him.

"The Psalm book was the sole material evidence of my mystical tie with Avital. What impelled her to send it to me on the eve of my arrest? And how did it happen that I received it on the day of my father's death? The reading of the Psalms not only reinforced our bond but also demystified their author. King David now appeared before me, not as a fabled hero or as a mystical superman but as a live, indomitable soul – tormented by doubts, rising against evil, and suffering from the thought of his own sins."

Towards the end of his autobiography, Sharansky writes about his very last moments of imprisonment, all those years ago, just before he stepped onto the plane that would take him to freedom:

"Where's my Psalm book?"

"You received everything that was permitted," answered the intellectual in an unexpectedly rough tone. He signaled to the tails to take me away. I quickly dropped to the snow.

"I won't move until you give me back my Psalm book. When nothing happened, I lay down in the snow and started shouting, 'Give me back my Psalm book!'

"The photographers were aghast, and pointed their cameras to the sky. After a brief consultation, the boss gave me the Psalm book. I got up and quickly mounted the ramp."

In a dark world of suffering and injustice, one small black book gave light to the imprisoned Sharansky. It was a reminder of his Jewish heritage. It was a reminder of his wife, Avital, who gave him the book before his arrest. It was what provided him with the strength to survive those most terrible times.

Nati Gabbay, 11.02.2018

Where am I Going?

Justice Oliver Wendell Holmes was at times absent-minded. Riding a train, he was asked for his ticket but couldn't find it. He searched everywhere – pockets, briefcase – but to no avail. Unable to find the train ticket, Holmes grew distressed.

The conductor, knowing the justice and his high reputation, told him not to worry. "Never mind, sit. When you find it, I'm sure you'll mail it in."

Justice Holmes wasn't reassured. "Mr. Conductor," he replied, "you don't understand. The question is not "Where is my ticket? The question is, Where am I going?"

We Are All Jews

Master Sergeant Roddie Edmonds of Knoxville, Tennessee, served in the US Army during World War II. He participated in the landing of the American forces in Europe and was taken prisoner by the Germans. Together with other American POWs, including Jews, he was taken to Stalag IXA, a camp near Ziegenhain, Germany.

In line with their anti-Jewish policy, the Germans singled out Jewish POWs, and many of them on the Eastern Front were sent to extermination camps or killed. In some cases, in the west, Jewish POWs were also separated from the others.

Sometime in January 1945, the Germans announced that all Jewish POWs in Stalag IXA were to report the following morning.

Master Sergeant Edmonds, the ranking officer of the American prisoners, and a Christian, ordered all the POWs – Jews and non-Jews alike – to stand together. When the German officer in charge saw that all the camp's inmates were standing in front of their barracks, he turned to Edmonds and said, "They cannot all be Jews." To this Edmonds replied, "We are all Jews."

The German took out his pistol and threatened Edmonds, but the Master Sergeant did not waver and retorted, "According the Geneva Convention, we have to give only our name, rank, and serial number. If you shoot me, you will have to shoot all of us, and after the war you will be tried for war crimes." The German gave up, turned around, and left the scene.

Paul Stern, one of the Jewish POWs saved by Edmonds, was taken prisoner on December 17, 1944, during the Battle of the Bulge. Stern and the other Jewish noncommissioned officers were fortunate and were taken to the nearby camp of Ziegenhain, while the other lower ranking Jewish POWs were sent to slave labor camps. It was in this second camp, Stalag IXA, where, thanks to Edmonds's courage, Stern and the other Jewish POWs were saved from another attempt to single out the Jewish POWs.

Stern told Yad Vashem that he had learned German in college, but did not reveal this to the Germans; he was able to listen to what the Germans were saying without them knowing that he understood them. Stern stood near Edmonds during the exchange with the German officer. The exchange between the German and Edmonds was in English. "

Another witness to the exchange was Lester Tanner. He told Yad Vashem that at the time, they were well aware that the Germans were murdering the Jews. They therefore understood that the order to separate the Jews from the other POWs meant that the Jews were in great danger.

"I would estimate that there were more than one thousand Americans standing in wide formation in front of the barracks, with Master Sergeant Roddie Edmonds standing in front of the formation with several senior noncoms beside him, of which I was one. (About 200 were Jewish.) There was no question in my mind or that of Edmonds that the Germans were removing the Jewish prisoners from the general prisoner population at great risk to their survival. The US Army's standing command to its ranking officers in POW camps was that you resist the enemy and care for the safety of your men to the extent possible. Edmonds, at the risk of his immediate death, defied the Germans with the unexpected consequences that the Jewish prisoners were saved."

After the war, Edmonds never discussed this story. It was only after his death in 1985 that his children began to uncover pieces of the heroic actions of their father that saved so many Jewish lives.

Eventually Yad Vashem in Jerusalem became aware of Edmonds's courage that day in Stalag IXA. On February 10, 2015, Yad Vashem recognized Master Sargent Roddie Edmonds as "Righteous Among the Nations," which is their project to acknowledge those who took great risks to save Jews during the Holocaust.

Yad Vashem: The World Holocaust Remembrance Center
www.yadvashem.org

♦♦♦

We Jews Control The Banks

A Jewish man in pre-World War II Europe sat on the train every day reading *Der Sturmer* – the Nazi newspaper.

Another Jew finally asked him, "Why do you read that garbage? Why don't you read a good Yiddish paper?"

The man answered, "When I read the Yiddish paper, I read about another pogrom, another antisemitic incident, how Jews are suffering. But, when I read this paper, I read how we Jews control the banks, how we control the media, how we control the government. Why shouldn't I read this paper?"

◆◆◆

Are You Ready for Act Two?

The date is June 24, 1859. Suddenly, there he is, atop a hill overlooking the plain of Solferino. The troops of Napoleon III (Louis Napoleon) prepare for battle with the Austrians below, and Henri Dunant has a box-seat view from his place on the hill.

Trumpets blare, muskets crack and cannons boom. The two armies crash into each other, as Henri looks on, transfixed. He sees the dust rising. He hears the screams of the injured. He watches bleeding, maimed men take their last breaths as he stares in horror at the scene below.

Henri doesn't mean to be there. He is only on a business trip – to speak to Louis Napoleon about a financial transaction between the Swiss and the French. But he arrived late and now finds himself in a position to witness first-hand the atrocities of war.

What Henri sees from his hill, however, pales in comparison with what he is soon to witness. Entering a small town shortly after the fierce encounter, Henri now observes the battle's refugees. Every building is filled with the mangled, the injured, the dead. Henri, aching with pity, decides to stay in the village three more days to comfort the young soldiers.

He realizes that his life will never be the same again. Driven by a powerful passion to abolish war, Henri Dunant will eventually lose his successful banking career and all his worldly possessions only to die as a virtual unknown in an obscure poorhouse.

But we remember Henri today because the Swiss humanitarian and activist was the first recipient of the Nobel Peace Prize (in 1901). We also remember him because he took his country's flag, a white cross on a red background, reversed the colors and founded what was to become a worldwide movement – the Red Cross.

Act One of Henri Dunant's life closed June 24, 1859. Act Two opened immediately and played the remainder of his 81 years.

Many people's lives can be divided into Act One and Act Two. The first performance ends when one decides to ultimately follow a new direction or passion. Henri's old life, driven by financial success, prestige and power, was no longer satisfied. A new Henri Dunant emerged in Act Two; one who was motivated by love, compassion and an overriding commitment to abolish the horrors of war.

For many people like Henri, Act Two begins with a defining moment – it may be an experience, an important insight or perhaps even a rite of passage, such as a birthday. However it comes about, Act Two begins when the "old self" is laid to rest and a new self is born. At its best, this new self is one governed by different priorities and a renewed passion to live differently.

Act One might be closing in your life. If so, are you ready for Act Two? Something exciting may be about to begin.

Steve Goodier

♦♦♦

Unless It Is Used

A rabbi and a soap-maker once went for a walk together. The soap-maker said to the rabbi: "What good is Judaism? After thousands of years of teaching about goodness, truth, justice, and peace, after all the study of Torah, and all the fine ideals of the Prophets, look at all the trouble and misery in the world! If Judaism is so wonderful and true, why should all this be so?"

The rabbi said nothing. They continued walking until he noticed a child playing in the gutter. The child was filthy with soot and grime.

"Look at that child," said the rabbi. "You say that soap makes people clean, but see the dirt on that youngster. What good is soap? With all the soap in the world, that child is still filthy. I wonder if soap is of any use at all."

The soap-maker protested and said, "But, Rabbi, soap can't do any good unless it is used!"

"Exactly!" cried the rabbi. "So it is with Judaism. It isn't effective unless it is applied in daily life and used!"

Jewish Folktale

♦♦♦

Shlomo's Scales

D ecember 1700. It was a cold winter in Poland, and a blanket of snow covered the entire country. The city streets were filled with people bundled up in fur coats, and the country peasants were busy warming their homes with wood and themselves with vodka. The holiday season was approaching, and everyone was in good spirits.

But in the Jewish ghetto in Krakow, gloom and fear filled the air and moaned from every corner. Persecuted by poverty and hate, the Jews of Krakow had but one source of worldly joy, and that too was being taken from them: the children were dying of smallpox.

It was the beginning of an epidemic. The doctors were helpless to stop it, and the various home remedies did nothing. Every day the town was visited with more heartbreaking tragedies. The only one they could turn to, as usual, was their Father in Heaven, and He didn't seem to be listening to their prayers.

The rabbi of the community had declared a fast day, then another, then three days of prayer and self-examination. But nothing seemed to work. A week of supplication was announced, but before it began, the elders of the community decided to make a *she'eilat chalom*, the "dream query" employed by the masters of the secret wisdom of the Kabbalah.

It was a drastic move, but they felt that they had no other choice. They purified themselves, fasted, recited Psalms all day, immersed in a mikvah, and then requested from Heaven, according to ancient Kabbalistic formulas, that they be given some sort of sign that night in their sleep.

And that night, they all had the same dream.

An old man in a white robe appeared and said: "Shlomo the butcher should pray before the congregation."

Early the next morning they met in the shul and related their dream to each other. It was clear what they had to do.

The twenty of them solemnly walked to Shlomo's home and knocked on the door. When his wife opened, she almost fainted at the sight of them.

"Ye--s?" she stammered, pushing her loose hair under the kerchief on her head.

"We want to speak to your husband. Is he home?" said one of them, smiling and trying to be as pleasant as possible. "May we come in?" asked another.

Shlomo came to the door, invited them all in, shook everyone's hand and ran around looking for chairs. When they were finally all seated, one of them began:

"Shlomo, we made a *she'eilat chalom* yesterday. We asked what to do about the epidemic, and we all had the same dream. We dreamed that you have to lead the prayers today."

Shlomo was dumbfounded. If it weren't such a serious matter, he would have thought that this was some kind of joke.

"I should lead the prayers? Why, I ... I can't even read properly. I can't ... I mean, what good will it possibly do?"

"Shlomo," the elders begged, "Just come and do what you can. You don't have to really lead, just pray in front of everyone. Maybe there will be a miracle. Just come and give it a try. We have summoned everyone to the shul. Just come and say a few words. Anything is better than what we have now."

So Shlomo, with no other choice, left his house and accompanied them. But as soon as they had entered the crowded synagogue and closed the door behind them, Shlomo suddenly broke away and ran back outside and down the street, out of sight.

What could they do? He'd disappeared. They didn't even know where to look. They had no choice other than to wait.

A few minutes later the door opened, and in came Shlomo, pushing a wheelbarrow covered with a cloth.

All eyes were on him as he went up to the podium, pulled off the cloth and lifted an old set of scales out of the barrow. He'd brought his butcher's scales into the shul!

The scales were very heavy. But Shlomo lifted them high above his head, his face contorted with the effort, tears streaming from his eyes.

"Here!" he yelled at the ceiling. "Here, God! Take them! Take the scales! That must be why You want me to lead the prayers, right? So take the scales and heal the children! Just heal the children. Okay?"

By now Shlomo was sobbing loudly, and the whole place was dead silent. A few men rushed over and helped him put the scales on a table in the front of the room, and the congregation began the prayers.

That evening, the children were already getting better.

You can imagine the joy and festivities that followed. They even made a nice glass case for the scales, and left the whole thing there permanently for all to see.

But after a few days, when the excitement died down, the elders had to admit that they couldn't figure it out. After all, there were tens of shops in the ghetto that used scales, and all of them were owned by honest, God-fearing Jews. What could be so special about Shlomo's scales?

The answer was soon in coming. When they went around checking all the other scales, they discovered that every one of them, without exception, was a bit off. Certainly never enough to constitute bad business, but inaccurate nevertheless. It seems that Shlomo checked his scales twice every day, while the others checked only occasionally. "That's what God wants," Shlomo explained.

Legend has it that these scales remained on display in that Krakow synagogue for over two hundred years, until the Germans destroyed everything in World War II.

Rabbi Tuvia Bolton, www.chabad.org

Become Yourself

Have we grown into the person we were meant to be? Have we realized our potential or betrayed it?

The story is told of the renowned scholar, Rabbi Hayim of Volozhin, that when young, he was an indifferent student. One day, he decided to abandon his studies and go to a trade school instead. He announced his decision to his parents, who reluctantly acquiesced.

That night, the young man had a dream. In it, he saw an angel holding a stack of beautiful books.

"Whose books are those?" he asked the angel.

"They are yours," was the answer, "if you have the courage to write them."

The dream changed the young man's life, and Rabbi Hayim of Volozhin was on his way to discover who he was meant to become.

Perhaps if we listen to our inner angels, we can do the same.

Rabbi David Wolpe

◆◆◆

They'll Find Us!

Sam and Esther were flying to Australia on a long holiday to celebrate their 50th anniversary. Suddenly, over the public address system, the Captain announces:

"Ladies and Gentlemen, I am afraid I have some very bad news. Our engines have ceased functioning and we will attempt an emergency landing. Luckily, I see an uncharted island below us and we should be able to land on the beach. However, the odds are that we may never be rescued and will have to live on the island for the rest of our lives."

Thanks to the skill of the flight crew, the plane lands safely on the island. An hour later, Sam turns to his wife and asks, "Esther, did we pay our Kol Nidre pledge to the Synagogue yet?"

"No, sweetheart," she responds.

"Esther, did we pay our United Jewish Israel Appeal pledge?"

"No, I'm sorry. I forgot to send the check."

"One last thing, Esther. Did you remember to send a check for the Jewish Care appeal this month?"

"Forgive me, Sam. I was so excited about our holiday that I didn't send that one, either."

Sam grabs her and gives her the biggest hug and kiss in 40 years. Esther pulls away and asks him, "So, why did you kiss me?"

Sam answers: *"They'll find us!"*

◆◆◆

Wisdom Is More Precious Than Gold

King Solomon, *Sh'lomo Ha-melekh*, was famous for his wisdom, and people used to travel from all over to seek his wisdom.

Once, three brothers came, asking how to become as wise as he is. They asked, "May we stay here and serve you and thereby learn?" This time the King agreed, but on condition that they stay for at least three years. So, for three years they sat in on his cases and watched and listened.

After three years, the brothers didn't feel that they had gained any additional wisdom, so they decided to return home, and asked for the King's permission to leave. Since they'd stayed for the three years, he released them from his service and offered them a choice of one hundred gold coins, or three wise sayings. Each brother decided to take the gold coins.

Shortly after leaving the palace, the youngest brother regretted his choice. Since they'd come seeking wisdom and not money, he wanted to return and ask for the King's wise words. His brothers laughed and left, while he returned to the King. The King was delighted at his change of heart and gave him three wise sayings:

- When you travel, journey only by daylight, and find your place to sleep well before dark.
- When you find a river swollen with water, wait and do not cross.
- When you return home, meet your wife and confide in her as a true friend.

The youngest brother caught up to his brothers, but said nothing of the King's advice. They rode until they came to an inn. While there was still a couple of hours of daylight until sunset, the youngest brother wanted to stop, but the other two brothers wanted to continue. They taunted him about whether this wasting of time was the kind of wise advice he had received. But the youngest brother followed the wisdom of the King and stayed at the inn, while his older brothers continued. Both his horse and he ate a good dinner and were nice and warm all night. The older brothers found themselves on the mountain when a sudden snow storm arose, and were trapped and froze to death.

The youngest brother left at dawn. On his way up the mountain he found his brothers' bodies. He wept, tried to bury them as best he could, recited a prayer over their bodies and continued. He decided to take the gold they had received from the King.

On the other side of the mountain he saw an overflowing river in the distance that he would have to cross, and the water was rushing and swirling. He remained on the mountain, deciding to wait until the water receded.

Two men on horseback driving several heavily laden mules were approaching the river. He yelled, trying to get them to wait, but his voice blended with the wind and water. Soon the men and their mules drowned.

When the water finally receded, he went to cross. On the way, he found the men's gold on the backs of the dead mules, and decided to keep it too.

After three days, he reached home and told his wife everything. When his sisters-in-law heard he was home, they immediately came over to find out about their husbands. They saw the bags of gold and wondered what had happened that he was home and they weren't.

He realized he had to tell them the story.

After they had heard, they accused him of murdering their husbands – his brothers – for their gold. They promised to take him to court. They were sure that he would be found guilty and be taken to the gallows.

His wife backed up her husband, saying he'd followed the King's advice. The sisters-in-law said of course she would back her husband so that she could keep all of the gold that rightly was theirs.

At this point, the youngest brother's wife suggested that they all travel to King Solomon's court, for he would surely know and be able to see into their hearts and thoughts. Which is what they did.

The King recognized the youngest brother, and said that he was the only one who had wanted to hear the King's wise advice. The King repeated what he told to the youngest brother. He then told the women that no one had murdered their husbands.

The fact was that their husbands had not understood the rules of nature and scoffed at his wisdom. But, because the youngest brother took the King's wise advice, he had survived the treacherous trip.

The King gave the widows the gold coins that he had given to their husbands, but that the rest of the gold belonged to the youngest brother, and added, "Remember, always seek wisdom, for wisdom is more precious than gold."

Peninnah Schram's version of this parable.

Only in Israel

Finally, a story, shared with me by a close friend, experienced on his return to Jerusalem, late at night from an overseas trip.

Asher, at the time, was saying *Kaddish* for his mother, and was hoping to find a *Ma'ariv minyan* upon his trip home from the airport. He asked his taxi driver if he knew of a synagogue that would have a late *Ma'ariv* service.

Sensing that his driver was secular, because he wasn't wearing a kippah, he knew the odds of the driver knowing of a *minyan* were slim, but he figured he would ask, anyhow.

"You need a *minyan?*" the driver asked.

"Yes," Asher answered.

"Don't worry," his driver assured him.

Asher wasn't sure what the driver had in mind, but they continued on the climb up the steep highway to Jerusalem. Shortly after entering the city, the driver pulled his taxi to the side of the road, took a well-worn kippah out of his glove compartment, got out of the cab, and told my friend, "wait a minute." The driver then proceeded to flag down eight cars, got the drivers to come out of their cars, brought them together, to make a late-night *minyan* on a Jerusalem sidewalk.

Where else could this happen, if not in Israel? The same land that bore witness to the return of a dispersed nation, would be the land where a total stranger would bring together a *minyan* of strangers, to be no longer strangers but fellow Jews on a mission, that of standing by each other at that moment of need, enabling true *kaddish*, true *kedushah* to triumph, in a world where holiness can often be hard to track down.

Rabbi Philip Scheim

Have Faith in What You Have

A century ago, Russell Conwell traveled the United States with a speech he called, "Acres of Diamonds." Of the many stories he told, one was of a young man who studied at Yale to become a mining engineer. Upon graduation, "gold fever" struck him and he set off to California to seek his fortune.

Yale had offered him a position as an instructor, which he turned down. He persuaded his mother to sell their Massachusetts farm and accompany him. But the trip was futile as he found no gold, and eventually accepted a job in Minnesota working for a mining company – at a lower salary than he would have received at Yale.

More interesting is that the man who bought the family farm from the widowed mother was harvesting potatoes one day. As he slid a heavy bushel through an opening in the stone wall, he noticed a shiny stone. He had it assayed and learned it was native silver. The farm was sitting on a fortune in silver!

Why had the mining engineer, who had undoubtedly passed by that same rock and others like it hundreds of times, not discovered the ore? Could it be that he never dreamed a treasure could be found so easily? Was it because he believed that one must go elsewhere to fulfill a dream?

A profound life truth is this: what we are seeking may be found right where we are. Think about it. Do you need to go somewhere else to find happiness? Chances are, if you were truly aware of what you have in your life now, you could be happy. Or do you think you'll find love if you only search for somebody else? Look more carefully, through appreciative eyes, at who is in your life today.

It's easy to miss what you have when you are busy searching someplace else. Sometimes it's just about changing our thinking. What you seek (happiness, security, fulfillment, challenge, love, meaning, purpose – the list is practically endless) may be right in front of you. You likely just don't see it. It may be hidden in plain sight.

Before you search someplace else, look carefully! You just might be amazed at what you see.

Steve Goodier

To Kill Curiosity

A professor became so enamored with giving outside lectures that he decided to tape his weekly remarks for his seminar group. When he unexpectedly returned early because of a canceled engagement, he went right to his classroom to see how his students were getting along.

As he opened the door, he heard his own voice coming out of the tape recorder – and in the students' places were 12 other tape recorders.

Impersonality in teaching tends to kill curiosity and initiative.

Dr. Harold Taylor, former president of Sarah Lawrence College

♦♦♦

One Minute Can Change A Life

He almost killed somebody, but one minute changed his life. During his college years, Sherman Rogers spent a summer in an Idaho logging camp. When the superintendent had to leave for a few days, he put Rogers in charge.

"What if the men refuse to follow my orders?" Rogers asked. He thought of Tony, an immigrant worker who grumbled and growled all day, giving the other men a hard time.

"Fire them," the superintendent said. Then, as if reading Rogers' mind, he added, "I suppose you think you are going to fire Tony if you get the chance. I'd feel badly about that. I have been logging for 40 years. Tony is the most reliable worker I've ever had. I know he is a grouch and that he hates everybody and everything. But he comes in first and leaves last. There has not been an accident for eight years on the hill where he works."

Rogers took over the next day. He went to Tony and spoke to him. "Tony, do you know I'm in charge here today?" Tony grunted. "I was going to fire you the first time we tangled, but I want you to know I'm not," he told Tony, adding what the superintendent had said.

When he finished, Tony dropped the shovelful of sand he had held and tears streamed down his face. "Why he no tell me dat eight years ago?"

That day Tony worked harder than ever before – and he smiled! He later said to Rogers, "I told Maria you first foreman in deese country who ever say, 'Good work, Tony,' and it make Maria feel like Christmas."

Rogers went back to school after that summer. Twelve years later, he met Tony again. He was superintendent for railroad construction for one of the largest logging companies in the West. Rogers asked him how he came to California and happened to have such success.

Tony replied, "If it not be for the one minute you talk to me back in Idaho, I keel somebody someday. One minute, she change my whole life."

Effective managers know the importance of taking a moment to point out what a worker is doing well. But what a difference a minute of affirmation can make in any relationship!

One minute. Have you got one minute to thank someone? A minute to tell someone what you sincerely like or appreciate about her? A minute to elaborate on something he did well? One minute. It can make a difference for a lifetime.

Steve Goodier
From Sherman Rogers' book, Foremen: Leaders or Drivers?

◆◆◆

But I'm Doing That Now!

There is a businessman who meets a Mexican fisherman while on vacation. The businessman notices several large yellow fin tuna in the fisherman's boat. He compliments the fisherman on the quality of the fish and asks how long it took to catch them.

"Only a little while," explains the fisherman.

"Well, what do you do with the rest of your day?" the businessman wanted to know.

"I play with my children, take a siesta with my wife, Maria, stroll into the village each evening where I sip wine and play guitar with my amigos."

The businessman just couldn't resist giving his advice. "Don't you know that if you spent more time fishing, you could buy a bigger boat, and then with the bigger boat you could catch more fish until you could buy even more boats? You could eventually catch so many fish that you could avoid the middleman and sell directly to distributors. You would get so large, that you could move to New York City where you would run the whole enterprise and then sell your company stock to the public. You could make millions!"

The fisherman asked: "How long will this take?"

The man replied, "Fifteen to twenty years."

The fisherman asked: "Then what?"

The businessman smiled and said, "Then you could retire in a small Mexican village where you could sleep late, fish a little, play with your children, take a siesta with your wife, and sip wine with your friends."

The confused fisherman replied: "But I'm doing that now!"

We often get so caught up in making a living that we forget about making a life!

◆◆◆

The Face Of Another Human Being

Rabbi Abraham Joshua Heschel asked a student he taught at the Jewish Theological Seminary, "how did you arrive at the seminary today."

The student answered that he walked.

Rabbi Heschel asked, "Did you see God as you walked?"

The student answered, "I did not take the beautiful path, through Riverside Park along the Hudson River. I was late so I walked along Broadway."

Rabbi Heschel responded, "You walked along Broadway, probably passing a few hundred people, and you did not see God?"

The story is clear. In Judaism, we see God when we encounter the face of another human being.

◆◆◆

Antisemitism – The World's Oldest Virus

Two Corona viruses are speaking. One says, "I have to find someone to infect. I need to make copies of myself."

The second says, "How about that man?"

The first answers, "He is not available. He has stayed home for over two years, having his groceries delivered to his front porch, never going outside and having no one visit."

The virus says, "How about that woman?"

The first answers, "She is not available. She has been social distancing, wearing a mask, using Purell, and washing her hands constantly."

The second finally says, "How about that man? He is out demonstrating with the crowds, not wearing a mask and not socially distancing. He is speaking out against immigrants, against blacks, and most vocally, against Jews. Look, he is carrying a sign saying, 'Jews will not replace us.'"

"I cannot infect him."

"Why not?"

"He already has a virus."

◆◆◆

It Made a Difference to that One

Whoever saves a single life – it is as if that person has saved an entire world. (Mishnah Sanhedrin, Ch 4, end)

There was a woman who used to go to the ocean to do her writing. She had a habit of walking on the beach every morning before she began her work. Early one morning, she was walking along the shore after a big storm had passed and found the vast beach littered with starfish as far as the eye could see, stretching in both directions.

Off in the distance, the woman noticed a young boy approaching. As the boy walked, he paused every so often and as he grew closer, the woman could see that he was occasionally bending down to pick up an object and throw it into the sea. The boy came closer still and the woman called out, "Good morning! May I ask what it is that you are doing?"

The young boy paused, looked up, and replied, "Throwing starfish into the ocean. The tide has washed them up onto the shore and they can't return to the sea by themselves. When the sun gets high in the sky, they will die, unless I throw them back into the water."

The woman replied, "But there must be tens of thousands of starfish on this beach. I'm afraid you won't really be able to make much of a difference."

The boy bent down, picked up yet another starfish and threw it as far as he could into the ocean. Then he turned, smiled and said, "It made a difference to that one!"

A story from Jewish tradition expresses the very same idea. Once, while Moses, our Teacher, was tending his father-in-law Yitro's flocks, a lamb ran away. Moses ran after the lamb until he reached a small, shaded place. There, the lamb came across a pool and began to drink. As Moses approached the lamb, he said, "I did not know you ran away because you were thirsty. You are so exhausted!" He then put the lamb on his shoulders and carried him back.

The Holy One said, "Since you tend the flocks of sheep with such overwhelming love – by your life, You shall be the shepherd of My flock, Israel." (Exodus Rabba 2:2)

By definition, since every human being is made in God's Image, every single human being is valuable. "Usefulness to society" is not a valid criterion. There is a certain arrogance to those who maintain that the mover-and-shaker, the orchestra conductor, or research geneticist is of greater importance than the cashier at TJ Maxx, the taxi driver, the UPS person, or the custodian at the synagogue.

God chose Moses because Moses cared about every single animal in the flock.

In the world of Jewish tradition, no one gets left out. By extension and possible analogy, a curious section of Jewish law hints at this.

For certain prayers to be recited, a minimum of 10 adults must be present. This quorum is called a *minyan*. In the Shulchan Aruch (Code of Jewish Law), section Orach Chaim, 55:6, it states: "...if one of them is asleep, even so, that person is counted."

Some commentators disagree, but the plain text says that, even asleep, the person is part of the minyan.

I have discussed this with several people and their interpretations vary:

(1) That there are many people in society who are, as it were, "asleep", unaware, or unresponsive...of their own volition or

involuntarily. They are most certainly part of our community.

(2) Perhaps the sound of the prayers themselves will awaken the person. Stories are legion about people in comas waking up from the most likely to the least likely stimuli... a piece of music, petting a dog, a familiar smell, a touch or stroke on the arm. It is all very mysterious, and, while not everyone is capable of "waking up", certainly many more are than we might initially assume.

(3) Medical personnel in operating rooms are ever-more-aware of how much an anesthetized person can hear and remember. While the person may not visually or aurally respond, clearly the person is definitely absorbing the words.

To summarize:

(1) Everyone who is alive is part of the community, and

(2) We can never know how little or how much or what in particular will "wake someone up".

My mother was in the hospital for about a month. Though she was unresponsive, I remember many occasions when her cardiologist, Dr. Warren Levy, – May he live a long, happy, and full life! – came in, and before examining her, would whisper into her ear, "Now, Edythe, I am going to check...." It was so gentle, so very, very moving. It was the perfect human touch.

Danny Siegel

Bis Hundert Und Tzvanzig

Sidney was called into court to testify. The attorney asked him his age.

"84 until 120," he answered."

"Please just answer the question, how old are you?

"84 until 120."

The judge jumped in. "Sir, please give us a simple answer. How old are you?"

"84 until 120."

Finally, the opposing attorney stepped forward. "Perhaps I can help. Until 120, how old are you?"

"84," answered Sidney.

The Pretensions of the Evil Inclination

One wintry day, after morning prayers, Rabbi Pinhas of Koretz sat in the *bet midrash* and heard a discussion of Hasidim about wiles of the Evil Inclination, which uses all kinds of tricks to capture people into its lair and seduce them to sin.

Rabbi Pinhas taught them:

I hate the Evil Inclination, not because it instigates and seduces, but because it deceives and fools people. Never have I heard that the Evil Inclination comes to a Jew and says to him: Commit such and such a sin. Rather when it wants to seduce someone away from the proper path, it comes and pretends to be righteous, and says: Do such and such a mitzvah. This man does not observe Shabbat properly, and you must chase after him until he does, etc. In other words, the Evil Inclination's method is to lie and cheat and pretend that it seeks the welfare of a person.

I'll give you an example. Today, I had dealings with the Evil Inclination. As is my custom I awakened before sunrise and I wanted to go and bathe in the mikveh. Along comes the Evil Inclination and tries to seduce me.

He says: How can you go bathe in this cold weather? It's freezing outside, there's snow and ice, the water in the mikveh is frozen, and bathing under these conditions is a sin, because it may endanger your life.

I said to him: If the air is so cold, how did you get here? Did you not stay in my house all night! Surely you feel very cold. Therefore lie down in my place in my warm bed, and I will go to the mikveh.

I went to the mikveh, I shattered the ice, went down and bathed. But when I looked around, I saw the Evil Inclination next to me in the water. He starts to praise and laud me. You are a true tzaddik; there is no one as great as you!

Again he is pretending to be a friend in order to bring pride to my heart.

Heart and Scroll: Heartfelt Stories of Hasidic Sages,
Ed. Simcha Raz; Translator: Rabbi Dov Peretz Elkins

◆◆◆

The Chief Rabbi of Israel and Napoleon's Throne

In the early 2000s, Rabbi Mordechai Eliyahu, the Chief Sephardic Rabbi of Israel, received an official invitation from the President of France, Jacques Chirac, to visit his country.

Chirac was known as a hard line pro-Arab leader, constantly pushing Israel to cede territories to the Palestinians.

Rabbi Eliyahu was very friendly. During a visit to the French national museum, the rabbi was shown the throne of Napoleon, and he asked if it was for sale, and if so, for how much, and how long ago did Napoleon live?

The tour guide explained that the chair of Napoleon was of great historical and national importance, and was certainly not for sale.

Later, returning to the office of the president for an official ceremony, Rabbi Eliyahu was asked to say a few words. He repeated his question about Napoleon's chair, and everyone laughed.

The members of the Israeli Embassy were in panic, certain that Chirac would storm out of the room in a fury.

Then Rabbi Eliyahu explained: three thousand years ago our King David and King Solomon secured the city of Jerusalem. Does it not make simple sense that just as you expect us to honor your heritage, so you should honor ours? If the chair of Napoleon is not for sale, then how can you expect us to sell parts of Israel and Jerusalem.

Then Chirac warmly shook the Rabbi's hand, and whispered something to one of his assistants. The man hurriedly left the room and returned in just seconds with a small velvet box. Chirac then announced, "This medallion is usually reserved for visiting heads of state, but I have never heard anyone speak such clever words like these. They so impressed me that I am presenting this to you." And when he finished speaking, the crowd gave the rabbi a standing ovation.

Yeshiva Ohr Temima

◆◆◆

Environmental Justice

There was once a goat who had horns so long and beautiful that when he lifted his head, he could touch the stars, and they would sing the most beautiful melody that anyone had ever heard. One day, a man walking encountered the goat, and a brilliant idea jumped into his head: "I could make my wife a gorgeous jewelry box for her birthday from a piece of one of the goat's horns."

The man approached the goat and explained, "I want to make a jewelry box from just a small piece of one of your horns. It won't hurt when I cut it off, and I'll just take a small piece. You won't even miss it!" The friendly goat lowered his head to accommodate the man's request.

The jewelry box the man made was indeed beautiful, and his wife adored it. Proudly, she showed it to all of her friends who soon wanted one just like it. Before long people inundated the goat with requests to "cut off just a small piece" of one of his horns. Soon, of course, the goat could no longer reach the stars, and that most beautiful melody was forever silenced.

In the Passover story, Pharaoh's advisors warned him before the plague of locusts ravaged the land: "Do you not yet know that Egypt is nearly destroyed." (Exodus 10:7) That warning should ring out to us across the millennia. Do we not realize that our earth is nearly destroyed?

Although it is too late for the goat to make the stars sing, it is not too late for us to save our planet and vouchsafe clean water, clean air, sufficient food, and a beautiful earth for future generations.

Rabbi Stephen Lewis Fuchs

♦♦♦

Don't Trouble Yourself

There is a beautiful story told of the Brisker Rav, Reb Hayyim Halevy Soloveitchik. Once a man arrived late at night in Brisk. All the houses were dark, except for one, so he knocked at the door. He was greeted warmly, and the host prepared a meal for him. Looking around, the man saw that the house was filled with sefarim, sacred books, and surmised that the man was learned, a Rabbi or a perhaps a *Dayan*, a judge.

The man became uncomfortable disturbing a scholar and said to his host, "You needn't trouble yourself." His host didn't answer but instead began to make the bed and the man said, "You needn't trouble yourself."

The next morning, the two went to synagogue together and the traveler discovered that his host was the famed Rabbi, who offered the man the honor of *hagbah*, lifting the Torah. As the man prepared to lift it, the Rabbi whispered, "You needn't trouble yourself."

Through his own example the Brisker Rav was teaching the beautiful lesson that we should take no less trouble for a human being than we would for a scroll of Torah. When another person needs us, it is not a burden but a mitzvah.

◆◆◆

Encouragement

A little boy who loved music was bitterly disappointed because he could neither play nor sing.

One day he told his disappointment to Amati, a violin-maker, who said, "Come into the house and you shall try. The song in the heart is all that matters, for there are many ways of making music. Some play violins, some sing, some paint pictures, some carve statues, while others till the soil and grow flowers. Each sings a song and helps to make the music of the world. You can make music too."

It was this encouragement which stimulated Antonio Stradivarius to become the world's greatest violin-maker.

◆◆◆

The Rabbi of Sasov Understood

How to love men is something I learned from a peasant. He was sitting inside an inn along with other peasants, drinking. For a long time, he was as silent as all the rest, but when he was moved by the wine, he asked one of the men seated beside him: "Tell me, do you love me?"

The other replied: "I love you very much."

But the first peasant replied: "You say that you love me, but you do not know what I need. If you really loved me, you would know."

The other had not a word to say to this, and the peasant who had put the question fell silent again.

But I understood. To know the needs of men and to bear the burden of their sorrow – that is the true love of men.

Rabbi Moshe Leib

◆◆◆

Decision Is Destiny

A little girl asked, "Mommy, what happens when a car gets too old and banged up to run?"

"Well," her mother said, "someone sells it to your father."

I think I have bought a couple of cars like that. Like most people, my life is punctuated by decisions that did not turn out the way I'd hoped. But we cannot always be expected to make the best decisions. Sometimes we simply don't have enough information. And other times, there just isn't a good decision anywhere to be found and we go with the lesser of several evils, hoping that we know a lesser evil when we see one. All we can really do is make decisions the best way we know how and act on them.

But making better decisions is important. Things change when decisions change.

Before his rise to political fame, Maryland Congressman Kweisi Mfume walked a path of self-destruction. He dropped out of high school. A few years later, he robbed a pedestrian in order to join a street gang. Mfume spent the following years drinking and trouble-making with the gang.

A turning point came one summer night when he abruptly decided he could no longer continue on his present course. He decided to earn his high school equivalency certificate and later graduated magna cum laude from Morgan State University in Baltimore. He then went on to earn a graduate degree at Johns Hopkins University.

When Mfume ran for Congress in 1986, his opponents tried to use his old mistakes against him. But his achievements since he left a troubled past behind captivated an electorate who voted him into office by an overwhelming 87 percent. He was on a collision course with total failure until he made an important decision.

That decision included getting an education and trying to improve the world rather than taking from it. And it was also a decision to make better decisions. He eventually became a representative to the US House of Representatives (twice), he headed up the National Associate of the Advancement of Colored People (NAACP) and served as the CEO of the National Medical Association.

What changes a life is not simply learning more, though education is important. What changes a life is making decisions – the best decisions you can make – and acting on them. It's been accurately said: "Your decisions determine your direction, and your direction determines your destiny." Or put another way, "The decisions you make... make you."

Steve Goodier

How to Criticize

Rabbi Gerson Cohen, past Chancellor of the Jewish Theological Seminary, tells of the time he was a child at Camp Ramah in Wisconsin. As he and his friends were playing basketball, the game got a little rough – as sports often do. Without warning, one of the scholars-in-residence, a Rabbi and professor of Talmud, intervened, scolding the boys that, "There is a Jewish way to play basketball. And this is not the Jewish way."

Rabbi Cohen remembers that they were stung by the remarks, and humbled. Instead of grumbling about it, however, they stopped their game and started a discussion about how they would try to play in the future. As the scholar was about to walk away, he said to the kids, "How wonderful, a group of boys able to receive rebuke."

The Man Who Joined the Search Party Looking for Himself

Muster the courage to examine the only place we can truly find who we are looking for – inside ourselves.

I didn't know if I should laugh or cry. I read the news item about a Turkish man who joined a search party for a missing person, not realizing the person everyone was looking for was him!

In the town of Inegol, northwest Turkey, Beyhan Mutlu, 51, went drinking with a buddy in a forest. He didn't return home and his wife reported him missing. She heard he had walked away from his friend, drunk.

While Mutlu was sleeping in a house in the forest, military forces and rescue teams were called in to search for him.

Mutlu woke up in the morning and came across members of the search party. He decided to help them find the missing person. Once he heard them calling out his name, it dawned on him that he was the focus of the search.

Mutlu told Turkish news that he told them he was in fact Beyhan Mutlu, the man they were looking for, but they continued to search. "They didn't believe me. The truth came out when my friend saw me." He spent more than half an hour looking high and low for himself.

It's hard to resist turning a story like this into a metaphor for life. *To find myself, I need to look within, not outside of myself.*

So many people are out there in the forest, joining the party and searching for themselves, without stopping to realize: I'm right here. To find myself, I need to look within, not outside of myself.

We hunger and yearn for connection, meaning and self-understanding. Driven to fill the void, we join the throngs of people, co-travelers who are also searching, and set our focus externally, too afraid to closely examine the only place we can find who we are looking for – inside ourselves.

We are masters at distractions, attempting to fill that inner ache through an endless stream of ersatz meaning – approval and attention from wherever we can get it, a bevy of addictions (food, films, fun, fantasy, drugs), external power and success – while we move further away from the person we're really looking for.

We need to hit the handbrake and stop (too bad that Facebook/Whatsapp/Instagram outage we experienced this week wasn't longer than six hours). In order to find the person we're looking for, we need to stop roaming the forest and muster the courage to look inside ourselves.

In his *48 Ways to Wisdom* series, Rabbi Noah Weinberg placed a huge emphasis on urging people to take the time to answer, with clarity and conviction, these questions: What am I living for? What are my priorities in life? What is my game plan to attain these goals? In order to answer these foundational questions, it's essential to spend time interviewing the most fascinating person you could ever meet in the world: yourself.

Rabbi Weinberg encouraged us to sit down with pen and paper, phones turned off, and take the time necessary to answer the following questions:

What are my primary goals in life?

Why did I choose this career? Am I satisfied with it?

For what do I want to be remembered?

How can I be happier and more fulfilled?

What are my secret dreams and ambitions? Why haven't I fulfilled them?

How can I be a better parent, spouse, friend?

Answering these questions play an important role in understanding who you are. Call off the search party. The person you're looking for is right there inside of you. Take the time, determination and focus to discover who you really are.

Rabbi Nechemia Coopersmith
Reprinted by permission, www.aish.com

◆◆◆

Kamtsa and Bar Kamtsa

The Talmud records a poignant story relating to the destruction of the Temple in Jerusalem by the Romans in 70 CE. Although historians describe various political, sociological, and military explanations for the Roman war against the Jews, the Talmud – through the story of Kamtsa and Bar Kamtsa – points to a moral/spiritual cause of the destruction.

R. Johanan said: The destruction of Jerusalem came through Kamtsa and Bar Kamtsa, in this way...

A certain man had a friend Kamtsa and an enemy Bar Kamtsa. He once made a party and said to his servant, "Go and bring Kamtsa." The man went and brought Bar Kamtsa. When the man (who gave the party) found him there, he said, "See, you tell tales about me; what are you doing here? Get out."

Said Bar Kamtsa: "Since I am here, let me stay and I will pay you for whatever I eat and drink."

The host said, "I won't."

Then Bar Kamtsa said, "Let me give you half the cost of the party."

"No," said the host.

"Then let me pay for the whole party," said Bar Kamtsa.

The host still said, "No," and he took Bar Kamtsa by the hand and put him out.

Said Bar Kamtsa, "Since the rabbis were sitting there and did not stop the host, this shows that they agreed with him. I will go and inform against them to the Government."

Bar Kamtsa went and said to the Emperor, "The Jews are rebelling against you."

The Emperor asked, "How can you tell?"

Bar Kamtsa said to the Emperor, "Send them an offering and see whether they will offer it (on the altar)."

So the Emperor sent with him a fine calf. While on the way Bar Kamtsa made a blemish on its upper lip, or as some say on the white of its eye, in a place where Jews count it as a blemish, but the Romans do not.

The rabbis were inclined to offer it in order not to offend the Emperor.

Said R. Zechariah b. Abkulas to them, "People will say that blemished animals are offered on the altar."

They then proposed to kill Bar Kamtsa so that he should not go and inform against them, but R. Zechariah b. Abkulas said to them, "Is one who makes a blemish on consecrated animals to be put to death?"

R. Johanan thereupon remarked, "Through the scrupulousness of R. Zechariah b. Abkulas, our House has been destroyed, our Temple burned and we ourselves exiled from our land." (Gittin 55b-56a)

The story reflects a lack of peace among the Jewish community in Jerusalem. The antagonism between the host and Bar Kamtsa is palpable. The unpleasant scene at the party was witnessed by others – including "the rabbis"; obviously, "the rabbis" were included on the party's guest list. They were part of the host's social network.

When Bar Kamtsa was ejected from the party, he did not express rage at the host. Rather, he was deeply wounded by the fact that rabbis had been silent in the face of the humiliation he had suffered: "Since the rabbis were sitting there and did not stop him, this shows that they agreed with him."

He might have understood the host's uncouth behavior, since the host hated him. But he could not understand why the rabbis, through their silence, would go along with the host. Why didn't they stand up and protest on behalf of Bar Kamtsa? Why didn't they attempt to increase peace? Bar Kamtsa was so disgusted with the rabbis that he decided to stir up the Roman Emperor against the Jewish people. If the rabbinic leadership itself was corrupt, then the entire community had to suffer.

Why didn't the rabbis speak up on behalf of Bar Kamtsa?

The rabbis kept silent because they thought it socially and economically prudent for their own interests. They could not muster the courage to confront the host and try to intervene on behalf of Bar Kamtsa. By looking out for their own selfish interests, the rabbis chose to look the other way when Bar Kamtsa was publicly humiliated.

Rabbi Marc D. Angel

◆◆◆

To Turn On The Lights In People's Souls

The Rebbe asked about my father and about my current occupation. I said, "I go to college."

"What are you studying? What do you want to become?"

"I'm going for a master's degree in education."

"Very good."

And then the Rebbe continued, "I went to college also."

"Where?" I asked.

"The Sorbonne," he answered

Wow! The Sorbonne University in Paris is a world-renowned university. And so I asked him what he studied there, figuring he would tell me something like theology.

"My field was electrical engineering," he replied. "But I prefer to turn on the lights in people's souls."

I remember those words precisely, and I will remember them to my dying day.

Len Weksler

◆◆◆

If I Had a Hammer

In his story, "Gooseberries", Anton Chekhov writes: There ought to be behind the door of every happy, contented man someone standing with a hammer continually reminding him with a tap that there are unhappy people; that however happy he may be, life will show him her laws sooner or later, trouble will come for him – disease, poverty, losses, and no one will see or hear, just as now he neither sees nor hears others.

But there is no man with a hammer ...

Even if you don't hear the tap of the hammer, let *Hessed* – doing of acts of kindness – guide you every day.

◆◆◆

That's The Kind Of Thing Sara Would Do

In 1966, an eleven-year-old black boy moved with his parents and family to a white neighborhood in Washington. Sitting with his two brothers and two sisters on the front step of the house, he waited to see how they would be greeted. They were not. Passers-by turned to look at them but no one gave them a smile or even a glance of recognition. All the fearful stories he had heard about how whites treated blacks seemed to be coming true.

Years later, writing about those first days in their new home, he says, "I knew we were not welcome here. I knew we would not be liked here. I knew we would have no friends here. I knew we should not have moved here ..."

As he was thinking those thoughts, a white woman coming home from work passed by on the other side of the road. She turned to the children and with a broad smile said, "Welcome!" Disappearing into the house, she emerged minutes later with a tray laden with drinks and sandwiches which she brought over to the children, making them feel at home. That moment – the young man later wrote – changed his life. It gave him a sense of belonging where there was none before. It made him realize, at a time when race relations in the United States were still fraught, that a black family could feel at home in a white area and that there could be relationships that were color-blind.

Over the years, he learned to admire much about the woman across the street, but it was that first spontaneous act of greeting that became, for him, a definitive memory. It broke down a wall of separation and turned strangers into friends.

The young man, Stephen Carter, eventually became a law professor at Yale and wrote a book about what he learned that day. He called it *Civility*.

The name of the woman, he tells us, was Sara Kestenbaum, and she died all too young. He adds that it was no coincidence that she was a religious Jew. "In the Jewish tradition," he notes, "such civility is called *hessed* – doing of acts of kindness – which is in turn derived from the understanding that human beings are made in the image of God." Civility, he adds, "itself may be seen as part of *hessed*: it does indeed require kindnesses toward our fellow citizens, including the ones who are strangers, and even when it is hard."

To this day, he adds, "I can close my eyes and feel on my tongue the smooth, slick sweetness of the cream cheese and jelly sandwiches that I gobbled on that summer afternoon when I discovered how a single act of genuine and unassuming civility can change a life forever."

I never knew Sara Kestenbaum, but years after I had read Carter's book, I gave a lecture to the Jewish community in the part of Washington where she had lived. I told them Carter's story, which they had not heard before. But they nodded in recognition. "Yes," one said, "that's the kind of thing Sara would do."

Rabbi Jonathan Sacks

♦♦♦

To Take Out The Trash

A newlywed student and his wife couldn't agree on who should take out the trash. Each one felt it was the other's responsibility, and the daily disagreement was escalating from bad to worse.

The husband decided to ask his rebbi, HaRav Mordechai Gifter, for advice. Rav Gifter listened in silence and didn't offer any comment.

The following Friday afternoon, while the couple was preparing for Shabbos, they had a surprise visitor... Rav Gifter. He told them that he came to take out the trash. Ouch!

The Rosh Yeshiva made his point. It is all part of our work. Helping one another is never beneath anyone. View it as a mitzvah, an opportunity to be helpful. To work on our middos, our character traits.

And how beautiful is that.

Chaya Sora Jungreis Gertzulin

♦♦♦

But There Are People There!

Sholom Aleichem wrote a story about a Jewish young man who was conscripted into the Russian army, and was trained how to use his rifle.

"At the firing line, the sergeant noticed Yechiel shooting up in the air instead of ahead; he poured a flood of curses and abuse on his head, with all the worst names for Jews in Russian to boot, and showed him where to aim his gun. A little later the sergeant again saw Yechiel aiming up in the air. This time he was flabbergasted: What, he wanted to know, was the matter with that crazy Jewish soldier? Hadn't he told Yechiel where to aim his gun?

"Yes," Yechiel replied, "but there are people there!"

This seemingly amusing story points to a serious truth. When people see each other as fellow human beings, it is difficult to shoot at them. To engage in violent action first requires a process of dehumanization of the victim. People need to be trained to hate the "enemy," to see the other as a villain unworthy of life.

Rabbi Marc D. Angel

◆◆◆

Doing A Favor To Others

Rabbi Kalonymus Kalman Shapira, the Grand Rabbi of Piascezno, Poland was interred among the hundreds of thousands of Jews living in inhuman conditions and dying of starvation and diseases in the Warsaw Ghetto. He devoted his life to inspire and bring hope to the desperate and downtrodden, the walking skeletons – the veritable Muselmann. His exceptional dedication was to the countless "little ones", the pre-bar/bat mitzvah children for whom he established a secret synagogue. He devoted day and night ministering to each one. He was father, mother and best friend to thousands of kids. The one message he constantly resounded and his undying legacy is "the greatest thing in the world is doing a favor to others!"

◆◆◆

Two Monks and a Woman

A senior monk and a junior monk were traveling together. At one point, they came to a river with a strong current. As the monks were preparing to cross the river, they saw a very young and beautiful woman also attempting to cross. The young woman asked if they could help her cross to the other side.

The two monks glanced at one another because they had taken vows not to touch a woman.

Then, without a word, the older monk picked up the woman, carried her across the river, placed her gently on the other side, and carried on his journey.

The younger monk couldn't believe what had just happened. After rejoining his companion, he was speechless, and an hour passed without a word between them.

Two more hours passed, then three, finally the younger monk could contain himself no longer, and blurted out, "As monks, we are not permitted a woman, how could you then carry that woman on your shoulders?"

The older monk looked at him and replied, "Brother, I set her down on the other side of the river, why are you still carrying her?"

We all go through times in life that lead us to hold onto things better left "on the other side of the river" and yet we still carry them and only hurt ourselves. What are you still holding onto that is better left?

Amanda Hunt

♦♦♦

The Rabbi's Gift and the Mashiah

Once, a synagogue had fallen on hard times. Only five members were left: the cantor and four others, all over 60 years old.

In the mountains near the shul lived a retired rabbi. It occurred to the five to ask the rabbi if he could offer any advice that may save the shul.

The cantor and the rabbi spoke at length, but when asked for advice, the rabbi simply responded by saying, "I have no advice to give. The only thing I can tell you is that one of you is the *Mashiah* (Messiah)."

Returning to the shul, the cantor told the four other synagogue members what the rabbi had said. In the months that followed, the elder synagogue members pondered the words of the rabbi.

"The *Mashiah* is amongst us," they each thought to themselves. As they considered this possibility, they all began to treat each other with extraordinary respect on the off chance that one among them might indeed be the *Mashiah*. And, on the off chance that each member himself might be the *Mashiah*, they also began to treat themselves with extraordinary care.

As time went by, people visiting the shul noticed the aura of respect and gentle kindness that surrounded the five old members of the small shul.

Without any apparent reason, more people began returning to worship at the old synagogue. They brought their friends, and their friends brought even more friends; within a few years the small shul had once again become a thriving congregation!

Indeed, each and every one of us is a potential *Mashiah* – and we can even start his work before he reveals himself to us.

The True Disciple

Two students studied with the same great rabbi. After the rabbi died, they separated and did not see each other for many years. One of them meticulously followed all he had learned from the rabbi. The other developed his own interpretations as well, and in many matters diverged from what they had learned.

After many years the two met. The first said to his former friend, "I don't understand. We had such a magnificent mentor. Why didn't you live as I have, and remain faithful to the teachings of our Master?"

The second answered, "I did. Indeed, I followed his way more scrupulously than you. You see, he grew up and left his rabbi. I grew up and left mine."

If we are fortunate enough to have figures in private or public life whom we admire, we will naturally share many of their teachings and inclinations. Yet, in the end, we must each forge our own path in this world. No one else can live our lives for us. We learn what we can from our teachers, and then leave them to become ourselves.

Rabbi David Wolpe

♦♦♦

Amazing!!

The story is told of a South African native with the unusual name of "Amazing." All his life, this modest, unassuming person felt embarrassed by his name, and so when he died, he asked that his tombstone omit his name and simply read:

Here lies a good man, who never said a bad word,
  never hurt or cheated anyone.
He raised a wonderful family, always wore a smile
  and loved each and every person he met.

And all the people who would pass by that stone in the cemetery would stop, read it, smile and say, "Amazing!!"

♦♦♦

Embarrassing

Psychologist and teacher, Rabbi Dr. Abraham Twerski was once traveling on a train, bearded and wearing his usual Hasidic garb of a long black coat and black hat. He was approached by a Jewish passenger who berated him, "Why do you have to dress like that?! Don't you know you're attracting attention and embarrassing other Jews?!"

Rabbi Twerski shot a look of incredulity at the man and coolly replied, "My dear fellow, I think you have made a mistake. I'm Amish, and this is the way our people have dressed for centuries."

The man was taken aback and began to apologize. "I'm terribly sorry," he stammered, "I meant you no ill will. I actually think it's commendable that you have maintained your traditions over such a long period of time."

Dr. Twerski abruptly cut him off and put him in his place. "Oh, so you think it's quaint and acceptable that the Amish keep up their traditions, but not us Jews?! Maybe you ought to come see me professionally, and we can work on your sense of self-esteem."

Three Wondrous Answers

One day it occurred to a certain emperor that if he only knew the answers to three questions, he would never stray in any matter.

- What is the best time to do each thing?
- Who are the most important people to work with?
- What is the most important thing to do at all times?

The emperor issued a decree throughout his kingdom announcing that whoever could answer the questions would receive a great reward. Many who read the decree made their way to the palace at once, each person with a different answer.

In reply to the first question, one person advised that the emperor make up a thorough time schedule, consecrating every hour, day, month, and year for certain tasks and then follow the schedule to the letter. Only then could he hope to do every task at the right time.

Another person replied that it was impossible to plan in advance and that the emperor should put all vain amusements aside and remain attentive to everything in order to know what to do at what time.

Someone else insisted that, by himself, the emperor could never hope to have all the foresight and competence necessary to decide when to do each and every task and what he really needed was to set up a Council of the Wise and then to act according to their advice.

Someone else said that certain matters required immediate decision and could not wait for consultation, but if he wanted to know in advance what was going to happen, he should consult magicians and soothsayers.

The responses to the second question also lacked accord.

One person said that the emperor needed to place all his trust in administrators, another urged reliance on priests and monks, while others recommended physicians. Still others put their faith in warriors.

The third question drew a similar variety of answers.

Some said science was the most important pursuit. Others insisted on religion. Yet others claimed the most important thing was military skill.

The emperor was not pleased with any of the answers, and no reward was given.

After several nights of reflection, the emperor resolved to visit a hermit who lived up on the mountain and was said to be an enlightened man. The emperor wished to find the hermit to ask him the three questions, though he knew the hermit never left the mountains and was known to receive only the poor, refusing to have anything to do with persons of wealth or power. So the emperor disguised himself as a simple peasant and ordered his attendants to wait for him at the foot of the mountain while he climbed the slope alone to seek the hermit.

Reaching the holy man's dwelling place, the emperor found the hermit digging a garden in front of his hut. When the hermit saw the stranger, he nodded his head in greeting and continued to dig. The labor was obviously hard on him. He was an old man, and each time he thrust his spade into the ground to turn the earth, he heaved heavily.

The emperor approached him and said, "I have come here to ask your help with three questions: When is the best time to do each thing? Who are the most important people to work with? What is the most important thing to do at all times?"

The hermit listened attentively but only patted the emperor on the shoulder and continued digging. The emperor said, "You must be tired. Here, let me give you a hand with that." The hermit thanked him, handed the emperor the spade, and then sat down on the ground to rest.

After he had dug two rows, the emperor stopped and turned to the hermit and repeated his three questions. The hermit still did not answer, but instead stood up and pointed to the spade and said, "Why don't you rest now? I can take over again." But the emperor continued to dig. One hour passed, then two. Finally the sun began to set behind the mountain. The emperor put down the spade and said to the hermit, "I came here to ask if you could answer my three questions. But if you can't give me any answer, please let me know so that I can get on my way home."

The hermit lifted his head and asked the emperor, "Do you hear someone running over there?" The emperor turned his head. They both saw a man with a long white beard emerge from the woods. He ran wildly, pressing his hands against a bloody wound in his stomach. The man ran toward the emperor before falling unconscious to the ground, where he lay groaning. Opening the man's clothing, the emperor and hermit saw that the man had received a deep gash. The emperor cleaned the wound thoroughly and then used his own shirt to bandage it, but the blood completely soaked it within minutes. He rinsed the shirt out and bandaged the wound a second time and continued to do so until the flow of blood had stopped.

At last the wounded man regained consciousness and asked for a drink of water. The emperor ran down to the stream and brought back a jug of fresh water. Meanwhile, the sun had disappeared and the night air had begun to turn cold. The hermit gave the emperor a hand in carrying the man into the hut where they laid him down on the hermit's bed. The man closed his eyes and lay quietly. The emperor was worn out from a long day of climbing the mountain and digging the garden. Leaning against the doorway, he fell asleep. When he rose, the sun had already risen over the mountain. For a moment he forgot where he was and what he had come here for. He looked over to the bed and saw the wounded man also looking around himself in confusion. When he saw the emperor, he stared at him intently and then said in a faint whisper, "Please forgive me."

"But what have you done that I should forgive you?" the emperor asked.

"You do not know me, your majesty, but I know you. I was your sworn enemy, and I had vowed to take vengeance on you, for during the last war you killed my brother and seized my property. When I learned that you were coming alone to the mountain to meet the hermit, I resolved to surprise you on your way back and kill you. But after waiting a long time there was still no sign of you, and so I left my ambush in order to seek you out. But instead of finding you, I came across your attendants, who recognized me, giving me this wound. Luckily, I escaped and ran here. If I hadn't met you I would surely be dead by now. I had intended to kill you, but instead you saved my life! I am ashamed and grateful beyond words. If I live, I vow to be your servant for the rest of my life, and I will bid my children and grandchildren to do the same. Please grant me your forgiveness."

The emperor was overjoyed to see that he was so easily reconciled with a former enemy. He not only forgave the man but promised to return all the man's property and to send his own physician and servants to wait on the man until he was completely healed. After ordering his attendants to take the man home, the emperor returned to see the hermit. Before returning to the palace, the emperor wanted to repeat his three questions one last time. He found the hermit sowing seeds in the earth they had dug the day before.

The hermit stood up and looked at the emperor. "But your questions have already been answered."

"How's that?" the emperor asked, puzzled.

"Yesterday, if you had not taken pity on my age and given me a hand with digging these beds, you would have been attacked by that man on your way home. Then you would have deeply regretted not staying with me. Therefore, the most important time was the time you were digging in the beds, the most important person was myself and the most important pursuit was to help me. Later, when the wounded man ran up here, the most important time was the time you spent dressing his wound, for if you had not cared for him he would have died and you would have lost the chance to be reconciled with him. Likewise, he was the most important person, and the most important pursuit was taking care of his wound.

"Remember that there is only one important time and that is now. The present moment is the only time over which we have dominion. The most important person is always the person you are with, who is right before you, for who knows if you will have dealings with any other person in the future? The most important pursuit is making the person standing at your side happy, for that alone is the pursuit of life."

Tolstoy's story is like a story out of scripture: it doesn't fall short of any sacred text. We talk about social service, service to the people, service to humanity, service for others who are far away, helping to bring peace to the world, but often we forget that it is the very people around us that we must live for first of all.

If you cannot serve your wife or husband or child or parent, how are you going to serve society?

If you cannot make your own child happy, how do you expect to be able to make anyone else happy?

If all our friends in the peace movement or of service communities of any kind do not love and help one another, whom can we love and help?

Are we working for other humans, or are we just working far the name of an organization?

Lev Tolstoy (related by Thich Nhat Hanh)

♦♦♦

If You're Not Loving Life

An efficiency expert once concluded her lecture with the comment, "Please don't try these techniques at home."
"Why not?" she was asked.
"I used to watch my husband prepare breakfast and wondered why he made so many trips to the table carrying only one item at a time," she replied. "One day I asked him, 'Wouldn't it be quicker and more efficient if you organized yourself to carry several things to the table at once?'"
"Did it work?" she was asked.
"Oh, yes, it worked," the expert replied. "It used to take my husband twenty minutes to prepare breakfast. Now I do it in seven."

Not all advice is readily received. And sometimes it is not heard the way it was intended. But neither should all advice be followed; rather, wisdom learns to separate kernels of truth from weeds.

Some advice worthy of consideration, though, comes from multi-billionaire Warren Buffett. These are some of his rules to live by.

1. Pay off your credit cards every month.
2. Put integrity first in your life.
3. Be smart about whose habits you decide to copy.
4. Don't do something just for the money. Happiness comes from loving the work.

I have a friend who believes in trying to do what you love. He says, "Seven years ago I decided to do what I loved most – loving people. Since that time, my cup has slowly been filled and is now flowing over the brim with love. Simultaneously, while seeking humility and significance, I lost pride and prominence. During those seven years I have had several mottoes. Probably the most significant one is: If you are not loving life, you are not living love."
I may never be a multi-billionaire like Warren Buffett. But if I get better at living love, I may just be about the richest person around.

Steve Goodier

♦♦♦

A Traveling Torah

A few years ago, a New York supporter of my Jerusalem synagogue volunteered to donate a Torah scroll to our community. I, of course, was thrilled with this kind offer and immediately agreed to bring the Torah back with me to Israel at the conclusion of my next visit to America. It was during this return trip – during this experience of transporting a Torah from New York to Jerusalem – that I learned an incredibly important additional lesson about holiness. Holiness, I came to understand, is not just about what I do as an individual – and what I personally consider valuable; it is also about with whom I do those holy things and with whom I share these values.

Allow me to explain.

The starting point for my New York to Jerusalem journey was my in-laws' Manhattan apartment. Our bags were packed and brought downstairs to await the arrival of a taxi to take us to the airport. I followed a moment later, taking hold of the Torah and covered it with a tallit, out of respect for the holiness of the scroll. As I exited the elevator, the building's doorman immediately approached me and offered to take the Torah out of my hands, and, to my horror, he volunteered to throw it away for me! He had never seen a tallit before and simply assumed it was some type of sheet used to cover the garbage.

A few moments later the taxi arrived. After loading all the bags into the trunk of the car, the driver suggested I throw my "laundry" in the trunk as well. The "laundry" of course was the Torah I was still holding in my arms. Given the fact that the tallit is an actual garment, the driver's suggestion was a little closer than the doorman's idea, but obviously still too far away to give me much comfort. I sat down in the front seat and held the Torah on my lap.

When we arrived at the airport, things began to change a little.

As I approached the El Al Airlines ticket counter, people began to murmur and point at me – at the covered Torah that is – with both knowledge of, and respect for, what it was. A few people asked me if it was in fact a Torah under there, and after I nodded yes, said: "Oh isn't that so nice, you're bringing a Torah to Israel."

As my turn in line arrived, I was greeted with an incredibly broad smile from the El Al ticket agent.

I was then treated like royalty. "Oh you're accompanying a Torah.

That's so special!" the ticket agent enthused. "Let's see if I can find you a nice seat with plenty of extra room. You know what, let's see if I can find you an extra seat next to you so you can put the Torah down rather than place it in the overhead bin – that wouldn't be respectful now, would it?" I, of course, could not disagree. I was loving this new found respect and desire to help. I may have let the moment carry me away too far as I then asked the agent if I would be receiving the extra miles for the seat the Torah was occupying. Her smile disappeared, but amazingly, just for a moment.

A little while later I boarded the plane, still holding the Torah firmly in my arms. Now, the increase in respect was palatable. As I walked down the aisle people on both sides stood up and – as is traditional in synagogue when the Torah passes by – reached out their hand to touch the Torah. Some even lunged forward and kissed the Torah directly.

During the course of the flight I became somewhat of a celebrity. People from all sections of the plane – even First Class – made pilgrimages to see the Torah and pay their respects. Parents brought children to me and held them over me so they could kiss the Torah on the seat next to me. Stewardesses responded to my requests.

Not only did this royal treatment continue once I arrived in Israel, but it increased. Taxi drivers began fighting with one another over who would have the honor of transporting the Torah – and me and my family – to Jerusalem. The winning driver proudly called his wife and told her of his victory as we began ascending to Jerusalem.

It was still day-time when we reached our home. I therefore decided to quickly drop off our bags in the house and carry the Torah the short distance to my synagogue a few short blocks away.

As I began my journey, a stranger on the street stopped me, kissed the Torah and asked me where I was going. He then asked if he could have the honor of accompanying the new Torah and me to the synagogue.

"Sure," I said. A few moments later another stranger joined us, and then another, and then several more. By the time I arrived at the door of the synagogue, we were not simply a diverse group of strangers; we were a loud and celebratory group of close friends singing and dancing around the Torah.

Returning home alone after safely depositing the Torah in the Synagogue – now, no longer with my entourage of singing minstrels

– was at first somewhat disappointing. I had grown accustomed to being the center of attention. But soon my disappointment turned to joy. This experience had taught me something special.

The closer I got to Jerusalem, the more people recognized and appreciated the holiness of the Torah. I thus began to think that perhaps part of the reason why Jerusalem is considered holy itself is because it is populated by people who *recognize* what holiness is!

Sure, Jerusalem is special because God said so, because God chose Jerusalem to be the place where God tested Abraham and where God commanded the Jewish People to build the Holy Temple. But maybe it's not just because of God's actions.

Perhaps Jerusalem's holiness is also inspired by the actions of its residents, people who are sensitive to matters of the spirit and brimming with the desire to honor symbols of learning (like a Torah).

Rabbi Ian Pear, The Accidental Zionist

When You're Dead in the Water

During the 1812 conflict between Britain and America, the crew of the USS Constitution, a 19th century American warship affectionately called "Old Ironsides", sighted what appeared to be several American ships blockading a harbor. Overnight the ship joined her supposed allies, only to find in the morning that she had closed up with five enemy British vessels. The worst thing was that there was no wind, making it impossible to sail away again.

With the Constitution in deep danger, her captain had to come up with another way of moving. For two days he and the crew crept slowly away from the British ships by sending an anchor ahead in one of the ship's lifeboats, dropping it, and then using the capstan to pull the ship towards safety. In this fashion, hour after hour, the ship inched ever-so-slightly away from the enemy. The arduous work of pulling up anchors from the bottom of the bay, loading them into small boats, rowing impossibly heavy boats toward open sea, wrestling the anchors overboard and towing the ship toward anchor must have been an excruciating and mind-wracking ordeal for the crew – and especially with the enemy so close.

The opposing captains soon realized what the Constitution was doing and employed the same tactic in pursuit. But the American ship had widened the gap just enough that, when wind finally returned, the British were unable to catch her.

In Sydney Smith's encouraging words, "It is the greatest of all mistakes to do nothing because you can only do little – do what you can." The crew of the Constitution did what little they could, though it may have seemed almost useless at the time.

Maybe you feel as if you are stuck – dead in the water. Maybe all you can do is barely move the ship of your life an inch at a time. Maybe it feels as if you are getting nowhere. And maybe it seems that the almost imperceptible movement forward is the hardest thing you've ever done.

But will you do nothing because you can only do a little? If one tiny step is all you can take, will you take it today?

Steve Goodier

Who I Am, Where Do I Come From, And Where I Am Going To

A Hasidic tale tells of a rebbe in a Russian village who used to take a dip in the river every morning. One day, the new local policeman on his first patrol just before sunrise, saw the rebbe diving into the frozen river. He ran to the strange old man, calling him to get out of the river and shouting, "Who are you? Where do you come from? And where are you going?"

The old rebbe smiled gently and asked the policeman: "How much do they pay you for this job?"

"Ten Kufeykas a day," answered the baffled young policeman.

"I'll tell you what," said the rebbe, "I'll pay you twenty Kufeykas a day if you come to me every morning and ask me who I am, where do I come from, and where I am going to."

Human beings are dynamic and ever evolving creatures, and just like our muscle system becomes atrophied if it is not stimulated enough, so does our moral and intellectual system. Hence, it is crucial we get asked those questions, about ourselves and our purpose, constantly.

◆◆◆

Sh'ma Yisrael

One cannot overestimate the importance *Sh'ma Yisrael* (Hear, O Israel) has in Jewish heritage throughout the generations. In many cases, these were the only "Jewish words" that Jews, who lived in remote places and who heard them from their ancestors, knew. The "marranos" in Spain and Portugal passed them on from parent to child, sometimes without knowing, their actual meaning but with profound understanding of their value. Many Jews, beginning with Rabbi Akiva, and up to the victims of the Holocaust recited the *Sh'ma* with their last breath.

The centrality and profound importance of the six words that comprise *Sh'ma Yisrael* could not be encapsulated in a short essay such as this (or in any form, to be honest). I will confine myself to one story, one that is documented in more than one version, and has to do with the special place that the *Sh'ma* had in the minds of young children.

After the Holocaust, Rabbi Eliezer Silver of Cincinnati went to Europe to look for Jewish survivors and especially for children who were hidden in monasteries during the war. The story tells that he entered a certain monastery in Krakow, where he heard that there were many Jewish children and asked the priest in charge if he could see the children for a couple of minutes before they went to bed. Standing in the large dormitory, he recited loudly, but tenderly, the words of *Sh'ma Yisrael*, the room was immediately filled with children's cries and excitement. Rabbi Silver looked at the priest and they both understood the meaning of this encounter. The children had recited these words every night with their mothers, who were no longer alive, before their world turned dark, and they were indelibly engraved in their hearts. And these words were the gate through which they returned to their people.

The *Sh'ma* verse and the response to it (*barukh shem kvod malkhuto l'olam va'ed*) are encased within two readings of love, as if they were a sacred sandwich of love – *Birkat Ahava* (the blessing of love) just before, and the rabbis teach us that one should not interrupt between the blessing and *Sh'ma Yisrael*, not even for saying "Amen" after the blessing, and *V'ahavta* (you shall love), the first portion of the *Sh'ma* – verses from Deuteronomy – just after it.

The *Ahava* blessing is a heartfelt thanksgiving for the abundant love God has for us. Note that in the morning we recite "*Ahava rabba*" (with abundant love) and in the evening "*Ahavat olam*" (with eternal love), both contain similar content. After the verse of *Sh'ma Yisrael* we continue with the command to ourselves to love Adonai our God, with all our heart, with all our soul and with all our might. In between these two declarations of love that stand as powerful guards, we find the words of the *Sh'ma*.

The words of *V'ahavta* contain the order to love God (and some may ask how can you force someone to love), but the demand is made, as it were, only after it guarantees God loves us and after mentioning the precious gifts that the Divine has given us – in the morning we mention God's "gracing us with surpassing compassion" and in the evening we are more specific thanking God for the "Torah and Mitzvot, laws and precepts" given to us.

The *Sh'ma* verse is a meeting point, an intersection, if you will, between God's love for us and our commitment to love God in return. Reciting it with our eyes closed we address not only our own soul but also our fellow Jews and remind ourselves that although our world seems dispersed and disintegrated, there is one unity behind it – "*Adonai ehad*", and it is our duty to find this harmony in a broken and suffering world.

Maybe the children in the Krakow monastery had a sense of it (probably without being able to explain it) on the night that Rabbi Silver gathered them before going to sleep.

Rabbi Dalia Marx

♦♦♦

Humility
Gam Zeh Ya'avor – **This Too Shall Pass**

Sometimes, it may seem, as though the good times pass faster than they should, and the bad times pass too slowly. But the reality is that it all passes the same. They're just ups and downs in this roller coaster of life.

There is a parable in which King Solomon realizes *Gam Zeh Ya'avor* – that this too will pass.

One day Solomon decided to humble Benaiah ben Yehoyada, his most trusted minister. He said to him, "Benaiah, there is a certain ring that I want you to bring to me. I wish to wear it for Sukkot, which gives you six months to find it."

"If it exists anywhere on earth, your majesty," replied Benaiah, "I will find it and bring it to you, but what makes the ring so special?"

"It has magic powers," answered the king. "If a happy man looks at it, he becomes sad, and if a sad man looks at it, he becomes happy."

Solomon knew that no such ring existed in the world, but he wished to give his minister a little taste of humility.

Spring passed and then summer, and still Benaiah had no idea where he could find the ring. On the night before Sukkot, he decided to take a walk in one of the poorest quarters of Jerusalem. He passed by a merchant who had begun to set out the day's wares on a shabby carpet.

"Have you by any chance heard of a magic ring that makes the happy wearer forget his joy and the broken-hearted wearer forget his sorrows?" asked Benaiah.

He watched the grandfather take a plain gold ring from his carpet and engrave something on it. When Benaiah read the words on the ring, his face broke out in a wide smile.

That night the entire city welcomed in the holiday of Sukkot with great festivity. "Well, my friend," said Solomon, "have you found what I sent you after?" All the ministers laughed and Solomon himself smiled.

To everyone's surprise, Benaiah held up a small gold ring and declared, "Here it is, your majesty!" As soon as Solomon read the inscription, the smile vanished from his face. The jeweler had written three Hebrew letters on the gold band: *gimel, zayin, yud*, which began the words "*Gam zeh ya'avor* – This too shall pass."

At that moment, Solomon realized that all his wisdom and fabulous wealth and tremendous power were but fleeting things, for one day he would be nothing but dust.

♦♦♦

Upside-Down World

A story is told of Rav Yosef, the son of Rabbi Yehoshua ben Levi, who became ill and was about to expire. When he returned to good health, his father asked him:

"What did you see when you were about to die?"

He said to him: "I saw an upside-down world (*olam hafuch*). Those above, i.e., those who are considered important in this world, were below, insignificant, while those below, i.e., those who are insignificant in this world, were above."

He said to him: "My son, you have seen a clear world (*olam barur*). The world you have seen is the true world, as in that world people's standings befit them."

Rabbi Yehoshua ben Levi asked: "And where are we, the Torah scholars, there?"

Rav Yosef responded: "Just as we are regarded here, so are we regarded there."

Talmud, Tractate Pesachim 50a

♦♦♦

The "Rocks, Pebbles and Sand" Story

There once was a philosophy professor who was giving a lecture. In front of him, he had a big glass jar, a pile of rocks, a bag of small pebbles, a tub of sand and a bottle of water.

He started off by filling up the jar with the big rocks and when they reached the rim of the jar he held it up to the students and asked them if the jar was full. They all agreed, there was no more room to put the rocks in, it was full.

"Is it full?" he asked.

He then picked up the bag of small pebbles and poured these in jar. He shook the jar so that the pebbles filled the space around the big rocks. "Is the jar full now?" he asked. The group of students all looked at each other and agreed that the jar was now completely full.

"Is it really full?" he asked.

The professor then picked up the tub of sand. He poured the sand in between the pebbles and the rocks and once again he held up the jar to his class and asked if it was full. Once again the students agreed that the jar was full.

"Are you sure it's full?" he asked.

He finally picked up a bottle of water and tipped the water into the jar until it soaked up in all the remaining space in the sand. The students laughed.

The professor went on to explain that the jar of rocks, pebbles, sand and water represents everything that is in one's life.

The Explanation

The jar represents your life.

The rocks represent the most important things that have real value – your health, your family, your partner. Those things that if everything else (the pebbles and the sand) was lost and only they remained, your life would still have meaning.

The pebbles represent the things in your life that matter, but that you could live without. The pebbles are certainly things that give your life meaning (such as your job, house, hobbies and friendships), but they are not critical for you to have a meaningful life. These things often come and go, and are not permanent or essential to your overall well-being.

The sand (and water) represents everything else – the small

stuff. Material possessions, chores and filler things such as watching television or browsing social media sites. These things don't mean much to your life as a whole and are likely only done to get small tasks accomplished or even to fill time.

The metaphor here is that if you start with putting sand into the jar, you will not have room for rocks or pebbles. This holds true with the things you let into your life. If you spend all of your time on the small and insignificant things, you will run out of room for the things that are actually important.

The Lesson

Make room for what's important.

Take care of the rocks first – the things that really matter and are critical to your long-term wellbeing and happiness. If you deal with the big issues first by putting the rocks in the jar first, the small issues can still fall into place. However, the reverse is not true.

Identify the important things in life (i.e. set your priorities).

Set aside the time you need to work on them. This is where your focus should be in order to live a meaningful life (without over-obligating yourself).

Then you can fill in the pebbles and sand, knowing it's okay to procrastinate a little on these things because they are not so important.

Anonymous

♦♦♦

The Apple Tree's Discovery

There was a tiny apple tree in the middle of a forest, surrounded by huge oak trees. Every night the tiny apple tree would peek up into the sky and see the millions of stars that appeared to be dangling from the branches of the oak trees. He would ask God, "Please, God, I would like to have stars on my branches."

And God would say, "But your blossoms smell beautiful and provide a pleasant scent for all who walk by, isn't it enough that you have something to give?" And the apple tree would say, "I only want stars on my branches so I can also feel special."

When the apples grew on the tree, people picked them and enjoyed the fruit, but the apple tree still looked up at night and saw the stars on the oak trees and asked God to please put stars on his branches, too.

And God would say, "But you provide delicious apples to those who are hungry, isn't it enough that you have something to give?"

The apple tree said, "No."

A great wind began to blow and the apple tree shook his branches and the shaking caused an apple to fall, and when it fell, it split horizontally down the middle. The apple tree looked down and inside he saw ... a star! And God said to the apple tree, "There have been stars on your branches all along."

We all have hidden "stars" inside us. Sometimes we have to approach things differently to help others find their "stars."

Penninah Schram

♦♦♦

Commitment

A salmon and a chicken were once walking down the street when they passed by a restaurant. On the window was a sign that read:

SPECIAL TODAY: LOX AND EGGS

The chicken turned to the salmon and said, "Hey, why don't we go in there and help these people out!"

The salmon vigorously shook his fins and said, "Nothing doing, chickadee! I'm not setting foot in that place – no how, no way!"

"Why not?" said the chicken. "We all have to do our part for the common good. Why won't you help?!"

"Because from you," replied the salmon, "they only require a contribution. From me, they require a total commitment!"

◆◆◆

Try Something Different

Writer Douglas Adams said, "Human beings, who are almost unique in having the ability to learn from the experience of others, are also remarkable for their apparent disinclination to do so." I sometimes wonder about my own disinclination to learn from experience. If you're like me, you may repeat an unpleasant experience a few times before figuring out that something needs to change.

Maybe you can relate to a couple of men who were avid moose hunters. Every year they chartered a plane to take them to the Canadian backcountry. This year, hunting was especially good and in a few days they each bagged a moose. They radioed for their pilot to come pick them up.

When the plane arrived, the pilot took one look at the animals and told the hunters they could not take such a heavy load along.

"But we spent all week hunting," they protested. "And besides, the pilot we hired last year wasn't worried about the moose's weight."

After much argument, the pilot finally relented and allowed them to load the animals. The heavy plane was only airborne for a few minutes when it lost altitude and crashed into the side of a mountain. As the men struggled out of the wreckage, one hunter asked, "Where are we?"

His friend answered, "About a mile farther than we got last year."

You've heard it said: Keep doing the same thing and you will keep getting the same results. Or repeating the same experiences.

What is not working well for you? A habit you are trying to break? A relationship with a parent or spouse or child or friend?

What is the source of on-going frustration? Getting around to that project you keep promising to complete? Running up against the same old walls at work?

And the big question: What needs to change?

If you don't like the way things are turning out, what are you willing to try differently? And what if you tried it today?

Steve Goodier

♦♦♦

Who Was Giving, and Who Was Receiving

Rav Eliezer Gordon, founder of Telz, studied for many years through the generous support of his father-in-law. Many times he wanted to take a rabbinic position, but his father-in-law convinced him to stay on a bit longer and continue his learning. Finally, Rav Gordon felt he must utilize his learning and share it by serving a community (the Eisheshok kehilla).

"I cannot allow you to continue to support me," Rav Gordon told his benefactor, who whispered under his breath, "I'm not sure who is actually supporting who!"

On the very day Rav Gordon finally moved to his new position, his father-in-law had a heart attack and died. It was then clear who was giving, and who was receiving.

Rabbi Stewart Weiss

♦♦♦

I Have Set The Lord Before Me At All Times.

A man stopped attending his usual synagogue and started frequenting another minyan. One day he happened to meet the rabbi of his previous synagogue, and the rabbi asked him where he was praying these days. The man answered: "I am praying at a small minyan led by Rabbi Cohen."

The rabbi was stunned. "Why would you want to pray there with that rabbi. I am a much better orator, I am more famous, I have a much larger following."

The man replied: "Yes, but in my new synagogue the rabbi has taught me to read minds."

The rabbi was surprised. "Alright, then, read my mind."

The man said: "You are thinking of the verse in Psalms, 'I have set the Lord before me at all times.'"

"You are wrong," said the rabbi, "I was not thinking about that verse at all."

The man replied: "Yes, I knew that, and that's why I've moved to the other synagogue. The rabbi there is always thinking of this verse."

Indeed, an authentically religious person is always thinking of this verse, either directly or in the back of his or her mind. Such an individual lives in the presence of God, acts with modesty and propriety. The Rabbi Cohen of the story was genuine; he was a spiritual person seeking to live a godly life.

The other rabbi in the story was "successful." He had a large congregation and external signs of prestige. But, he lacked the essential ingredient of being authentically religious: he did not have the Lord before him at all times. He was busy trying to make himself popular, get his name into the newspapers, rub elbows with celebrities. Even when he prayed, his mind was not on God, but on how he could advance himself in the world.

Rabbi Marc D. Angel

◆◆◆

Rabbi Dr. Abraham Twerski
and Actor Danny Thomas

When I decided to go to medical school, I was married with two children and a third on the way. I held a low paying position as an assistant rabbi and my father helped support me and my family.

The tuition for medical school was formidable, but I was able to manage for a while using donations from my congregation and some loans. However, by the middle of my third year, I was in debt up to my ears and unable to go on. I wrote to foundations that gave scholarships to medical students but I was turned down. What to do?

I usually called home during the day to see how my wife was feeling and one day she said, "What would you do if you had four thousand dollars?"

"I'd travel around the world." Can't she see I'm busy, I said to myself. "I have no time for daydreaming," is what I said aloud.

"This is not a daydream. There's a check for four thousand dollars on its way to you."

"Did you forge it?"

"No, Danny Thomas is giving you four thousand dollars."

I had no idea who Danny Thomas was and wondered if perhaps my wife's pregnancy was making her a little strange. But after we had gone back and forth about this check, she read to me the following story out of the Chicago Sun Times.

At a meeting with officials from Marquette University, the officials told Danny Thomas about the plight of a young rabbi who was having a difficult time financing his education.

"How much does the rabbi need? " Danny Thomas asked.

"About four thousand dollars," the Marquette officials said.

"Tell your rabbi he's got it." Like it happened all the time, I thought. But sure enough several days later I received a call from Danny Thomas who affirmed that the money was coming in a few days."

For the rest of Danny Thomas's life we were in touch. I have no idea what Danny Thomas received spiritually from his generosity to strangers. I do know that I received a medical degree as well as a confirmation of my belief and pride in humankind.

One material return Danny Thomas received, came about many years later and I am forever grateful for having been a part of it.

Danny traveled around the country raising money for the hospital he had built that specialized in treating leukemia, the Shrine of St. Jude. He came to Milwaukee to raise money and I contacted people on his behalf asking that they attend a fundraising dinner.

That evening I was given the opportunity to make a presentation to Danny Thomas of the pledges we had raised for the charity which meant so much to him. At this time I shared with everyone what Danny had done for me. I was embarrassed by my tearfulness and avoided looking out at the group. But finally as I presented Danny with a gift, I had to look up and that's when I found many of those in the room weeping the same tears of gratitude I and admiration for this great, kind man. I also gave him a beautiful volume of the Bible with a silver filigree cover inscribed with this verse from Micah: "For what does the Lord God ask of you, but to act with kindness, do justice and walk humbly with your God."

Mitzvahs not only bind but also break through barriers, bringing people together as the brothers they should be. Who would think of a less likely combination: a Lebanese Christian and a Hasidic rabbi?

Rabbi Dr. Abraham Twerski

Lessons from the Shoemaker

O ne night, Rabbi Yisrael Salanter walked past the shoemaker's home. Despite it being very late, he noticed that the shoemaker was still busy, working by the light of a candle.

"Why are you still working?" Rabbi Salanter asked him. "It is very late and soon the candle will go out."

The shoemaker replied, "As long as the candle is still burning, it is still possible to accomplish and to mend shoes."

Rabbi Salanter notes the wisdom of this encounter: As long as our candles are still burning, we can still accomplish much and mend our mistakes (and our world).

What are you still waiting to accomplish? How will you mend yourself (*tikkun atzmi*) and mend our world (*tikkun olam*)?

♦♦♦

Two Simple, Little Words

L ecturer Charles Hobbs tells about a woman who lived in London over a century ago. She saved what little money she could working as a scullery maid and used it one evening to hear a great speaker of her day. His speech moved her deeply and she waited to visit with him afterward. "How fine it must be to have had the opportunities you have had in life," she said.

"My dear lady," he replied, "have you never received an opportunity?"

"No. I have never had a chance," she said.

"What do you do?" the speaker asked.

She answered, "I peel onions and potatoes in my sister's boarding house."

"How long have you been doing this?" he pursued.

"Fifteen miserable years!"

"And where do you sit?" he continued.

"Why, on the bottom step in the kitchen." She looked puzzled.

"And where do you put your feet?"

"On the floor," she answered, more puzzled.

"What is the floor?"

"It is glazed brick."

Then he said, "I will give you an assignment today. I want you to write me a letter about the bricks. Learn as much as you can about the bricks in your kitchen, then teach me."

Against her protests about being a poor writer, he made her promise to complete the assignment.

The next day, as she sat down to peel onions, she gazed at the brick floor. That evening she pulled one loose, took it to a brick factory and asked the owner to explain to her how bricks were made.

Still not satisfied, she went to a library and found a book on bricks. She learned that 120 different kinds of brick and tile were being produced in England at the time. Now curious, she discovered how clay beds, which existed for millions of years, were formed. Her research captivated her imagination and she spent every spare moment learning more. She returned to the library night after night until she became something of an expert on bricks.

After months of study, she set out to write her letter as promised. She sent a 36-page document about English bricks and, to her surprise, she received a letter back. Enclosed was payment for her research. He had published her letter. And along with the money came a new assignment – this time he asked her to write about what she found underneath the brick.

For the first time in her life she could hardly wait to get back to the kitchen. She pulled up the brick and there was an ant. She held it in her hand and examined it.

That evening, she hurried back to the library to study ants. She learned that there were hundreds of different kinds of ants. Some were so small they could stand on the head of a pin; while others were so large one could feel the weight of them in one's hand. She started her own ant colony and examined ants underneath a lens.

Several months later she wrote what she learned about ants in another long letter. It, too, was eventually published. For the first time, she began to think that she might be able to do something different with her life. She was thrilled to discover that her future was not predetermined. And in time, the woman quit her kitchen job to take up writing.

Before she died, she had traveled to distant lands and had experienced more than she ever imagined possible.

Two of the saddest words in the language are "if only."

...If only I had a chance.

...If only I had the time.
...If only I had more education.
...If only I had connections.
...If only I had more money.
...If only things were different.
If only...

And two of the most inspirational words are "I can."
...I can try.
...I can learn.
...I can adjust.
...I can heal.
...I can change.
...I can grow.
I can do it.

Two simple, little words. Yet they can change a life.

Steve Goodier

♦♦♦

Do Someone Else A Favor

Shlomo Carlebach, a renowned rabbi, shared this powerful story about a great rabbi in Poland who perished during the Holocaust. This particular rabbi focused on children and ran an amazing school. All his life, Rabbi Carlebach had wanted to meet one of those children. It was only in his later years that Rabbi Carlebach met an old hunched over man sweeping the streets of Tel Aviv and discovered that this man was once a student of the holy teacher.

"Please share with me something that you learned from the rabbi!" Rabbi Carlebach begged.

After some coaxing, the man replied, "This is what the rabbi said to us over and over again: 'The greatest thing in the world is to do somebody else a favor!'"

The old man continued, "When I was in Auschwitz, I wanted to end it all and kill myself. But then I would hear my rabbi's voice say, 'The greatest thing in the world is to do somebody else a favor!' Do you know how many favors you can do in Auschwitz at night? People are lying on the floor crying. I would walk from one person to the other and ask, 'Why are you crying?' I would listen, hold their hands and cry with them. Then I would walk to the next person. And it would give me strength for another day."

The man continued, "I'm here in Tel Aviv and I have no one in the world. Sometimes I'm at my end, but then I hear my rabbi's voice saying, 'The greatest thing in the world is to do somebody else a favor.' Do you know how many favors you can do on the streets of the world?"

Friends, today and every day, do someone else a favor. It truly is the greatest thing in the world!

Yael Eckstein

♦♦♦

Planning A Trip

Come with me to a third grade classroom... There is a nine-year-old kid sitting at his desk and all of a sudden, there is a puddle between his feet and the front of his pants are wet. He thinks his heart is going to stop because he cannot possibly imagine how this has happened. It's never happened before, and he knows that when the boys find out, he will never hear the end of it. When the girls find out, they'll never speak to him again as long as he lives.

The boy believes his heart is going to stop; he puts his head down and prays this prayer, "Dear God, this is an emergency! I need help now! Five minutes from now I'm dead meat."

He looks up from his prayer and here comes the teacher with a look in her eyes that say he has been discovered.

As the teacher is walking toward him, a classmate named Susie is carrying a goldfish bowl that is filled with water. Susie trips in front of the teacher and inexplicably dumps the bowl of water in the boy's lap.

The boy pretends to be angry, but all the while is saying to himself, "Thank you, Lord! Thank you, Lord!"

Now, all of a sudden, instead of being the object of ridicule, the boy is the object of sympathy. The teacher rushes him downstairs and gives him gym shorts to put on while his pants dry out. All the other children are on their hands and knees cleaning up around his desk. The sympathy is wonderful. But as life would have it, the ridicule that should have been his, has been transferred to someone else – Susie.

She tries to help, but they tell her to get out. "You've done enough, you klutz!"

Finally, at the end of the day, as they are waiting for the bus, the boy walks over to Susie and whispers, "You did that on purpose, didn't you?"

Susie whispers back, "I wet my pants once too."

May God help us see the opportunities that are always around us to do good.

◆◆◆

No Regrets

Not many people have heard of Bill Havens. But Bill became an unlikely hero of sorts – at least among those who knew him best. Here is his story:

At the 1924 Olympic Games in Paris, the sport of canoe racing was added to the list of international competitions. The favorite team in the four-man canoe race was the United States team. One member of that team was a young man by the name of Bill Havens.

As the time for the Olympics neared, it became clear that Bill's wife would give birth to their first child about the time that the US team would be competing in the Paris games. In 1924, there were no jet airliners from Paris to the United States, only slow ocean-going ships. And so Bill found himself in a dilemma. Should he go to Paris and risk not being at his wife's side when their baby was born? Or should he withdraw from the team and remain with his family?

Bill's wife insisted that he go to Paris. After all, competing in the Olympics was the culmination of a lifelong dream. But Bill felt conflicted and, after much soul-searching, decided to withdraw from the competition and remain home where he could support his family. Just four days after the games (at which his brother Bud Havens and the rest of the U.S. canoe crew won three gold, one silver, and two bronze over six events), his son Frank came into the world.

People said, "What a shame." But Bill said he had no regrets. For the rest of his life, he believed he had made the better decision.

However, there is an interesting sequel to the story of Bill Havens....

Frank, the child born to them that year, grew to love canoeing as much as his father did. And at 28-years-old, in 1952, Frank sent his father a cablegram. It came from Helsinki, Finland, where the Olympic Games were being held. The message read: "Dear Dad, thanks for waiting around for me to get born in 1924. I'm coming home with the gold medal you should have won. Your loving son, Frank."

Frank had set the new world record and took home the gold in the solo 10,000-meter event. He came home with the medal his father had dreamed of winning. Like I said – no regrets.

Thomas Kinkade eloquently said, "When we learn to say a deep, passionate yes to the things that really matter, then peace begins to settle onto our lives like golden sunlight sifting to a forest floor." Saying yes to the things that really matter might mean you say no to something else you want... but it's a way to have no regrets.

Steve Goodier

♦♦♦

What Really Matters Is Helping Others Win

This is my favorite story that came from the Seattle Special Olympics? Well, for the 100-yard dash, there were nine contestants, all of them so-called physically or mentally disabled. All nine of them assembled at the starting line, and at the sound of the gun, they took off. But not long afterward, one little boy stumbled and fell, hurt his knee and began to cry. The other eight children heard him crying. They slowed down, turned around, and ran back to him. Every one of them ran back to him. One little girl with Down Syndrome bent down and kissed the boy, and said, "This will make it better."

The little boy got up, and he and the rest of the runners linked their arms together, and joyfully walked to the finish line. They all finished the race at the same time. And when they did, everyone in that stadium stood up, and clapped, and whistled, and cheered for a long, long time.

People who were there are still telling this story with great delight. And do you know why? Because deep down, we know that what matters most in this life is more than winning for ourselves. What really matters is helping others win, too. Even if it means slowing down and changing our course.

Fred Rogers, Minister

A Deep Teaching

A beautiful question-and-answer in the name of the Gerer
Rebbe: When strangers come to visit Abraham (Genesis
chapter 18), the Torah tells us that Abraham, who was in God's
presence, rushes out to visit the strangers. The Talmud comments
on this that we learn it is more important to greet strangers than to
bask in the Divine presence.

The Rebbe asked – we learn this lesson from Abraham, but how
did Abraham know? How did he have the chutzpah, the audacity, to
walk away from God to greet the strangers?

His answer: It is actually *because* Abraham was in God's presence
that he went to greet them. To feel the *Shechina*, the Divine presence
is to be moved to do a mitzvah. God's will is expressed in our conduct
toward one another.

In the Jewish tradition, devotion to God is less a theological
question than a behavioral one. Closeness is exemplified through
a life of mitzvot, in prayer that moves one to action, in ritual that
is reflected in community and kindness. Abraham was uplifted by
encounter to open his home and his heart.

Rabbi David Wolpe

◆◆◆

He Wrote the Check

Sammy is on a holiday in Israel and goes to a concert at the Cohen Family Auditorium. When he gets to his seat, he looks around and is very impressed with the architecture and the acoustics.

After the concert is over, Sammy asks one of the employees, "I was wondering for which Cohen family is this magnificent auditorium named? Is it the family of David Cohen, the famous biblical scholar?"

"No," replies the worker, "It's not."

"Oh, well is it named after the family of Dr. Nahum Cohen, the Nobel Prize winner in Medicine?"

"No, not that one either."

"Oh well, then surely it must be named after Walter Cohen, the great conductor of the New York Philharmonic?"

"No, not that one either."

"OK, I give up," Sammy says. "Which Cohen family is the namesake of this beautiful auditorium?"

The employee says, "It's named for the family of Brian Cohen of Minneapolis, the famous writer."

"Oh, I've never heard of Brian Cohen. What did he write?"

The employee says, "He wrote the check."

♦♦♦

Then We Are the Chosen People

In the concentration camp, the SS guards taunted and teased the Rebbe, pulling his beard and pushing him around. They trained their guns on him as the commander spoke.

"Tell us, rabbi," sneered the officer, "do you really believe that you are the Chosen People?"

The soldiers broke out in sinister laughter, but the rabbi stood up and answered loud and clear, "most certainly I do!"

The officer, enraged that a Jew would talk back, lifted his rifle and sent it crashing into the rabbi's head. The Rebbe fell to the ground and the German asked again, "Do you still think you are the Chosen People?!"

Once again, the rabbi nodded his head and said, "Yes, we are."

The officer, infuriated, kicked the Rebbe in the chin and repeated, "Stupid Jew, you lie here on the ground, beaten and humiliated, in a puddle of blood. What makes you think that you are the Chosen People?!"

With his mouth gushing blood, the Rebbe replied, "As long as we are not the ones kicking, beating and murdering innocent people, then we are the Chosen People."

Deuteronomy 7